WIDOW IN MISTLETOE

Brides By Chance
Regency Adventures
Book Seven

Elizabeth Bailey

WIDOW IN MISTLETOE

Published by Sapere Books.

20 Windermere Drive, Leeds, England, LS17 7UZ,
United Kingdom

saperebooks.com

ISBN: 978-1-80055-175-6

CHAPTER ONE

The muffled clop of hooves disturbed the eerie silence of the snowbound countryside. Chloe looked across the banked white mounds to the barely visible ribbon of the road below, but no vehicle was yet in sight. No doubt someone with a pressing reason to be travelling on such a day.

She plodded on along the path that ran parallel to the road, setting her booted feet into fresh snow. Easier to crunch anew than to risk slipping in the prints already made by early wayfarers, including her own going in the opposite direction. At least her basket was now empty, the provisions she'd taken to old Mrs Trott having been heavier than usual. She'd packed in double the amount in case the snow became too bad for her to venture out in safety. Her companion Agatha had set up a protest, saying she ought rather to send one of the servants.

"Let Jemima or Tibby go, my dear Mrs Quilter. It is not fit for you."

"It's not fit for those poor little overworked maids either. Whatever should we do if one of them were to fall and break a limb?"

Miss Flook became agitated. "Then send the footman, or Nat, I do beg of you."

Chloe laughed. "To see to Mrs Trott? She would shriek in horror, poor thing. Don't worry about me, Agatha. I will take the greatest care."

Miss Flook had wrung her hands. "If I was not so unsteady on my legs, I would go myself."

"Well, we certainly don't want you laid up, Agatha. Come, I'm fit as a fiddle and will come to no harm for a trifle of snow."

She was also young and strong enough to be capable of making so unadventurous a trip, but she refrained from saying so. Her elderly companion tended to look at the world from her own perspective, which had been melancholy enough until Chloe had hired her to lend respectability to her widowhood. She'd hoped for a more congenial companion than a retired governess whose years of tutoring girls into becoming young ladies of gentility had left her with a marked tendency to treat her employer as if she were a pupil. But Chloe had been touched to realise the anxious creature who came for the interview was eking out a miserable existence in a dingy lodging, and engaged her on the spot. Not that Agatha had complained. But snippets had slipped out, and it had not taken much imagination for Chloe to put together a picture of her life. She'd known enough of poverty to recognise the signs.

The hoofbeats grew louder, pulling her out of her thoughts. A vehicle came into sight around the bend, its pace adapted to the condition of the road. A curricle? In this weather? Drawn by four horses too.

It was then she noticed the abandoned cart standing directly in the path of the approaching vehicle. It looked as if it had ploughed into a drift in the ditch, for it was pitched at a crazy angle, the wheels in the air. It must have been left last night for it was covered in snow, making it difficult to spot.

Apprehension sent Chloe stepping at a greater rate. Should she try to warn the driver? A wild idea of running and yelling was no sooner thought of than discarded. She would only distract him.

At least he was not driving too fast. The chances were he would see the obstruction and draw up in time. She could not yet make out more than an unformed figure inside the hood.

Looking back to where the cart had been so recklessly left, Chloe tried to discover if there was room for the curricle to pass. She visualised in her mind's eye the narrowness of the road without its covering of snow, but could not recall it well enough. She'd passed by here on numerous occasions, but had clearly not paid enough attention to such a detail.

Meanwhile, the curricle was coming on its inexorable way. Chloe stopped walking, peering at the driver, who was a trifle clearer now. She could make out his hat and one of those many caped greatcoats the fashionables wore, which made his shoulders look enormous. There was another figure beside him, coated to be sure, but more modestly. A groom? Surely he must see the danger?

Chloe's heart was pattering in her chest. She saw a pointing hand come out and a voice cut into the still air. Yes, he'd seen it!

Within yards of the wreck, the horses swerved out to the right to avoid it. Why did he not stop? But the driver's evasive action took the curricle wide; the horses steadied and picked up the pace slightly as they went by the cart.

At which point, the wheels must have slipped in the snow. The curricle swung further to the right, much too close to the far verge of the road. Chloe saw the driver struggle with his reins, and then a horrid crunch sounded. The vehicle bounced back. There was the crack of splintered wood, the plunging of the horses as the curricle teetered crazily on the edge of overturning and the occupants were thrown out.

Dropping her basket, Chloe stepped off the path and made the best of her way towards the mound at the edge of the road, as fast as she could without endangering herself. Her head was in chaos, her pulse out of rhythm, but she knew exactly what had happened. Too late her mind presented her with the picture of the road and the milestone on the other side, which had lain concealed ready to trap the unwary driver.

She scrambled down the bank and hurried towards the spill. She could see the man who'd been a passenger had managed to get himself up and run to struggle with the horses. The driver was lying unmoving at some distance on the far side of the curricle, which had settled at an angle.

Chloe's heart leapt into her mouth. "I'm coming to help," she called to the groom, who seemed unhurt.

He was at the lead horses' heads, grasping their bits, evidently trying to calm them as they shifted and tossed their heads. But he turned at her call. "Can you check on my master? I daren't leave the cattle!"

No indeed! One of the rear horses whinnied, making a spirited attempt to kick out of the traces.

"Yes, of course. I'll help you presently."

Stomping her way around the unhappy horses, Chloe made for the prone figure lying face up, half buried in a flush of snow that had fallen upon him from a shrub, exposing a batch of mistletoe.

He was alarmingly still, his countenance pale as death. With a shaft of horror, Chloe saw a trickle of blood creeping down his cheek, emanating from under the dark of his hair. He was bareheaded and the greatcoat was awry, but at least it was protecting him from the cold.

Chloe knelt at his side and grasped his gloved hand. Stripping off her own glove, she slipped her fingers under the heavy sleeve of the coat, feeling for his wrist. The pump of a pulse rewarded her after a moment and she let out a relieved breath.

"He is alive," she called to the groom, "but I fear he has injured his head."

She heard an expletive from the man, but paid no heed, moving to examine the gentleman's scalp. Threading her fingers into his hair, she found a sticky patch to the side of his temple. He must have knocked it as he fell or when he hit the ground.

Had he hurt himself in any other way? His limbs did not look to be crooked or awkwardly placed, but it was impossible to tell if he had broken anything or cracked more than his head.

"We must get him into the house," Chloe said aloud, "and fetch Doctor Goodleigh to him as soon as we may." She was about to rise when she saw his eyelids flutter. She leaned over him as they opened and a pair of green eyes blinked up at her.

"Clarissa?"

"No, I'm Chloe," she said. "You've suffered an accident."

He did not seem to hear her. A faint smile quivered. "Is that mistletoe? Then you owe me a kiss."

A surprisingly strong hand caught Chloe about the neck and pulled her close. Cold lips pressed against hers for an instant. Then the pressure released, the hand fell and the lids sank over the startling eyes.

Flustered and a little amused, Chloe eyed the creature's face for a moment. It was, despite its pallor, a pleasing one, with a lean cheek, a straight nose and those impertinent lips well sculpted.

"Sir? Can you hear me?"

He did not wake again and anxiety claimed Chloe. She struggled up and brushed the snow from her coat.

The groom had succeeded in persuading the horses to remain still.

"How can I help?" asked Chloe.

"Do you think you could hold them, miss? I've to get them out of the traces."

"I could, but I think it more urgent to bring succour to your master. My house is very close. Let me rush home and I will bring help for you and the means to carry him to safety."

The groom thanked her, urging her to hurry. "For they'll take cold and his lordship will murder me if his horses come to harm!"

The title caught Chloe's attention. "His lordship?"

"Lord Pettipher, miss."

"Well, I doubt his lordship will be in any state to do any murdering yet awhile."

"Ha! Alive, ain't he?"

Chloe could not forbear a laugh, but she promised to come back as quickly as she could. Indeed she must, she thought, as she hurried across the road and struggled up the bank, pushing through the mound of snow as quickly as she might. It was not only the horses who would take cold. And the gentleman's danger was more than a mere chill.

She made better speed once she hit the path, her mind already running on arrangements. By the time she clicked the latch on the gate, she had her keys out. By good fortune, her groom Nat was busy sweeping the path to the house with a birch broom.

"Leave that, Nat! There's been an accident on the road."

"Accident, mistress?"

"A curricle and four hit the milestone."

Nat flung away his broom as his eyes lit. "Four horses? That'll be a spill and a half, that will!"

Aware that her groom chafed at having to double as gardener and secretly longed for better than a gig and a couple of hacks, Chloe urged him to hurry down to assist.

"The vehicle did not quite overturn, but they're restive and the groom needs to get them out of the traces. You'd best bring them to the stables."

Nat was already halfway out of the gate when she called after him.

"Tell him I'm sending others for his master!"

Nat nodded and sped off. Chloe entered the house and set up a shout for Basil, moving to catch up the hand bell from the hall table and plying it with vigour. As she anticipated, the racket brought not only her butler, puffing through the servants' door, but both Jemima and Tibby tumbled down from the upper regions and the footman ambled in from the dining parlour, clad in the green apron he wore for polishing the silver.

"What's to do, mistress?"

"There's been a carriage accident on the road and a gentleman injured. Basil, you and Jack must take a hurdle of some kind and bring him here."

Mutterings of surprised anxiety broke out all around, but Chloe had no time to waste. The stolid butler, as might have been expected from one who had taken her in charge when her father died and resolutely sorted her future, went into immediate action.

"We've that old gate still out by the stables, Miss Chloe, that'll do it. Jack, put off your apron and come with me."

"It's right below the path, almost opposite us, Basil. You can't miss it," Chloe called as he hurried back through the door protected with green baize, closely followed by the burly Jack, stripping off his apron as he went.

By this time, Miss Flook had joined the party and begun to twitter. "What is it? What's happening?"

"An accident, Agatha. We're going to have an injured guest, I'm afraid."

"Gracious me! Who —? What —?"

"Never mind who or what for the moment. Would you help Jemima to make up a bed for him in the big spare room, if you please? And Tibby!"

The older and more experienced of the maids started off towards the stairs, but Miss Flook did not immediately follow. Little Tibby, who was indeed of small stature, bobbed about on her uneven legs with all the eagerness of extreme youth.

"Yes, mistress? Shall I help Jemima?"

"No, dear. Put on your coat and go down to the village to Doctor Goodleigh's house." The little maid started to hurry off, but Chloe grabbed her arm. "One moment, dear. You don't know what to tell him yet, do you?"

Tibby blushed. "Oh, no, I doesn't, mistress, do I?"

Chloe tamped down her impatience and smiled. Her late husband Oswald would have said Little Tibby was two sheets short of a blanket, but she was so willing Chloe could not bear to dismiss her. But this task was not beyond her.

"You must tell the doctor's housekeeper that he is needed up at Derry Lodge. And say it's urgent. Can you remember that?"

"Needed up at Derry Lodge and it's urgent," Tibby repeated carefully, nodding a couple of times.

"Off you go, and don't forget your coat."

"Needed up at Derry Lodge and it's urgent," intoned Tibby as she dot-and-carried up the stairs as fast as she could.

Agatha hurried to the bottom of the stairs and called up after her. "Be careful in the snow, girl!" She turned to Chloe. "She'll likely fall and we'll have two injuries on our hands. But, my dear Mrs Quilter, what are you thinking? You said him. A man? You cannot house a man!"

"I don't have a choice, Agatha. He'll do me no harm." Remembrance of that stray kiss caused a flitter of doubt. No, why? The creature was barely conscious.

"But your reputation, dear Mrs Quilter!"

"What would you have me do? Send him to The Bear? He won't be properly cared for by Mrs Buller. She's a mean piece."

Miss Flook wrung her hands. "But you know how people will talk, Chloe dear. And that horrid Mrs Jolliffe is only waiting for an excuse to blacken your character, you know she is."

Chloe gave the elderly dame a little push towards the stairs. "It can't be helped, Agatha. Now, go on up and do your part, if you please. Poor Jemima will be struggling to make that room habitable, and I know I may trust you to see all right."

"But where are you going?"

"Back to the scene of the accident, of course. Now, do not argue with me, Agatha, for there is no time to lose."

Lord Pettipher struggled out of a cloying dream. His eyes hurt as light hit them and instinct brought his hand up to try to shade them.

"That's too bright for you? I'm sorry."

The light disappeared. He sought for the source of the soft voice and found a shadow leaning over him.

"Don't try to talk. I'm going to raise your head."

A hand slipped under his head and it was gently lifted. Pain streaked through it and he winced.

"I dare say it hurts like the devil. Try to sip this. It will help."

He felt the edge of a glass at his lips and opened them. Bitter liquid slid into his mouth and he choked. The glass was removed.

"Slowly, if you please. Now, let's try again."

He felt the cool of the glass and this time was ready for the liquid. He swallowed. He found he was thirsty, wanting more despite the acrid taste. His fingers groped for the glass to try and tip it to make the liquid come faster, but it was at once removed.

"A little at a time, my lord."

"My lord?" He muttered it, could make no sense of it, abandoned the effort. "Thirsty."

"Are you? Well, that is a very good sign. I have some barley water for you once you have finished this dose the doctor left."

The glass was again put to his lips and he took the remainder of whatever was in it.

"Oh, well done, my lord. You are a very good patient."

Was he? Patient? He peered up at his nurse. He supposed she was a nurse. His eyes had become a little more accustomed, but she was against the light and he could only make out a silhouette and a pale oval of a face as she turned back to him, holding another glass.

"Here is your reward, sir. You may drink as much of this as you can take."

Was that a smile in her voice? But the question became unimportant as the fresher taste came in his mouth and he drank eagerly.

"Gently, sir, gently. We don't want you choking again."

The chiding note amused him. As if she was addressing a child! But he obediently lessened the speed of imbibing and drank until his thirst was quenched. Then he pushed the glass away.

"There, that is better. You have taken almost half the glass."

Was that all? He felt he'd had a pint at least.

"You may sleep now."

His head came to rest on the pillows and the hand slid out from underneath. The suggestion seemed good to him and he closed his eyes, sinking back into slumber.

When he next awoke, it was daylight and an elderly female with a pair of spectacles perched on her nose was peering at him.

"Oh, you are awake! How do you do, my lord?"

He blinked at her. "Where is she?"

"She? Oh, you mean Mrs Quilter?"

"Do I?"

"She's laid down upon her bed, sir. Resting, I hope. She insisted upon sitting up half the night with you. Highly inappropriate, but Chloe can be stubborn when she is determined upon a course." The mutter, for it was little more, ceased. Faint colour came into the withered cheeks. "I should not talk so. Forget I said it, pray."

He could not remember much of what she'd said in any event. He was tired and his head ached. He recalled his nurse — Mrs Quilter, didn't she say? — had given him something bitter.

"It must have made me sleep."

"What must?"

"She made me drink it, I remember."

"Oh, you must mean the dose the doctor left. I'm afraid you may not have another until he comes again. He will be here this morning."

It already looked like morning to him. "What time is it?"

"A little after six."

Not that it mattered. He drifted off again and was woken by a man's voice.

"Slept all night, did he? That's the ticket." A face, bewigged and frowning, appeared above him. "Awake are you, my dear sir? Well, well, you look to be better than I'd hoped for. Let's take a look at that wound of yours, shall we?"

The bass tones echoed in his head and he winced. He managed a dry croak. "My head aches."

"That does not surprise me, my dear sir. You took quite a knock."

Fingers were shifting in his hazy vision, and he felt them against his head. Removing a bandage? A knock? "What's that you say?"

Another voice spoke, a touch gentle on his hand. "Don't let it trouble you, my lord."

He slid his eyes to the other side of the bed. A pretty face, framed with golden curls, vaguely familiar. "Surely I know you?"

It smiled. "You do now."

The fingers probing his head touched a nerve and he hissed in a breath. "That hurts."

"Aye, it will do for a day or two yet," returned the doctor. He supposed the fellow was a doctor. The man spoke across him, addressing the female. "Well, it is healing as it should, Mrs Quilter. My only concern is a possible concussion."

Ha! He felt as if he'd been battered. Concussion? Had some ruffian set about him?

"How will we know?"

Really, she was a vastly sensible creature. Capable too. He liked her better than the old one who was here before.

"Some confusion may be expected, but as long as he is not in a delirium, we may count ourselves satisfied there is no serious damage."

"Damage?" What did that mean?

The doctor's eyes rested on his. "None, my dear sir, if you will remain quiet and rest. Now, I am going to place another compress to the wound and give Mrs Quilter a powder for the pain."

Yes, but she didn't need it! "Hey! I'm the sufferer."

A gurgling laugh pleasurably assailed his ears and he glanced towards it. His pretty nurse twinkled at him. "It's for you, my lord, never fear."

He kept his eyes on her face, trying to think how he knew her. So familiar, yet so elusive. A wave of sadness washed over him and his vision blurred.

Things became hazy again. He thought he drank at her command, but could not be sure. Pain in his head prevented much thought beyond the wish it would stop. Visions twisted in his mind.

He was travelling at breakneck speed in stark whiteness and Clarissa was begging him to go faster. He lost the way and was walking in the empty streets, trying to find her, calling her name. She was slipping in the cracked ice and he seized her wrist, trying to drag her back as the winds pulled her from his grasp. He screamed her name.

"There, now, there, my lord. All is well. You are safe."

He opened his eyes and found her face leaning over him. "Clarissa?" He sought for her hand. Found and gripped it. "I lost you."

A grimace passed across her face. "All is well. Rest now."

"You won't run away again?"

"I will be here when you wake. Sleep." Her fingers stroked his forehead. "Sleep now, my lord."

The puzzlement rankled. "You keep saying that."

"Sleep, you mean?"

"My lord… I don't know why."

"Never mind it now. Sleep a little and all will be well. Hush, now. Sleep."

The gentle tone soothed him and he allowed his heavy lids to droop over his eyes. Her face followed him into his dreams.

The groom was evasive, but Chloe persisted. Upon enquiry, he had given his master's full credentials and she learned she was housing none other than Lancelot Ravensthorp, Earl of Pettipher. Yet on the matter of Clarissa, the fellow proved reticent.

"Rowley, I cannot help Lord Pettipher as well as I may if I don't know what is troubling him."

He looked undecided, twisting his hat in his hands. Chloe had summoned him to the book-room, which constituted both library and study where she kept her papers and accounts in the roll-top desk Oswald had bought her. That, and the chairs and chaise longue in the small back parlour were the only pieces of furniture she had brought from The Great House at Mortain, since they were her personal property and not part of the estate that fell to her stepson. She believed her stepdaughter Matilda begrudged her even these few items, never mind the house Oswald had left to her. It was not part of the entail and there was no dower house, but that did not prevent Matilda from objecting to Chloe inhabiting it. But then her stepdaughter objected to her very existence, she believed. What she would say when she found out Chloe was housing an injured earl she dared not contemplate.

"All I am trying to do is establish the identity of this Clarissa, Rowley. Is she betrothed to Lord Pettipher, perhaps?"

The groom sighed. "She were, ma'am."

"I see. But no longer? That is a pity. I was rather hoping we might send to her."

The groom looked still more unhappy. "Impossible, ma'am." He drew a breath and looked her in the face at last. "The lady's been dead these many years."

Shock hit, then pity, and was swiftly succeeded by realisation. "That explains it, then! He spoke of having lost her, you see." Chloe recalled his mistaking her for the dead woman more than once, and immediately upon the first occasion, the one involving the kiss. "Rowley, do I resemble her in any way?"

A startled expression came into the groom's eyes. "Beg pardon, ma'am?"

Chloe sighed. "He thinks I am Clarissa. Which is worrying, for Doctor Goodleigh warned me to watch for delirium."

The groom began twisting his hat again, his features creased with concern. He eyed her in a covert fashion. "Well, ma'am, she were fair like you. I can't say as I recall exactly what she looked like." He brightened suddenly. "He carries a miniature. Fashioned into a fob, it is. He wears it mostly."

No, she was not going to pry into his personal belongings beyond necessity. It was fortunate he'd had a portmanteau stowed in the curricle, for Jack and Basil had been able to dress him in his own nightshirt. She had sent Jack in to attend to his lordship's ablutions, having located his shaving gear and toiletries.

She returned to the more pressing matter. "You said you were on your way to Lord Pettipher's estate for Christmas. Is there anyone there who might be asked to come to him?"

"Well, Finch should have reached Ravensthorp by now, if the coach ain't foundered like us. Only I don't know as a messenger would get through."

"Yes, but if he did? Who is Finch?"

"His lordship's valet, ma'am."

"But is there no one else? A suitable female whom he might recognise, perhaps. His mother? Or a sister?"

The groom shook his head. "Not as would come. His lordship's sister has two nippers and lives at a distance from Ravensthorp besides. My lady Pettipher died two years back. There's only his old aunt otherwise, and she's an invalid."

Chloe sighed. "You must not think I am unwilling to nurse him myself, Rowley. I'm only too happy. But the thing is, I fear his memory is affected. I don't think he knows who he is."

CHAPTER TWO

The experiment of bringing the groom into the bedchamber did not answer. Lord Pettipher was freshly shaved and washed, as well as Jack could manage it as the footman had explained on a note of apology, but he was barely conscious. He blinked up at Rowley's face.

Chloe, watching him from the other side of the bed, saw no recognition flash as she'd hoped. "Talk to him," she urged in a low murmur.

The groom looked unhappy, almost in tears, Chloe guessed. He cleared his throat. "You took a toss, my lord."

"A toss?"

The faintness of his voice caused the groom to falter, casting a glance at Chloe. She nodded at him to answer.

"Curricle overturned, my lord. It weren't your fault. Mrs Quilter here says it were a milestone hidden in the snow."

Blankness was all the response in the green eyes, though Chloe saw him frown. In an effort of memory?

"Snow … ice … a crack in the ice."

"No, my lord, there weren't no ice."

Lord Pettipher's head turned and he looked directly at Chloe. "He's doing it too."

The groom became agitated. "My lord, don't you know me? It's Rowley."

"Go away."

"You got to know me! Been with you since you were a stripling, remember?"

The sufferer did not turn his eyes from Chloe's face. "Tell him to go away. I can't…"

She leaned over him and patted his shoulder in a soothing fashion. "Never mind it. I dare say it will come back to you presently. Rest easy now, just as the doctor ordered."

"But, my lord —"

Chloe put a finger to her lips and shook her head at the man. She watched his lordship's lids sink over the green eyes and waited until his even breathing betrayed that he was asleep again. Signalling to the groom, she tiptoed away from the bed and ushered him out of the room, bringing the door to behind her but leaving a crack through which she could still hear in case her patient woke.

"I should not have tried to force it, Rowley, forgive me. It is too soon, I suspect."

The groom dashed a hand across his eyes. "I been with him so long, ma'am. I can't believe he don't know me."

"The doctor fears he may have a concussion. We will consult him about his lordship's memory when he comes this evening." She smiled at the man. "Come, Rowley, we need not yet despair. Why, it is barely four and twenty hours since the accident." With deliberation, she changed the subject. "How are his horses faring?"

"Oh, nowt wrong with them, bar a graze or two." With a sigh, the groom embraced the less disturbing subject. "Which is as well. If we'd been going faster, it might have been different."

"Have we enough fodder?"

"For a day or two yet, ma'am. Though if we've to purchase more, I can get his lordship's purse for it, ma'am."

"Certainly not. I will tell Nat to get a good supply from Farmer Gare. Are you well housed yourself, Rowley?"

"I am that, thank you, ma'am. Mr Basil, or rather Mr Clinch, I should say —"

"Everyone calls him Mr Basil," Chloe broke in, smiling. "He's seen to your needs, I hope."

"I was going to say, ma'am, as he's done me proud. I can't tell you how grateful I am, ma'am, especially as you've taken his lordship under care. He'll be thankful for it when he comes to himself — if he does."

"Well, of course he will. We must give him time."

With which, she dismissed the man and went back into the spare bedchamber. Lord Pettipher was lying with his eyes open, staring at the tester above him.

Chloe went to the dresser now operating as a table for the invalid's needs and poured barley water from the jug. She brought the glass to the bed and sat on the edge. "How is your head?"

His gaze turned on her, registering puzzlement. "This is not my bed."

"No, indeed. You are a guest in my house, sir."

"How very odd." His voice was stronger and he sounded a trifle indignant.

Chloe smiled and held the glass to his lips. "Drink, if you please."

He sipped obediently, but the frown persisted, his gaze travelling from Chloe to the landscape on the wall, the press near the window, and ending at the mantel where a cheerful fire burned. "Winter, that's it."

"Yes, indeed, and a very bad one too. We've had snow for several days now. A little more, sir." She urged the glass upon him, but he pushed it away.

"Talk to me."

The imperious tone both amused and irritated. Chloe raised her brows. "What would you wish me to talk about?"

A sudden smile lit his wan features. "Anything. I just want to look at you."

A feather brushed across her heart. Was this because he took her for his lost love? She was tempted to quash the mistake, but dared not interfere with the process of remembering. If she told him this Clarissa of his was long dead, would he become distraught? Doctor Goodleigh had instructed it was imperative he remain quiet. She sought for an innocuous subject.

"I'll tell you about the carnival in Italy, if you wish."

He did not answer, continuing to regard her in an unnervingly steady fashion.

Chloe rose from the bed and set down the glass.

"Come back."

"Very well."

She sat down again and he groped for her hand. She allowed him to find it and felt heat in his fingers. Was he feverish? Concerned, she reached to touch her free hand to his forehead and found it warm, but not overly so.

Relieved, she sat upright again and found him still watching her, but his lids were beginning to droop. She kept silent, waiting until his eyes closed and his fingers slackened on hers and she was able to withdraw them.

The door opened and she looked round. Agatha's bespectacled face appeared in the aperture. Chloe put her finger to her lips and rose with caution, checking to see that her patient did not wake before gliding to the door with soft steps. She did not speak until she had joined Miss Flook in the corridor. Her companion looked anxious.

"You look tired, my dear Mrs Quilter. But I've come to relieve you as agreed. Is he any better?"

"In body, yes, but not in mind." She had necessarily shared her fears with Miss Flook, although she'd passed lightly over the Clarissa business. That, however, was becoming a trifle difficult. "He may object to my absence if he wakes. You must tell him I've gone to consume a luncheon."

"Which will be perfectly true. Mrs Vaughan has prepared a sustaining broth and you must go down directly."

"Thank you, I will. Have you eaten?"

"I took a bowl before I came up. But go down, my dear Mrs Quilter, before it grows cold."

With which, she opened the door and tripped into the bedchamber, closing it behind her. Chloe found herself reluctant to leave Lord Pettipher in any hands but her own, but that was perfectly nonsensical. And she must eat. Indeed, she was excessively hungry and the thought of the warming soup made her turn her steps for the stairs.

The doctor listened to Chloe's account with a frown and pursed lips. She held nothing back, except the kiss, though she told him Lord Pettipher had taken her for Clarissa at the outset.

"He slept through the afternoon, but he knew nothing more when he woke. Which is why I've waylaid you before you go in to him. Is there anything we can do?"

Doctor Goodleigh shook his head. "I doubt it, if he did not even recognise his own groom. We must allow nature to take its course."

"Yes, but what if he does not regain his memory?"

"It is likely he will do so, in fits and starts at first, I suspect." Doctor Goodleigh regarded Chloe over the top of his pince-nez, his face serious in the candlelight. "Have you denied to him that you are this Clarissa?"

"No, for I feared it might upset him. I told him once that my name was Chloe, but that was right at the start when I rushed to help after the accident."

"And you say he objects to being addressed as 'my lord'."

"He does not precisely object, but he mentions it, as if he cannot understand why we use the term. I've stopped doing so, by the way."

"Very wise. Yes, you would do better to allow him to come to terms with the situation in his own time. Do not argue with him, but on the other hand, I suggest you adopt a little distance. Your presence may hold him in the past."

Chloe was surprised to feel dismay at the notion of withholding herself from his lordship. It was odd, for though he was a stranger to her, his assumption of her identity as Clarissa had induced a sense of intimacy. Ridiculous. She hardly knew him, and he most certainly did not know her. At least, not for who she truly was.

"If you think it may be beneficial, doctor, I shall of course take your advice."

He gave a prim smile. "I dare say the imposition is a burden upon your household. You might employ a nurse, perhaps, to alleviate it?"

"Mrs Prettejohn, you mean?" Chloe knew the dislike was in her voice.

"She is a competent nurse."

She was well aware the doctor had no other woman in the village to call upon for such services. But Chloe had seen Mrs Prettejohn at work when she attended old Mrs Trott, and had been unimpressed. "She may be competent, doctor, but she is very rough and ready." She did not add that the woman's breath smelled of alcohol. "I'll not subject Lord Pettipher to her ministrations, I thank you. We will manage."

"As you wish. Now, perhaps I had best visit my patient?"

Agatha was on duty by the bed when Chloe led the doctor into the spare bedchamber. She came towards them at once, a wagging finger by her lips, her voice a whisper. "He is restless. I have not been able to quiet him."

A riffle of alarm within her, Chloe went immediately to the bedside, where the bedclothes were in motion as Lord Pettipher's limbs shifted beneath them. His arms were on top of the quilt, plucking at its folds and though his eyes were closed, his head jerked, a low mutter issuing from his lips. Chloe listened, but the words were incomprehensible.

"Let me come there, Mrs Quilter."

Chloe gave way to allow the doctor access, but remained close enough to watch, unable to wholly relinquish her patient into his charge. *Her* patient? She brushed the thought away and concentrated on Doctor Goodleigh's fingers, which were about his lordship's wrist. He laid it down after a moment.

"His pulse is tumultuous."

Well, she could see that for herself! It must be, since he was thrashing about in such a fashion. Chloe strove for calm. "Is he feverish, do you suppose?"

The doctor was checking the patient's forehead and cheeks. He lifted the quilt and felt the chest beneath the nightgown. "There is no sign of heat, though he is sweating a little. And his pallor does not indicate fever. No, I'm afraid the trouble may be in his brain."

Chloe's alarm intensified. "What does that mean, if you please?"

A grave look came into the doctor's face. "The wound may have bled into the brain, causing unseen stress. In which case, Mrs Quilter, I fear there is little I can do for him."

"But if it isn't so? Is there no other reason he could be like this?"

Doctor Goodleigh pursed his lips. "Pain can induce nightmares, of course. And anxiety is to be expected with concussion. But he has not woken with being touched, which leads me to believe he is deeply unconscious."

Panic coursed through Chloe. She fought it. "Then let me try and wake him. He responds to my voice."

He put out a hand to prevent her getting to the bed. "That would be most unwise, Mrs Quilter."

"Why?"

"Waking too suddenly may shock him. You may try talking gently to him and see if he quietens to your voice. But by no means attempt to shake him into wakefulness or shout or anything of that nature."

"I would not do that in any event." Even as she spoke she knew her panic would have tempted her to take just such foolish measures.

"I will leave you a draught which should calm him. You may administer it at once when he wakes — if he wakes."

The rider sent a flutter of fury into Chloe's breast. He would wake! She would see to that. She kept her tone even. "Thank you, doctor. Under the circumstances, I will continue to nurse him myself."

Doctor Goodleigh was rummaging in his bag, which he had left on the dresser. He glanced up, peering at her over his spectacles. "You are thinking of my advice to you concerning this Clarissa business. Indeed, it might be kinder to allow him his delusion in this extremity."

Chloe could not let this pass. "I am determined it will not prove to be an extremity, doctor."

A smile came and his gaze softened. "That does not surprise me. I am well acquainted with your crusading spirit, dear lady."

Chloe's ruffled feathers smoothed a little, and she returned the smile. "Well, Mrs Trott is doing a great deal better, as I am sure you must know. And Little Tibby got you here in excellent time, did she not?"

"She did, though I was surprised you sent her out in these conditions."

"My dear sir, the whole essence of my strategy is to treat her as if she had no disability. And she managed very well."

He handed her a vial and closed his case. "Two drops in a little water. You may repeat the dose at four hour intervals, and we must hope it will answer. Send to me if he worsens, otherwise I will return in the morning."

Chloe thanked him and signalled to Agatha, who had remained in the room at a distance. She never interfered in the presence of others, reserving her opinion for her employer's private ear, a practice Chloe regarded with mixed feelings.

"Miss Flook will see you out, doctor."

He took her proffered hand and gave her a measured look over his pince-nez. "I brought that girl into the world, you know. Her father despaired of her, but Tibby's mother regards you in the light of an angel."

Chloe had to laugh. "I am certainly not that."

"Yes, you are."

The voice came from the bed. Chloe turned sharp about and hurried to Lord Pettipher's side, the doctor on her heels. Her patient's eyes were still closed and his aspect did not appear to have changed, though Chloe thought he was shifting less.

The doctor's voice, dropped to a murmur, reached her. "Perhaps he is not as deeply unconscious as I supposed. A hopeful sign."

She matched his tone. "Do you think so indeed?"

"Only time will tell, but it is a blessing he responds to your voice." He nodded. "I must go."

She hardly noticed him leave, her attention on Lord Pettipher. She sat on the bed and reached for one of his hands. Wholly forgetful of the doctor's instructions, she caught it up and held it fast. "Don't you die on me, Lancelot Ravensthorp, do you hear?"

The thrashing ceased at once. He did not wake, but his fingers curled into hers and a murmur reached her. "Clarissa."

He was crawling across the ice. He would have run, but the voices of caution penetrated the horror in his heart.

"You'll go down too, Lance, don't be a fool!"

"They are fetching ladders. Wait!"

How could he wait? He had to get to her before it was too late. He dropped to his knees and flung himself forward.

"Careful! It's cracking, Lance!"

Too late! It had cracked already, swallowing his love into the depths. He pulled himself along on his elbows, digging the toes of the skates in for purchase. He was going as fast as he could, but the blackness ahead was as far away as ever. It seemed to withdraw before him, taking her further and further from him.

The shouts receded into the distance. He could hear his own rasping breath, see it in steaming clouds before his face. He pulled himself along more swiftly, dread heavy in his mind and chest, taking his strength.

He could see the opening. Beneath him the ice shivered, a crazy line of cracks appearing. Panic froze him for a space and the shouts and calling impinged.

"Don't move, Lance!"

"They are coming along the bank! They have the ladders!"

The shadow in the ice caught his questing eyes. Danger drifted into the mist of things unregarded. He resumed his crawling progress, drawn by the mesmerising shadow.

Vague in the background of his mind, he heard them calling. Nothing could reach him now … as he stared through the ice at the angel face beneath … wide blue eyes, golden hair streaming, in death as beautiful as the first moment he'd seen her…

"Don't you die on me, Lancelot Ravensthorp!"

Confusion wreathed his brain. Alive? The ice vision faded. He remembered he was in his bed and she was nursing him. He curled his fingers into the hands holding his. He wanted to ask how she had escaped, but tiredness claimed him. He spoke her name and his mind drifted.

When he woke again, it was dark and he was alone. He saw shadows of furniture in the flickering light from a fire. Why he was sleeping with his curtains open was a mystery. Finch was scrupulous when he put him to bed. Then it dawned on him that this was not his bed. His gaze flicked around the shadows. It was not his room. Where in the devil's name was he? Some inn somewhere? And who the deuce was the old woman sleeping in the chair by the door? A guttering candle on the little table at her elbow enabled him to judge her elderly, but she was a complete stranger to him.

His eye caught a jug on the dresser. Was that a glass beside it? Lord, but he was thirsty!

He struggled onto his elbow. Why was he so weak? He put a hand to his aching head, regretting the brandy. Had he lost control and drunk too much again? All too possible, for he'd been at Wintringham with Vince. No, that didn't fit. Fellow was sober as a judge these days, besotted with his Lily. Nice girl too, the lucky dog.

He became aware his fingers were feeling other than his skin
and hair. A bandage? What the deuce? Dear Lord above, was
he injured?

His throat was dry. Must get to that jug. He thrust off the
covers and swung his legs to the floor. Dizziness hit him and
he had to grasp the mattress either side, dropping his head. He
heard movement and a twittering voice.

"Oh, dear me! No, no, my lord! You must not get up!"

He forced his head up and looked into a shadowed anxious
face. "I'm thirsty. Wanted to get at that jug."

"Yes, yes, I will fetch it to you, but get back into bed at once,
if you please."

He found himself obeying, though a protest rose up. "God's
teeth, woman, do you take me for an infant?"

But the elderly dame was at the dresser, pouring from the jug
into the glass. She brought it across to him where he was now
sitting up in the bed, and he saw her hand was shaking.

Amusement rippled through him as he took the glass. "Beg
pardon, ma'am. I didn't mean to swear at you."

"Oh, it makes no matter. Drink up, do."

He put the glass to his lips and drank deeply. An innocuous
concoction that tasted of God knew what. "What is this?"

"Barley water. You may have as much as you wish."

He held out the glass for a refill. Not that he wished to drink
the stuff, but he still felt parched. Barley water indeed!
"Anyone would take me for an invalid."

The creature had the jug ready and had begun to pour,
holding the glass steady. Was it his hand shaking, then?

"Well, indeed you are an invalid, sir, just at the moment."

"Good God, am I?"

"Yes."

She said no more and he drank again, more interested in quenching his thirst than the curious notion she'd raised. He handed her the empty glass.

"Who are you? I don't mean to be rude, but…"

She held up the jug. "Have you had enough?"

"Thank you, yes."

"Then it will be best if you lie down again."

Rebellion revived. "I don't want to."

She looked nonplussed, as far as he could see in the dim light. Then she set down the jug. "Let me bank your pillows at least. I cannot think it right for you to be holding yourself up in this way." She busied herself in plumping up and adding to the pillows behind him. "There, sir. That should be more comfortable."

As indeed it proved. He rested against them with a sigh of relief, only now recognising the effort it had cost him to hold himself upright. "I'm as weak as a cat," he complained.

"That is to be expected, sir."

Puzzlement wreathed his mind. "Why am I here? And you did not tell me who you are."

"I am Agatha Flook, but that will mean nothing to you."

"Yes, but I don't understand. I don't know you, nor this place. I don't know what I'm doing here."

"Mrs Quilter had you brought here after it happened."

He eyed her, a dull sensation sifting into his brain. He had no recollection of sustaining an injury. "After what happened?"

"Oh, dear, I don't think… I'd best fetch Mrs Quilter, my lord."

More puzzling still. An odd way to address him. He watched her hurry away, slipping out of the door like a wraith. His mind grew hazy. He was lying in the ice. No, the snow. No, it was a bed, was it not?

But he could no longer see the room, its shadows creeping into his mind like a blanketing mist where flickers of images came and went.

Presently he heard whispering.

"Are you sure he was back to himself?"

"Well, he was unlike he has been, my dear Chloe. He seemed to know he was in a strange place. But when he asked about the accident…"

"Hush! Doctor Goodleigh said we must allow him to recall it all in his own time."

He knew that voice. "Clarissa?"

The whispers ceased.

She glided towards him. The candle in her hand showed him her golden hair tumbling about her shoulders, a frothy wrapper concealing her curves. A thing he might have expected her to wear on the wedding night that never happened. A miracle?

She sat on the bed, her smile as warm as he remembered. "You look a degree better."

That voice of honey. How could he forget? It belonged to a woman, not the girl he'd lost. The last high-pitched squeal of laughter that lay coiled in the deeps of his heart. His mischievous Clarissa, disobedient to the last.

"Do you age in heaven, then?"

Her pale brows drew together, the eyes beneath registering concern. "Heaven?"

He put out his hand and let his fingers caress a limb beneath the silky fabric of her dressing-gown. "You feel real, but you can't be. A trick of the mind, perhaps."

She did not answer. He watched her turn her head towards the hovering old woman. He'd forgotten her name.

"Go to bed, Agatha. I'll sit up with him."

"But your time does not begin for another hour yet."

"I won't sleep now. Better if one of us is rested tomorrow."

The woman Agatha nodded and he watched her leave, an unwelcome thought surfacing.

"If you were alive, she'd have to stay. Propriety and all that." He glinted at her, expecting the roguish twinkle. It did not come.

"I am very much alive, as you see." She sounded perfectly serious and she was not smiling.

"It can't be, my lovely one. How did you escape from the ice?"

She set the candle down on the bedside table and he could no longer see her face as clearly. A sigh came. "I was never in the ice, sir."

Had he dreamed it, then? No! He remembered it all. The thunderous crack. The stark horror as the ice opened. The speed of her vanishment. There one moment. Gone in an instant.

"It did happen, Clarissa! I tried to get to you. I found you. Too late, my love, too late!" He caught her fingers as his vision blurred.

Her voice came then, soft and soothing, honey sweet. "Never mind, it is over now. Rest … rest and all will be well."

The murmurs were meaningless, without power to assuage the rage of grief rising to choke him. He turned on his side, away from her, unwilling to look upon the dream, the angel presence calling to his heart.

Lance! Lance, watch me! See, I can spin like a top!

Clarissa, no! Be careful! Stop! Come back, you little fool!

But she was spinning away, spinning and spinning, whirling across the ice, unheeding when he called to warn of the weak spot just there…

Blackness invaded his mind and the images dispersed into roaming figures. He could hear the horses whinnying, felt again the disorientation of the fall, helpless in the air … like Clarissa, spinning, spinning … and then he was overtaken by the black emptiness of night.

CHAPTER THREE

"How did she die?"

The groom sidled in discomfort. He'd regarded Chloe warily as he came into the room. Did he fear her questions? Or was he too disconcerted by the evident resemblance to the dead girl? Chloe stood up, moving out from behind the desk to confront him, dropping her tone to a plea.

"Rowley, I am at a loss. The doctor expressly advised me not to dismiss his lordship's notion that I am his betrothed. But when he begins to think I am a wraith of some kind, it is beyond a joke, my friend."

She regretted the curtness that crept in, but she could not deny it was galling to be held in this invidious position. She could not address the error as she wished, telling Lord Pettipher that she was not this Clarissa. In lieu of that, at least she ought better to understand the circumstances.

The groom looked decidedly unwilling to pursue the matter. Chloe pushed. "As far as I can ascertain, it was a skating accident, yes?"

Rowley nodded. A sigh escaped him and he capitulated. "See, she were doing a twirl, and the master says she didn't realise as she was skating where the ice were thin. She went through, ma'am. I saw it. We all did. There were an almighty crack and she just dropped through the ice. Disappeared, just like that."

"God in heaven!" Chloe felt the icy shock that must have attacked all those present. "Did they find her?"

"Master did. She'd drowned, but her body rose up and he could see her through the ice."

Creeping horror assailed Chloe's breast. How in the world was a man to get over such a tragedy?

The groom, having begun, seemed ready to spill the whole story, though now she was less eager to hear. "We got her out at last, though it were a trial to do it. She were frozen like a board. The doctor said as she likely were dead of cold before she could drown. My master too. He'd crawled across the ice and his fingers were like to break with frostbite. We'd to get him to bed. They warmed him with blankets and hot bricks, but he were raving, crying as he'd to get to her before she drowned. It were a day or more 'til he understood she'd gone."

"When was this, Rowley? When did she die?"

He dabbed at wet eyes, the memory clearly almost as painful to him as to his lordship himself. "It's near ten years gone. She were just eighteen, and his lordship were only a year older. He's nine and twenty now, and I was dang sure he were over it."

Chloe felt battered. "But he never married?"

Rowley shrugged. "Keeps saying as he must and will, for he owes it to the line. Her ladyship were on to him all the time, and he paid no heed. But when she went, he started saying as she were right and he ought to knuckle to it. To my knowledge, he ain't shown no interest in no female since it happened." He flushed. "Not in the way of marriage, I mean, ma'am. And there's many a cap been set at him, I can tell you."

"So I should imagine. He must be eligible indeed." She noted how the revelation had left the groom despondent and did her best to cheer him. "Don't despair, Rowley. There is progress. Miss Flook says he woke quite as himself and his questions were pertinent. I am given to hope his memory is coming back. But we must give him time."

Rowley nodded. "We're causing you a deal of trouble one way and another, ma'am."

"You need not regard it. I could not do other than what I have done." She turned the subject. "It looks to be thawing a little, don't you think? Would it be possible soon to send to his lordship's home?"

"They won't think nothing beyond his lordship has had to take shelter in an inn somewhere, ma'am. There ain't no one waiting on him, excepting his old aunt as I mentioned, and she'll only trouble herself about him when it comes to Christmas."

Chloe would have liked to ask more about the earl's background, but she'd been away from Lord Pettipher's bedside for long enough. "I must go and see how he does. Thank you, Rowley."

The groom touched his forelock and left the room. Chloe did not follow him immediately, instead moving to the window and looking out across the lawns behind the house. White still largely covered them, but here and there a smattering of grass was showing and the naked branches were beginning to appear in the trees.

She had not been out for the previous two days, her attention wholly on caring for her patient. She felt decidedly restless, hankering after her usual pursuits. She'd told Rowley she was content with the situation, but the truth was she felt as if her peace had been invaded. In more than one aspect.

Her thoughts were interrupted by the opening of the door and her butler appeared in the aperture. He regarded her from the doorway for a moment, and then shut the door and moved into the room.

"Blue-devilled, eh? Just as I suspected, Miss Chloe."

A warm glow chased away the sombre mood. He still called her that in private, the pose of correct butler dropping away, revealing the old friend who'd been more father to her than her own. She drew in a breath and sighed it out.

"Oh, Basil, I don't know. I've no reason to be."

"Yes, you have, when the place is turned upside down to accommodate this here lord and you're spending your days in a sickroom. Enough to send anyone into the hips."

"It isn't that."

She turned back to the window, seeing in her mind's eye the carriage overturn and his lordship's body flying into the air, and then the startling green eyes when they opened and began this horrible farce. *Clarissa, Clarissa.* She wished she'd never heard the name.

"If you must have it, I am finding it galling to be mistaken for this dead creature."

Basil came to join her at the window, setting an avuncular arm about her shoulders. "He'll come to his senses again and realise you're someone else entirely."

"Yes, but when? And Doctor Goodleigh has made it clear I must not disabuse him, though I feel like yelling at him that I'm Chloe, not Clarissa."

Basil squeezed her arm and released her. "You won't do that. Not in your nature to be unkind, else you'd have had a thing or two to throw at those stepchildren of yours years back."

Chloe laughed. "Stepchildren! When Matilda is ten years my senior and Bernard is over forty. It's ridiculous."

"Won't be so ridiculous if that witch gets wind of a lord biding in the house."

"Don't! Agatha said as much in the first place, and of course she's right, but what could I do?"

The butler grinned at her. "Just what I'd have expected of you, Miss Chloe. Kitten, lord or Little Tibby, it's all one."

Chloe smiled but reminded of her self-imposed duty, threw off her megrims. "Speaking of lords, I'd best get back to him, if Jack has finished with his ablutions."

"He came down a few minutes ago."

"Good. Has Mrs Vaughan made the broth?"

"She has. I'll send Jack up with a tray."

Chloe thanked him and hurried out of the study and up the stairs. She had not tried Lord Pettipher with food, but Doctor Goodleigh had sanctioned a sustaining broth when he visited earlier in the morning.

The patient was awake, sitting up against his banked pillows and looking fresher than he'd done when the doctor visited.

Chloe smiled at him. "Are you hungry?"

He was regarding her with a look of puzzlement. "Are you the landlady?"

Taken aback, Chloe knew not what to say for a moment. Did this mean he no longer took her for Clarissa? She did not dare ask. "No indeed, for this is a private house."

A frown creased his brow. Without the bandage, which the doctor had said he no longer needed, and with his hair combed, he looked different. Chloe found it disconcerting.

"That fellow who came to shave and wash me…"

"Jack, yes. He's my footman."

"Not a valet, then?"

"I'm afraid there isn't one on the premises."

His gaze drifted away from Chloe and wandered about the room. Had he forgotten his mistaking her identity? She did not know what to make of his present mood. She opted for her role as nurse.

"How is your head?"

His eyes came back to her. "Better, thank you."

Come, this was a much more normal mien. Was it possible he was indeed coming to himself?

"I hope you are hungry. Jack is bringing up a bowl of broth."

"Thank you."

He fell silent and Chloe found the change unnerving. She did not know what to make of it and felt disoriented. Only last night, she'd been Clarissa to him. Now it appeared he regarded her as he might a stranger.

He had been acquiescent during the doctor's visit, only responding with a wince when his wound was probed. He'd looked gaunt then, paler than he was now, though his cheeks were still a trifle sunken and there were dark smudges under his eyes.

A knock at the door brought Jack with the tray, and Chloe was relieved to have something to do. "Set it down on the dresser, Jack, and then help me to arrange things so that it is comfortable for the gentleman."

She was aware Lord Pettipher watched her as she directed the footman to set another pillow behind him and a cushion on his knees to steady the tray. When it was set in place and a napkin laid to catch drips, however, it became obvious his lordship could not manage to feed himself.

He stared at the bowl and a wavering hand picked up the spoon, digging it into the soup in a rough manner that caused it to splash over the edge. He let go of the spoon and looked up at Chloe. "I'm not very handy, ma'am."

She smiled. "Then I will help you."

Nodding dismissal to Jack, she took up the spoon, careful to fill it with a small quantity of the thin broth, and presented it at his lordship's mouth.

"Open, if you please."

The green eyes twinkled, but he did as she asked and swallowed the broth. Chloe was conscious of a flutter at her bosom as she continued to feed him. The twinkling look was all too attractive. She was relieved when his hunger quickened and his concentration focused more on taking the brew than the fact he was being fed like an infant.

That was all she needed. To be drawn to a man who took her for his tragic and long lost love.

He had finished nearly all the soup when at last he pushed her hand away as she presented the spoon. "Enough, thank you. I was hungrier than I knew, but that is enough."

Chloe set down the spoon and handed him the napkin. He wiped his mouth and gave it back. She got up and removed the tray, setting it upon the dresser.

"I suppose I may not have a glass of wine?"

Chloe laughed as she turned. "You suppose correctly, sir. But if you are tired of barley water, you may have tea, if you wish."

"Coffee?"

The plea in his voice was hard to withstand. Likewise the boyish look of mischief, as if he sought to cajole her.

"I dare say coffee will do you no harm, though I think you would find tea more refreshing."

He grimaced. "I hate the stuff."

"In that case, I suppose I must let you have your way."

She crossed to the bell and pulled the cord. His eyes followed her and she became conscious again. Not knowing if he still thought of her as Clarissa was more disturbing, she realised, than knowing he did. She took comfort from the hope his attitude betokened he was much more himself — if she knew what that was.

She forced a smile as she returned to the bed, but he did not return it.

"And now you will go away and send the old one back to sit with me. What's her name, Flook?"

"Miss Flook, my companion."

"Do you need one?"

"I'm a widow, sir. It wouldn't be seemly to live without one." Realising she'd said more than she should, given the doctor's instructions, she added, "And I am remaining with you for the moment."

He gave a small sigh. "I'm so glad."

His eyes drooped. Chloe went to the head of the bed and removed a couple of the pillows. "There. You may lie a little more comfortably, sir, and sleep if you feel so inclined."

He settled back, but his tone became peevish. "I wish you will call me Lance."

Startled, Chloe eyed him. He knew his own name? How much more did he know? She could hardly ask. Or might she get at it indirectly?

"How did you come to be named after a knight of Camelot?"

He frowned. "Am I?"

"Lancelot?"

"Ah, I see what you mean." The twinkle appeared. "I have no notion. A conceit of my mother's, perhaps?"

"Had she read Sir Thomas Malory's *Le Morte d'Arthur* then?"

He shrugged. "Beats me, ma'am. I don't remember."

It was the first time he'd spoken outright of his lack of memory. Did he know then that it was affected? Chloe dared not ask. That he called her ma'am indicated he did not at present think of her as Clarissa. Relief swept through her.

She went to fetch the chair placed against the wall near the door. She set it down by the bed and sat, once more aware of the watching eyes. "I could read to you, if you wish?"

"No need. I'm content to look at you."

Warmth crept into her face and she cursed in her head. Then he had not abandoned this ridiculous notion of her being the wretched Clarissa female.

As if he read some of her thought, he gave her a smile that was all too charming. "You're beautiful, didn't you know?"

She lifted a hand to her cheek, sure she was flushing. "You are embarrassing me horribly, Lance."

He laughed. "Why? Don't you enjoy compliments?"

"Well, yes, but…" She could scarcely put into words her reasons for wishing him to remain silent upon the point.

"I won't say it, if you don't wish to hear it, but it won't stop me thinking it."

Worse and worse. She strove to find an innocuous subject to introduce. Difficult, when anything she said or asked might endanger his recovery. To her relief, a knock at the door brought Jemima in answer to the bell.

"Will you ask Mrs Vaughan for a pot of coffee for our guest, if you please, Jemima. And two cups." She might as well take some herself. "Do you take cream and sugar, sir?"

His brows rose. "I don't know. Do I?"

Oh, stupid! She must be more careful. "It makes no matter. Bring both, Jemima."

"Yes, mistress."

"And take this tray with you, if you please, dear."

The maid picked up the tray and hurried off and Lance gave her an odd look.

"Mistress?"

She laughed. "It's what they all call me. Except for Basil, of course."

"Who is Basil?"

"My butler. But indeed he is more a friend." She caught herself up. "But I must not run on. You seem to be doing a deal better. Has your headache gone?"

He frowned. "You're fobbing me off."

"I don't mean to. But your welfare is my concern."

"Is it? I'm glad of that."

How in the world was she to respond to such a remark? Really, this was becoming excessively difficult. She was tempted to send to Doctor Goodleigh, but it could scarcely be termed an emergency. And he would be back tonight. She determined to beard him and ask how she should deal with this new manifestation.

Lance's eyelids were drooping. She kept silent therefore and watched him slip into a light slumber. The opening of the door and the rattle of a tray woke him a while later when the coffee arrived. Chloe did not know whether to be glad or sorry that he was once more conscious and able to disconcert her at will.

The worry of where he was receded while she was with him. He gathered he had sustained some sort of accident, but his head no longer ached and when he was not plagued by hazy dreams, he felt lazily inclined to drift with events.

She was pouring coffee. Every motion she made gave him pleasure. The delicacy of her fingers, the sway of her hips, the ripple and flow of her arms, of her whole body were mesmerising. And yet when she sat motionless, her beauty shone like an image drawn by a master.

"Shall we try you with cream and sugar?"

There was that sweet smile, like an angel. Her words penetrated.

"Whatever you wish."

He would take vitriol if it was given by her hand. He watched the deft movements as she poured a little cream into the cup and dropped in a cube of sugar and stirred with a gentle motion of the spoon. That was her charm, Lance thought. Her gentleness showed in everything she did. That and a sensual grace which contributed to her allure.

She came to the bed, holding out the cup. "I will spare you a saucer to manage as well."

"You think of everything." He took the cup and brought it to his lips. The hot sweetness was soothing and he drew several sips. "This is highly satisfying."

A gleam of humour came into her eyes. "You are easily pleased. I think I said before what a good patient you are."

"What then should I say of my nurse?"

She wafted a hand and returned to the coffee pot. "That is quite another matter and we need not address it at this moment."

He did not pursue it. She had shown already how she balked at compliments. Because she was a widow? She had said as much. She sat down in the chair again, armed with her own cup and saucer. He was drinking again himself, but over the rim of his cup he watched her sip. After, her tongue slid over her lip and response echoed in his loins. Beautiful, desirable and as sweet as an angel. What more could a fellow wish for?

"Will you marry me?"

She choked. Lance could not but smile at the startled look in her eyes as she sought his. He was sorry for her sputtering and coughing, however.

"I do beg your pardon. That was a silly thing to do."

"And a very silly thing to say!" Indignation sounded under the husky note, presumably engendered by her coughing.

"Why is it silly?"

"You don't know me, nor I you!"

"Marriage will remedy that."

"Don't be absurd!" She rose and set down her coffee on the tray. "This is delirium of a high order, Lance. You are not thinking straight."

He remained unperturbed. "I was never more earnest."

"Then I must beg you not to continue in a proposition I could not consider."

"Why could you not consider it?"

She stared at him speechlessly. He waited, enjoying the fluctuations of colour in her cheeks, the changing expressions in her fine eyes as she thought of and discarded a number of reasons. He supposed that was what she must be doing.

At length she visibly pulled herself together. "Enough of this, if you please."

He began to feel rueful. "I've put you out of countenance. Forgive me."

"Yes, you have indeed! I set it down to your condition, so I suppose I must forgive you."

He said no more. Was it because of his condition? Whatever his condition was. He knew he was not entirely in his right mind. His name he knew, but little else. It did not seem to matter very much while she was by.

"Please sit down and drink your coffee in peace. I promise I won't disturb you again."

In proof of this, he addressed himself to his own drink and sipped, taking his eyes off her for the moment. In the periphery of his vision, he saw her hesitate and then fastidiously clean the saucer before pouring a little more of the brew from the pot into her cup. She looked round at him, the pot poised.

"A little more, sir?"

He smiled, glad to be free to look at her again. "If you please."

She took his cup and refilled it. He could watch her fingers at work forever. He wanted to stay here and do nothing but observe her doing whatever she must do for as long as he might.

He took the coffee with a word of thanks and indeed it was good on his tongue. To his joy, she sat down, her air of careful restraint a source of amusement.

"This is very cosy."

The smile at last. "I'm glad of that."

For a while she sipped in silence and Lance refrained from saying any of the things that came into his head. Things to which she was sure to object since they solely concerned her attributes and his ardent desire to remain in her company for the rest of his life.

Perhaps she was right, and it was a product of his illness, if such it was. He felt as if his life began anew, for he had no notion what had gone before. Without thinking, he voiced the thought.

"You do realise I have no recollection of anything before my sojourn in this place?"

A faint grimace passed across her face. Concern? "Is it so indeed?"

He smiled. "You are the beginning of my life."

She eyed him with a look of doubt, though the colour crept into her cheeks again. Then she leaned a little forward and the gentle note was back. "It will come back to you, Lance."

"Can you help me at all?"

"The doctor advised against it. He believes it is better for you to recover it at your leisure."

Hope lifted. "Then do I remain here until it comes back to me?"

Was that discomfort as she shifted in the chair?

"You are welcome for as long as you need."

Then let that be for life. But he did not say it. She would balk. And the last thing he wished was to unnerve her again. An unwelcome thought occurred. "I suppose it is possible I have responsibilities elsewhere? A wife even?" She looked hesitant. She was going to evade the issue. "Is that why you rejected my offer?"

"No, indeed."

His heart soared. "Then I am unmarried!"

"I did not say so." Again she dithered. He waited, anxiety creeping in. "Your groom is here. He was with you when…"

"Don't stop now! When —?"

"When you had the accident. You are aware you had an accident?"

"I supposed it must be something of the sort. What kind of accident?"

Again, the hesitation. He began to feel frustrated. Why had he embarked upon this? He was feeling perfectly comfortable and happy in his ignorance, and now…

"I think that may be one of the things I should not tell you," she said at last, disappointing him. She smiled, and there was a little of apology in it. "Shall we wait for the doctor's next visit? We will ask him what it is safe to reveal."

He agreed to it, but the prospect of dropping back into the cloud he'd inhabited failed to quiet the little demon that had risen inside. He let it go for the moment, sinking back against his cushions, watching the tendrils of blonde curl that escaped from her hair confined under a neat cap. He wished she would not wear it.

"When we are married, you can leave off that thing and wear your hair loose."

Consternation appeared in her eyes, but she remained steady this time.

He had not meant to say it. Rueful, he reached out towards her. "I'm sorry. I seem to have little control over what I should or should not say."

She appeared to accept this, for she said nothing. He was encouraged that she did not look away. Yet instead, the odd expression of puzzlement did not please him.

"What troubles you?"

Her brow cleared. "Why should you think anything troubles me?"

If he spoke his mind he would say he was beginning to know every change of expression, every curve of her cheek or lip. Indeed, he felt as if he had always known, her features were so very familiar to him. "I feel it," he said instead.

She set her cup down in the saucer. "I was wondering if that is a symptom of your condition."

He frowned. "You speak of my condition as if it is something you understand, but you will not explain."

She brushed a hand in the air as if to waft this away. "I mean only the fact that you have lost your memory through injury. I cannot think of a more suitable word, for you are not ill as such."

He finished his coffee and she immediately took the cup from him, rose and set it down along with her own. He had a horrid premonition that his boldness would make her find an excuse to leave and sought for a way to make her stay. "If you cannot tell me of my own affairs, can you speak of your own?"

She turned her head at that, a frown in her eyes. "In what respect?"

He smiled. "Well, your name would help a great deal."

She hesitated, biting her lip, eyeing him in an odd way he could not interpret. At last she appeared to make up her mind. "I am Mrs Quilter."

Her tone was repressive, and the formality chilled him. "Should I not have asked?"

She seemed altogether conscious, breathless even, if he was any judge. Her bosom shifted with her breath. "No … of course — it makes no matter." She smiled, but with an effort, as it seemed to him. "Lance, will you excuse me for a space? I will send Agatha in to you. Household chores demand my attendance."

She was going. He had blundered. He knew not how to stay her, unless he begged her never to leave him. But that would cause her to withdraw the more.

"You'll come back again?"

"Of course."

The smile looked more natural. He watched her pick up the tray and cross to the door. He made to get up. "Here, let me open it for you."

She turned, seemingly horrified to see him half out of the bed. "Good heavens, stay where you are, Lance! You are too weak to get up." She came a step or two back towards the bed.

Prudence gave him pause, and then a rise of dizziness made it imperative to lift the leg he'd set to the floor and lie back again.

Mrs Quilter was setting down the tray again. She came back to him and fussed with the bedclothes, smoothing them over his legs. "That was silly indeed," she scolded, as if to a child.

He could not prevent a grin creeping into his face, though he felt a trifle sheepish. "Did I give you a fright?"

"Yes, you did, you wretch! I wish you will behave!"

"Well, I will, for you were entirely right. I felt dizzy at once."

"You've been on your back for nearly three days and you've eaten very little, besides having a knock on the head. What else do you expect?"

He rejoiced at the easy way she talked to him again and resolved to refrain from causing her to retire behind that formal front he so much disliked. There seemed little he could say, though, without touching on matters she did not care to hear him speak about.

She straightened, the bedclothes evidently tidied to her satisfaction, and gave him a look of severity. "I will open the door myself first, so you may be easy."

Saying which, she crossed to the door and did as much, returning for the tray. He watched her leave the room, afraid to open his mouth in case he said something to wound or annoy her. She likewise did not speak, and she left the door open.

He could hear her steps retreat along a corridor and then descend some stairs. For the first time, he wondered about the accoutrements of the house beyond the walls of his room. He wished to know them, since she walked freely among them. And so would he, unless the gulf in his mind refilled with those escaped memories.

A sensation of isolation overcame him as that peace he'd cherished proved fragile.

CHAPTER FOUR

It was some time before Chloe could calm the disordered state of her mind. Never had she been so much in need of an excuse to escape. She took refuge in the book-room once she had disposed of the tray and sent Agatha to relieve her at the patient's side — with a warning not to satisfy him should he ask awkward questions, and on no account to give him her Christian name.

The latter sprang from instinct. His proposal could not possibly be meant for her, not as herself. The confusion of his inner mind must surely have caused him to think himself again in love with a present manifestation of his Clarissa. Whether he knew it or not, the identification he had made must have driven the notion. Not for a second did she entertain the belief he had actually succumbed to her charms, such as they were.

Even Oswald had never spoken of her in such terms. Such admiring looks as she had received from gentlemen of his acquaintance had been reserved, even avuncular. Chloe was more in the habit of attributing such looks to an expression of surprise at the oddity of Oswald having espoused a woman forty years his junior. Although he had assured her, when she demurred at his offer, that it was not uncommon and no one would think anything of it.

In this he had erred, for both his children thought a great deal of it, in no way complimentary to herself. Though Oswald had shielded her from the worst, he could not prevent the lashings she endured from Matilda's tongue when he was not by. Nor the darting dislike and jealousy exhibited by Bernard's wife Harriet. She supposed she must do Bernard the justice to own that he never said to her face what his wife claimed he said of her in private.

Be that as it may, to hear herself proclaimed a beauty was a novelty. To hear it from Lord Pettipher was hard to withstand. Not merely because of those attractive green eyes and the face to which the epithet handsome would not be misplaced once he had regained his former health and strength. Though she could not now recall how it had originally struck her directly after the accident, too overlaid was that image with so many more.

No, it was rather the enforced intimacy of their situation that put Chloe's emotions at risk. Thank heavens she had the sense to realise her danger and guard against it. To allow her heart to be touched by Lancelot Ravensthorp, like a giddy girl, would be too foolish. She was flurried by the distortion of mind that made her an object of close interest to him, which was not to be wondered at. Nor was it surprising he should fix upon her when he had no real memories to call upon. The unlucky chance of her resemblance to the dead girl was a complication, but it need not prove damning. As he regained his past, he was bound to recognise her as a stranger to him.

Recalling Lance's assertion that his life began with her, Chloe felt a resurgence of the patter in her pulse that had attacked her then. She strove to suppress the feeling. It would not do.

At the least let her persuade Doctor Goodleigh to allow her to set him right about her name, style and condition. The more differences she could lay before him between herself and Clarissa, the likelier he would be to separate them in his mind. At least, she hoped so.

She did not return to the bedchamber until the doctor arrived. Instead, she sent Jack up to relieve Miss Flook, with orders to remain once he had done whatever Lord Pettipher needed of those private functions which had fallen to the footman's lot. Jemima went up with a tray for his dinner, which consisted of minced chicken and a soft roll, and on Chloe's orders instructed Jack to assist the gentlemen to eat.

It took a great deal of resolution not to give in to temptation and attend to his meal herself, but Chloe had determined on remaining out of his way until she'd had speech with the doctor. A sneaking notion of teaching Lance a lesson entered at the back of her mind, but Chloe dismissed it. That was not her object, though she supposed her absence might anger or disappoint him. Perhaps he would indeed attribute it to his ridiculous offer and be more circumspect for the future. Which would be no bad thing.

She listened out for the sound of his arrival and waylaid Doctor Goodleigh in the hall. "Can you spare me a moment or two before you go up, doctor?"

He eyed her over the top of his pince-nez. "You look concerned, Mrs Quilter. What is amiss?"

"In private, if you please." She beckoned him into the book-room and closed the door. "Lord Pettipher is asking questions," she said without preamble, "and I need to know how and with what I may answer him. It is excessively awkward to be obliged to refuse to give him any information."

The doctor pursed his lips and frowned. "What sort of questions?"

Chloe shrugged. "Whether he is married and has responsibilities, that sort of thing. And he wants to know my name, which I was fearful of giving beyond Mrs Quilter because of his confusing me with Clarissa. He knows he has no memory prior to his accident. Oh, and he wanted to know the nature of the accident. I ventured to tell him his groom is here, with the notion he might ask questions of Rowley, but I could not introduce the man again without your sanction."

It was a moment before Doctor Goodleigh answered. He took an aimless turn about the room, his head down.

Chloe waited in growing impatience while he pondered, wondering at his hesitation.

"It is a tricky point," he said at last, looking up. "I have been reading up on the subject, for I have had no personal experience with it before this. The general opinion of my colleagues in such cases, as far as I have been able to ascertain, is that one may with advantage answer direct questions with the truth, but refrain from introducing facts unasked."

"Why such distinction?"

"Because a train of thought set up in his own mind may lead to a jog of the memory if he is given a correct answer, but an unregarded fact out of the blue is likely to confuse."

Chloe was conscious of a measure of relief. "Yes, that makes a lot of sense. Thank you. I can use that to make a judgement. What of the groom? If I asked him to wait upon his master for some purpose of serving him, perhaps? Would that answer?"

The doctor gave this his consideration. "Well, unless he is concerned for his horses, would his groom wait upon him in his bedchamber?"

"I suppose not." Chloe was regretful, but then rallied as a thought occurred. "But if he should ask about the accident, I might bring in the groom to give his account."

"Or he might ask about his horses then. As long as it is a natural introduction, following upon some query. Remember, our object is to avoid confusion."

Chloe agreed to it and then accompanied the doctor upstairs to his lordship's room. She nodded dismissal to Jack, who was sitting in the chair near the door, and glanced across to the bed.

Lance was sitting up, staring into space. He looked round as she and the doctor approached and she perceived, with a swoop of dismay, that his aspect was sombre. No smile of welcome came, and after one inimical glance he turned his attention to the doctor.

"Well and how do you do this evening, sir? You appear to be a little stronger at least."

The hearty manner appeared to grate on Lance, for his jaw tightened. "I am better, thank you."

"I hear you have been persuaded to take some sustenance, which is a very good sign."

Lance said nothing. The doctor turned to Chloe briefly with a flick of his eyebrows heavenwards, and tried again.

"Your appetite may be poor to begin with, but I feel certain it will quicken now you have begun to eat again."

The green eyes surveyed him coldly. "Will you inform my nurse that I may have wine, if you please?"

Chilled by both manner and tone, Chloe intervened. "I would not let him have it without your permission."

"Quite right, Mrs Quilter. However, I dare say a glass or two will do no harm."

A triumphant look was cast at Chloe and a spark of indignation leapt up. How dare he behave in this fashion?

"But a glass or two is your limit, sir," came on a severe note from the doctor. "Indulgence in liquor will not help you to recover your memory."

The reminder served to bring a sulky pout to Lance's mouth. Really, he was behaving like a spoilt child!

"I might as well soak my brain in liquor for all the help it is to me. I can squeeze nothing from it, try as I will."

"Then do not try, sir."

"What the devil else have I to do?"

A grunt issued from Doctor Goodleigh. "If you want employment, I am sure Mrs Quilter has books enough for you to read. Or a pack of cards, perhaps?"

Chloe forced a smile. "Certainly. I'm sure I can find occupation suited to my patient's needs."

She directed a meaningful look at Lance as she spoke and was both surprised and gratified to see a flicker of interest lighten his moody expression. That would teach him to sulk! Let him wonder what she had in mind. Not that she knew herself, except to let him understand she was not best pleased with his manner.

The doctor took care to examine the injury to Lance's head, pronounced it to be healing just as it should, recommended Chloe to administer a dose of the sleeping draught left in the bottle, if the wine did not do the trick, and prepared to take his leave.

"No, no, Mrs Quilter, there is no need to see me out. I will not call in the morning, unless you send to me. But I will come again at the same time tomorrow evening, if that suits."

She thanked him, shook hands and closed the door behind him, turning to confront Lance. "Is this petulance of yours meant to punish me?"

The frown descended onto his brow. "Is this upbraiding meant to make up for neglecting me?"

"Neglecting you? Merely because I have been busy —"

"You've not been so busy you could not have popped in to see how I did." His voice was a snap, matched by a spark at his eyes. "Don't lie! I discomposed you and you were too embarrassed to face me, isn't that nearer the truth?"

Taken aback, Chloe eyed him for a moment. Why she should find his reproaches unpalatable she did not know. She owed him no particular allegiance. "Nearer, but not all the truth," she said on a more moderate note.

A muscle twitched in his cheek. "Well, do you mean to tell me what is the truth?"

She was nettled. "No, I don't believe I do. My thoughts are my own."

"Not when they concern me."

"What makes you think they were wholly concerned in you, pray?"

A faint smile came. "Oh, so haughty, Mrs Quilter? Confess now. You stayed away from me on purpose."

Without will, she took a step or two to the bed. "Yes, I did, and I shall do so again if you persist in behaving like a thwarted child."

"That will bring me to my senses, won't it?"

"Not noticeably in the present case."

He laughed, and his tone became rueful. "Your absence made me wretched."

"So I perceive." She sighed and moved to pull the bell. "I'll have your wine brought up. Perhaps that will put you in a better frame of mind."

He regarded her, a mixture of plea and speculation in his gaze. "Will you stay and take a glass with me?"

Chloe curtsied. "As your lordship pleases."

His expression changed. "Am I a lordship? Truly?"

She hesitated, cursing herself for the slip. On the other hand, she was permitted to answer a direct question truthfully. "Yes, you are a peer of the realm."

His brows snapped together. "An earl?"

A flutter of excitement leapt within her. "Yes! Oh, well done, Lance!"

He looked surprised, then gratified, and a laugh escaped him. "You look as delighted as a little girl with her first pony."

She had to smile. "I am delighted. You've remembered something pertinent. Doctor Goodleigh said it would happen if you were permitted an answer to jog your memory."

He was regarding her in a fashion she could not interpret. "You've been discussing me with him?"

"Only to discover what I may or may not say if you asked me something." Why in the world should she feel guilty? Naturally she must discuss her patient with the doctor. "Do you object?"

"You might have asked him in my presence, don't you think?"

Good heavens, no! But she refrained from saying as much. "Perhaps. Nothing untoward was said, I assure you. He is unfamiliar with cases such as yours, but he said he has been reading material from colleagues."

Jemima's entrance interrupted her, and Chloe could not be sorry.

"Ask Basil to bring up two glasses of the claret, if you please, dear."

The maid's eyes widened and she cast a surprised glance at the invalid before bobbing a curtsey. "Yes, mistress."

She sped off and Chloe took the available chair to the bedside and sat down. She smiled at Lance, trying for a resumption of their former ease. "Since I am now at liberty to answer your questions, you may ask them with impunity, my lord."

He emitted a sound of exasperation. "For God's sake, don't start my lording me, woman! We're too intimate for that."

Intimate? Good heavens! She ignored the word, feeling unequal to respond to any overtures he might make should she show she had taken notice of it. He had demonstrated himself capable of utter indiscretion in his dealings with her, and she did not wish a return to the earlier disturbing subject of his nonsensical offer.

"Very well, Lance, if you prefer it."

"I do prefer it. But I have yet to learn how to address you."

Again she hesitated. If she gave him leave to use her name, would it complicate matters further? Would he take instant advantage of the added *intimacy*?

"You wish to distance me, don't you?"

The attack was sudden, and all too accurate. She succumbed to instant remorse. "My name is Chloe."

A slow smile spread across his face and it softened altogether from its former stiffness. "Thank you, Chloe. I've wanted to thank you, and I don't think I yet have."

She felt herself colouring and tried for a neutral tone. "Thank me for what?"

"For taking such good care of me. For having me cluttering up your spare bedchamber. For putting up with my megrims and bad temper, like the angel you are."

"Oh, stop! I am nothing of the kind. And as this is the first instance of temperament I have been obliged to deal with, I can hardly be said to have much to put up with. In general, you are a model patient."

He gave a tiny grunt. "Patient. I don't want to be a patient."

"I'm afraid you must be for a space. Patient, at least, in allowing your memory to reassert itself."

A lightning grin appeared. "I've made a start, Chloe, have I not?"

"You have indeed." She turned on the opening of the door. "Ah, and here comes the wine, just when we have something to celebrate."

He watched her pour the wine, conscious of anticipation for its taste even as he relished her presence. He was resolved to be circumspect. He'd driven her away and had missed her sorely.

"I deserved your scolding," he said as she handed him a glass.

She gave a faint smile but chose not to answer. He waited until she re-seated herself, and raised his glass in a silent toast. "To what are we drinking?"

She did smile at that. A warm smile that sent a flurry through him. She raised her glass. "To memory!"

He echoed her words and brought the wine to his mouth. Its aroma, heady and rich, penetrated his nostrils and he breathed it in, closing his eyes. "Now this I know. Too well, perhaps. Oh, but it is altogether welcome. Thank you, doctor!"

He sipped. The taste was momentarily alien on his tongue and then quickly familiar. He savoured it, sipping slowly, feeling the warmth of it all the way down his throat and spreading in his chest. He sighed out in satisfaction and opened his eyes to find Clarissa watching him with a lurking twinkle.

"You rogue, Clarissa, you are laughing at me!"

The twinkle vanished. Consternation leapt in her eyes and her colour rushed up.

Dismayed, he stared at her. "But what have I said?"

She shook her head, hiding in the glass as she drank from it.

"Chloe!" The glass came down and she stared at him, eyes wide. Dismay turned to alarm. "For heaven's sake, say something! What have I done that you should look at me as if I've run mad?"

She looked away and back again, bit her lip and then took a breath, her face becoming resolute. "My name is Chloe. You called me Clarissa."

Shock swept through him. Clarissa? Good God, he had not thought of Clarissa properly in years! "I did?"

"Just now, yes. And it is not for the first time."

He caught the edge in her voice and wondered at it. He hastened to explain. "Clarissa was my betrothed, many years ago. We never married."

"No, I know."

"You know?" He struggled with the implication. "Then I've done it before? I've miscalled you?"

Her colour seemed to fluctuate. She looked pale now. "You were confused, I believe. It is not surprising, for the knock you received was severe. Don't let it worry you, Lance, I beg."

"But it worries you."

Her lips twitched. "Shrewd of you, Lance. But I've noticed this in you. It's unusual in a man, you know."

He laughed. "Is it? Perhaps I recognise your changing moods because you are all I have." He had not meant to fluster her, but it was plain he had.

She gave him one of those mechanical smiles he disliked. "Shall we return to enjoying the wine?"

He was nettled. "Why must you always avoid the issue?"

"Because such discussions as these can only retard your progress."

"How, when this in particular has enabled me to remember I was once betrothed?" He realised the truth of what he'd said and grinned. "I did remember, didn't I?"

This smile was genuine and he rejoiced at it. "You did indeed."

He wanted to please her, appease her, if he could. He raised his glass. "To you — Chloe!"

She eyed him, her expression now unreadable. Then she raised her own glass. "To you — Lance!"

He sipped again at the wine, relieved to have overcome the awkwardness of the moment. But it rankled. What had made him call her Clarissa? He tried to summon an image of his former love to mind, but it came up blank. He spoke without thinking. "I don't remember what she looked like."

"Clarissa?"

It was a low-toned utterance, hesitant even. He wondered briefly why, but his thoughts went too fast for him. "I ought to recall her face, but I can't. I remember only the fact of her, and that we were betrothed. Also that it came to nothing. I don't know why."

She said nothing. Waiting for more? Then she smiled again. "It will come. Don't try to force it."

She sipped her drink and he followed suit, finishing what was left in his glass.

Chloe stood up. "A refill?"

He studied the empty glass. "No, thank you. I enjoyed it, but it's enough. Like Wintringham, I have moderated my intake of liquor."

She stood poised to take his glass, but did not move, question in her face. "Wintringham?"

"A friend of mine." He proffered the glass with a smile. "Thank you for drinking with me."

She took it and set it down along with her own. He feared she was going to leave him, but equally feared her irritation if he importuned her to stay. To his relief, she sat down again.

"Tomorrow I will see what I can find to interest you on my bookshelves."

He grinned. "Anything will do, since my tastes are unknown to us both."

"Well, perhaps a selection may help to determine your tastes. We might also play at backgammon or chess, perhaps?"

The faintly questioning note amused him. "Do you suppose I may recover an expertise of some kind? For all we know, I may be a virtuoso at the pianoforte or a versifier. Shall I write an ode to your fine eyes, Clarissa?" He heard the echo of his own voice before he noted the change in her expression. "Oh, Lord, I did it again! Forgive me. Chloe? Yes, Chloe. May I call you Chloe? You've not yet given me permission to use your name, and I certainly have not forgotten you are Mrs Quilter."

Aware he was gabbling, he closed his mouth on the tumbling thoughts, instead cursing in his head at the foolish error. He must learn to distinguish her name and not allow himself to fall into error again. For some reason, into which he dared not enquire, it troubled her that he called her Clarissa. He was sure of it. Was it pride? She would poker up if he asked, and he could not bear it if she withheld herself from his chamber again.

She was faintly smiling. "I doubt it matters whether I give you permission or no, for I'm sure you will use my name in any event. Do you suppose it is the aristocrat in you that makes you do just as you choose, regardless of anyone else?"

He had to laugh. "Doubtless. Am I horribly recalcitrant and high-handed? But you said I was a model patient!"

"Yes, when you were unable to make shift for yourself. However, it's said to be a good sign when a patient becomes difficult to manage."

"Is it? Why?"

"Because it shows improvement. Though in your case, I am rather at a loss to descry any — in conduct at least."

He could not resist. "Ah, but that is not to the point, if my health is improved."

"Not to the point for you, perhaps. Very much to the point for those who must endure your insolence."

He burst into laughter and put out a hand. "You must make allowances for me, Cla—" He checked himself and continued smoothly, "Chloe, for you are my whole dependence. What in the world should I do without you?"

"I dare say you would do very well, better than you suppose."

"And be miserable into the bargain."

"Then you'd best behave, had you not?"

Mischief prompted him. "But where would be the enjoyment in that?"

She fell into laughter, to his delight. "Wretched creature! I should leave you this instant."

He was at once penitent. "No, don't."

"I must soon, however."

"Not yet."

"Very well. I dare say I can endure to be plagued a little longer."

The insouciance of her tone was balm to him. He had succeeded in recovering the former ease between them and must strive to keep it so. He sought for an innocuous subject of conversation.

She forestalled him. "You spoke of a friend, did you realise it?"

"Wintringham?" He said it before it registered. The image popped into his head and he rushed to impart its substance. "I have it! Vince and his wife. Now, there's a virtuoso, if you like.

She plays exquisitely. Lucky dog! I was staying with them, I think. Yes, that is it. A short sojourn before going home for Christmas." He looked at Chloe, eagerness in his breast.

She was intent, leaning forward. "Why lucky? Lucky dog, you said?"

"Oh, because he had no expectation of happiness when he married." He looked at the thought and found it good. "How did I know that? It's true, though I cannot recall why it should be so."

Chloe wafted a hand. "Never mind it. You have regained a part of your life, Lance. It is an excellent beginning."

True enough. But if he remembered the past, would he lose this bittersweet present?

CHAPTER FIVE

Reading by the light of her bedside candle had become a pleasurable habit since her widowhood. Chloe disliked the cocoon of curtains to which she'd been obliged to accustom herself throughout the years of her marriage. The stifled feeling kept her wakeful, along with the sound of Oswald's heavy breathing and occasional snores whenever he chose to visit her at night. She was in the habit of leaving the curtains open at one side at least, benefitting from the candlelight to indulge her love of books.

This was the first night since Lance's accident she'd been able to resume reading her current volume of *Belinda*, but she found it hard to concentrate for the niggle of worry at the back of her mind.

He had assured her he could manage well enough alone. "I cannot have you sitting up with me when it's no longer needful."

Though she had read reluctance in his aspect when she said goodnight. She slipped into Agatha's room to tell her she need not take a turn at minding the patient.

"Is he well enough to be left, my dear Mrs Quilter?"

"He says so. I will slip in to check upon him in the night, but I think he will rest well enough. He's had a glass of wine and I think he may sleep."

Miss Flook was clearly relieved. "It will be strange not to be obliged to stay up, but I confess I can do with a full night's rest myself."

She was right. It was altogether strange. Chloe could not settle to her book and found she'd read several pages without taking in the sense of Mrs Edgeworth's tale. She laid it down and sat back against her bank of pillows, contemplating Lancelot Ravensthorp.

His image danced in her head, with its rapidly changing expressions. His smile, coupled with those attractive eyes, was beguiling. How in the world had he not been snapped up? From his groom's account, she knew him to be approaching thirty, and it was — what, ten years? — since the unfortunate accident that had taken Clarissa from him. Yet no female had managed to pluck him from the memory to a fresh affection. Until now.

No, Chloe Quilter. Do not be tempted to fool yourself. His vaunted admiration was not for her, but for Clarissa whom he saw in her. It had nothing to do with who she was. His being unable to distinguish between them proved that. He had called her Clarissa or Chloe impartially this night, without being aware of having done so.

It troubled her that he no longer recalled Clarissa's death, as he had done in those first hours when he'd mistaken her for a ghost. Or an angel. When the memory surfaced, would he feel again all the old grief? It was evident he had never truly overcome the loss, or he would be married by this time.

She could not but recognise the truth of this. No female had succeeded in ousting Clarissa from his mind and heart. He might have taken a wife for the purpose of securing the succession to his earldom. He need not love her. Chloe understood it was the practice of the aristocracy to marry for advantage. Had not her own father done precisely that when he ran off with an heiress? Not that it had done him the least good.

She brushed away the remembrance. She preferred to think as little as possible of the man who'd dragged her through

Europe from one meagre lodging to the next. She was not now concerned with Simon Kittisford, but with Lord Pettipher, a much worthier object for her care. Although he was recovering fast. She had thought it would be many weeks before he was well enough to return to his normal life. But his improvement even in the last four and twenty hours was astonishing.

A noise in the corridor interrupted her musing. Chloe sat up, listening.

A low muttering reached her. Then a decided thump. Even as she threw off the covers and hastened out of bed, groping for her dressing-gown, a series of bangs sounded from without.

Lance! It must be!

Seizing her candlestick, she hurried to the door and flung it open, stepping out into the corridor. Light from her candle fell upon sagging limbs and a splash of white which proved to be the edge of a nightgown. She started forward, a scolding note at once entering her voice.

"What in the world are you doing, foolish man?"

He had staggered against the wall and was holding on to it, his head resting against the panelling.

Chloe caught him about his back. "Here, lean on me!"

He pulled away, staggering across the corridor and catching at the baluster that marked the beginning of the stairway. Alarmed, Chloe set her candle down on the floor and went to him, catching him as firmly as she could about the torso and trying to drag him away.

"Do you wish to fall down the stairs, you idiotic creature? Come away at once!"

He held to the baluster, resisting. "Where am I? I don't know where I am!"

There was anguish in his voice and Chloe heard it with a streak of guilt. "Dear God, I should never have left you!"

To her relief, she heard footsteps coming from above and the beginnings of light.

"What is amiss? Mrs Quilter, is that you?"

"Basil, thank heavens! Come quick and help me!"

The light increased as her butler came hurrying down the stairs, his steps augmented by another set or more behind him.

"What is this place?"

Lance was turning, flailing his arms, in imminent danger of a fall. Chloe held on to him for dear life.

"Basil, hurry! I cannot hold him!"

He had begun to struggle. She heard Basil's voice.

"Jemima, take this!"

And then, thank heaven, he was with her, seizing hold of the struggling man. "Stand back, Miss Chloe! Jack and I will manage him."

Chloe was glad enough to relinquish her place to the burly footman, who had evidently followed Basil down, together with the maid. In the augmented light, she saw Lance's eyes were wild, his face tormented. His cries never ceased.

"Where am I? Don't touch me!" This to the men who now had hold of him. "Let me go! Where are you taking me? No, no, no! I won't go there! Who are you?"

Distressed, Chloe snatched up her candle again and followed as they manhandled him back into his chamber. She set down her candle as the butler and footman were attempting to put him back to bed, Basil trying to soothe.

"Now then, sir, no need to fuss. We'll do you no harm, but you must go back to bed. Come now, no one will hurt you."

"No, I won't, I won't! What do you want with me? Who are you people? What is this place?"

"It's Mrs Quilter's house, sir," said Jack, loud over Lance's protests. "Remember me, sir? I've been serving you these three days. I'm Jack, sir, remember?"

Arrested, Lance stilled, much to Chloe's relief. She was engaged in preparing the sleeping draught by the light of her own candle and the one Jemima was holding, but her fingers were shaking so much she had to slow her movements for fear of spilling the mixture.

"Jack?"

"Yes, sir, it's Jack. Now let Mr Basil and me get you into bed, sir. It won't do to be wandering about the house like you were."

They had succeeded in getting him to sit on the bed, but he put up his hands to push Jack's away. "Wait! I don't understand. I need to understand. Where am I? Why am I to go to bed?"

Seeing how he addressed the footman, Basil stood back, casting a glance at Chloe, who now had the glass ready. "Not yet," he murmured, and she nodded. Jack was endeavouring to calm the patient with soft words.

"You've been ill, sir. You're not yet well enough to walk about."

"Ill? How ill?"

"You took a knock on the head, sir."

Lance put up a hand to his head, feeling it as if he sought to find the wound.

While his attention was thus engaged, Chloe touched the sleeve of Jack's nightshirt, lowering her voice to a murmur. "See if you can get him to take this."

Jack nodded and took the glass, leaning down to Lance. "Here's a draught for you, sir."

Lance did not take it, eyeing the glass as if it contained poison. "What is it? What are you giving me?"

Jack threw a questioning look at Chloe, who stepped forward, adopting the gentle tone that had soothed him before. "It is to help you sleep, Lance, that is all."

His distraught glance passed over Jack's face and came to rest on her. In the dim light she could not be sure, but she thought a measure of recognition entered his eyes. He lifted a hand and took the glass, grimacing as he brought it close to his mouth. His glance passed across all three of the anxious persons at his bedside, and flicked back to Chloe.

"Wine," he said and blinked rapidly.

Was he recalling their earlier drink together? She would swear to it he knew neither her nor anything of their earlier conversation. She smiled at him. "I am your nurse, you see. Will you drink it? To please me?"

He looked doubtful, but he sipped a little of the liquid. Distaste curved his mouth. "It's bitter."

"It's best to swallow it quickly."

He looked into the glass and then put it to his lips and tipped it back. Making a disgusted face, he handed back the glass.

Chloe took it. "Excellent. Now, if you please, will you get back into bed?"

She nodded at Jack to help him, and he allowed his legs to be lifted in and submitted as Jack encouraged him to lie down and covered him over with the bedclothes.

"Thank you, both. I can manage him now."

"I'd best stay for a bit, mistress," Jack said in a low tone, "in case he takes it into his head to get up again."

She nodded and gestured for him to retire to the chair by the wall. She kept her eyes on Lance, but heard the footsteps as Jemima and Basil took their leave. Her heartbeat, which had been racing, was returning to normal. She took her candlestick from the dresser and set it on the bedside table so that it threw light on Lance's face. Then she sat on the bed and set her fingers to his wrist, feeling for his pulse.

Not much to her surprise, it was tumultuous and uneven. She saw sweat on his brow and got up to locate one of the cloths set ready on the dresser, with which she wiped away the beads of moisture.

His eyes had been closed, but he opened them at this, looking directly into her face. "Chloe?"

"Oh, thank heavens," she said on a sigh. "You know me!"

He groped for her hand and she curled her fingers about his. "Don't leave me."

His lids sank again and she thought he was falling asleep. She sat on the bed again and prepared for a long wait. Remembering the footman, she turned and found him patiently sitting by the door.

"I think you may go now, Jack."

"Are you sure, mistress?"

"He recognised me. I think he has returned to himself."

The footman nodded and rose, no doubt only too glad to be able to return to his bed. Chloe had no expectation of being able to do the same.

Lance opened his eyes again, and his fingers moved on hers. "I didn't know where I was. The place was alien to me."

"Were you dreaming?"

He sighed. "I don't recall. There were shapes, mountainous shapes. Snow? Yes, a good amount of snow. Is it winter?"

"Very much so, I'm afraid, but the thaw has set in these two days."

"I am glad. I dislike snow."

His voice was sinking, along with the lids over his eyes. Presently, his even breathing betrayed that he slept and his fingers slackened on hers. Chloe slid her hand away and he did not react. She sat quite still, watching him, at last at leisure to wonder what had set him off.

He had been thrown quite out of kilter. By what, he clearly did not know. It was worrying, for he was evidently not as well recovered as she'd supposed. Should she send for Doctor Goodleigh in the morning? It must depend on how he passed the rest of the night, she supposed. And whether he was himself again when he woke.

She fetched the chair from near the door and made herself as comfortable as she could, preparing for a long night.

Mountains towered over him, the horses were huge and noisy, and the face of the angel laughed. He tried to speak and could not. His throat had closed. His head felt light, empty, and the pain was gone.

He was searching through the woods. Snow was everywhere, hampering his progress. He could hear someone calling, but the words made no sense. His horses. He had to find his horses. Someone tried to tell him they were unharmed, yet still he must find them. He had to see for himself. He could hear the whistling distress from their overburdened lungs. And the snow kept falling.

He could not move for the mountains of snow that held him down. Somehow he could breathe beneath it, like the fish in the water swimming towards him, hair golden, spreading, flowing in the water, captured under the ice forever.

He woke with a start, disoriented, blinking into the dimness of a guttering candle. A white form bulged in his vision, hunched in the chair beside his bed. His hazy gaze pierced towards it, trying to make it out. Gradually it took shape in the form of a blanketed body. Recognition flashed.

"She's fallen asleep."

He was only half aware he said it aloud, hushed in tone nevertheless. She did not wake.

For a while he watched her, unable to see her well in the poor light of the flickering candle. A shape curving down her cheek proved to be tendrils of hair escaped from the encompassing nightcap. Lance was conscious of an almost overmastering wish to lean towards her and pluck the thing from her head, allowing the golden hair to fall about her shoulders. Gladly would he lose himself in those tresses, draw her close against him and caress her curves until she yearned for him as much as he did for her.

His body responded to the wish and his heartbeat accelerated.

As if his desire had communicated to her in some way, she shifted, sighed out a breath and opened her eyes. He lay still, willing control upon his unruly body lest he seize her to him in a frenzy of need. She yawned and her gaze met his. Her eyes widened. For a breathless instant, Lance thought she answered him with fire of her own. Then she seemed to wrench her eyes away as she sat up in a bang, her blanket falling away.

"You're awake! Are you feeling all right?"

No, he was feeling all wrong, but he dared not say so. "Yes, thank you."

She rubbed her eyes and rose, her curves vanishing as the night clothes fell about them. "Would you like a drink? There is barley water."

She went to the dresser and poured from a jug. He struggled up onto his elbow, accepted the glass and drank deeply, hoping the coolness might induce his arousal to subside. Though truth to tell, it was already fading with the resumption of normality.

"This candle is done with, I fear."

She blew out the flame, sending a point of smoke into the air from the wick. With some surprise, Lance found he could still see in the greyness that ensued.

"Is it morning?"

She smiled. "Dawn, I think. I will open the shutters."

He watched her glide to the window and pull them back, increasing the light. Then she crossed to the fireplace and bent, poking at the embers. The oddity of her being here struck him. "I thought you meant to leave me to myself last night."

Her head turned, a frown creasing her brow. She set down the poker and got up, moving to the other side of the bed. "You don't remember what happened?"

"When?"

"Last night."

Puzzlement wreathed his brain. "I remember waking to find you in the chair."

"You got up, Lance. You were wandering in the corridor outside. We had to get you back to bed for fear of you falling."

"I don't remember that."

She smiled. "Well, perhaps it is not surprising. You were a little disorientated."

His bewilderment increased. "You mean I was sleepwalking?"

"No, you were awake."

"Then what?"

Chloe came around the bed again and settled into the chair. Her voice took on the tone he recognised as that of his soothing nurse. "Don't let it trouble you, Lance. You were merely a trifle confused."

He began to feel agitated. He sat up in the bed. "But why should I be? And why don't I remember? I know I have lost my past life, but I cannot lose this one too!"

"Hush, now, there is no need for this dismay," she said, rising and coming to bank his pillows.

He seized her wrist. "Don't prevaricate! Tell me!"

She sat on the bed, making no attempt to free herself, though her tone became sharp. "Very well, but you are hurting me, Lance!"

He let go. She rubbed her wrist, and he at once felt remorseful. "Forgive me, Chloe!"

Her warm smile appeared. "You are absolved."

"But you won't explain."

She hesitated and then gave a little sigh. "You did not know where you were last night. Nor did you recognise any of us to begin with."

"Then I did lose my memory of you!"

"Only temporarily. I don't think it surprising. You have had a severe injury and we must expect the odd setback."

"Setback! What if I'm losing my mind altogether?"

"No such thing! Don't be absurd. You know me this morning, do you not?"

An anger he knew to be unreasoning swept through him. "You are Mrs Chloe Quilter and you won't marry me. That much I remember well enough."

She did not flinch, but her cheeks flew colour and he was ashamed of himself. But the well of resentment would not admit of apology.

"Then let that satisfy you. Your present memory is clearly intact."

"It doesn't satisfy me. If you must know, I am bursting with fury, though I have not the faintest notion why I should be."

She seemed to study him for a moment. He met her gaze, determined not to yield to the little voice that bade him retract, beg, woo and gentle her into submission. A faint smile crossed her face and she rose from the bed.

"I am going to get dressed. I dare say the servants are stirring. I will send Jack to bring up your hot water."

He wanted to prevent her from going, but the demon inside him kept him from speech. He watched her leave the room, aware of a constriction in his chest. Why should he feel like a beast on a chain? What was wrong with him? Or was this his true being at last coming through? What in Hades kind of a man was he?

While she washed, Chloe's mind was churning. She'd been glad of the excuse, needing to get away from Lance's disturbing presence. It was not merely the oddity of his unprecedented mood, perhaps brought on by his wanderings of the night. She could not dismiss the very different fire in his eyes at the instant of her waking.

They had glittered in the meagre light put out by the candle, seeming to burn at her out of the pale oval of his face on the pillows. Heat had flushed in her depths and she'd known a brief violent want that set up a series of impossible images in her head. With difficulty, she'd dismissed them, ignoring the hot pulsing which — thank heavens! — had dissipated as she assumed a prosaic attitude that bore no relation to the truth within. Evidence, for it was no less, the wretched creature had succeeded in enticing her with his nonsensical proposals.

Or, if she was honest, that she'd been drawn to him at the outset. Had it not been for Clarissa…

Useless to think of that, for there was Clarissa somewhere in the background of his mind, who had disposed him in Chloe's favour. Whenever she surfaced, Clarissa ousted Chloe, and it would ever be so.

She stripped off her nightgown and splashed the now lukewarm water on her body until she began to shiver. Effective and salutary, and so it must be. Muscles ached from sleeping in the chair and she rubbed at them vigorously as she towelled her person, forcing her attention away from Lance's effect on her and onto his moodiness.

He'd said he did not know himself why he was attacked by such feelings. Which troubled Chloe. It argued that his injury was to blame. Could it be that it would leave him subject to unreasoning tempers? Should she send for Doctor Goodleigh at once? No, for Lance had not lost control this morning. Yet, what if he became unmanageable as he had last night? She could not have her servants in constant attendance, having to leave their duties to pander to a recalcitrant and temperamental invalid. It would be both distressing and unfair upon them all.

Ought she to send for his people? As soon as he was well enough to travel, they could remove him to his home at Ravensthorp. She must discuss the matter with Rowley this morning.

She knew the groom had been to Bedford to arrange for the curricle's repair. It was presently standing in one of the outhouses, having been dragged thither by Farmer Gare's sturdy horse and several of his workers. Rowley had paid them for the service out of Lance's supply of money. But the horses were well housed and eating their heads off in her stables. Rowley could ride one to Ravensthorp, could he not?

She was still pondering the problem when she entered the dining parlour where Miss Flook was already seated at the table, engaged in pouring tea.

"Goodness, Mrs Quilter, I had not expected you to be up this early. I made sure you would be abed after such a difficult night."

"If you must have it, I fell asleep in the chair."

"Oh, no! I wish you had called me to replace you. Let me give you a cup of tea, poor dear, you must be exhausted."

Chloe took her place at the table, ignoring Miss Flook's anxious twittering, and accepted the proffered tea. "Thank you."

"You must eat, Mrs Quilter. A baked egg, perhaps? Or a little of the ham?"

Chloe took a warm roll from under the wraps in the basket and began to butter it. "Presently, when I've had my tea."

Miss Flook pushed the covered silver dishes nearer, pressing Chloe to take something, but was persuaded at last to return her attention to her own plate.

"Your egg will grow cold, Agatha. Pray eat and don't trouble your head about me."

The ritual was repeated almost daily. Agatha had never lost that consciousness of inferiority engendered by years of drudgery and her anxiety to please could be trying. But Chloe could never bring herself to repulse her efforts. Instead, she turned the subject.

"I am thinking it is time we sent to Lord Pettipher's people, Agatha."

Miss Flook was instantly diverted. "Indeed, yes, dear Mrs Quilter. Imagine how anxious they must be by this time. But how shall you manage? Though I dare say the posts are getting through now."

"The posts have likely been getting through all along, but I'm thinking of sending his groom. He may arrange for a coach to be brought that his lordship may be moved thence as soon as he is able to travel."

Miss Flook's eyebrows flew up. "But that may be many days, Chloe. After last night, I cannot suppose him anywhere near capable of setting forth for some little time."

But she needed him gone. Chloe did not say it aloud. How explain to Agatha the complexity of her feelings? The fear of growing too fond of a man who thought her a replica of his lost bride? She prevaricated.

"I do not mean them to take him up at once. Naturally he must remain until he is physically recovered."

"Indeed, yes, for he was scarcely able to remain upon his feet. Not that I thought well of his being brought here at the outset, but in Christian charity, one cannot turn the poor man out in his condition."

"I have no intention of turning him out!"

Miss Flook at once lost herself in a flurry of apology. "Oh, no, I did not mean… I know you would never … my dear Mrs Quilter, I had no wish to —"

"No, I know." Chloe struggled to control her irritation. "Pay no mind to me, Agatha. I am tired, that is all."

"Indeed, I am sure you must be. Still, I had no right…"

Summoning a smile, Chloe put up a placating hand. "Don't, Agatha. You said nothing at all out of the way. We are in perfect agreement. I confess it is becoming a little irksome to have the house in turmoil —"

"Gracious, yes, it is indeed!"

"— but I don't mean to complain. However, it will do no harm to put a future arrangement in hand. And, as you have said, his people are no doubt in quite a worry by this time."

Her resumption of her customary manner appeased Miss Flook and she subsided, addressing herself to her breakfast again. "I think I will take a roll and a little of the blackberry preserve. Mrs Vaughan makes it so very well."

Relieved, Chloe drank her tea in a measure of peace. She was contemplating taking a portion of ham when Miss Flook chose to harp on the invalid again.

"Do you desire me to send to the doctor? He was so very wild last night."

"I presume you are talking of our patient rather than Doctor Goodleigh," Chloe said, smiling, and went on over Agatha's reassurances, "I did think of it, but his lordship is himself again and the doctor is coming this evening. I will inform him of the episode then. Will you go up and sit with him this morning, Agatha?"

"Of course, if you wish it."

"He probably won't sleep and he was finding his confinement tedious yesterday. You could take him a book to read, or read to him, perhaps? Unless he would prefer a pack of cards. He could play at Patience, or you might engage him in a bout of German Whist or another game for two players. Or draughts?"

Miss Flook was all immediate willingness to do what she might to alleviate the patient's supposed boredom, even going so far as to suggest the childish game of Fox and Geese.

Chloe left it to her companion's imagination, reflecting ruefully that Lance was unlikely to consider anything provided for his entertainment of interest if she was not herself his partner in the pastime. It could not be helped. He must make shift to do without her, for she meant to hold a little more aloof if she could.

A thread of apprehension crept in, however, when she recalled his moodiness. She did not wish his unruly temper to fall upon Agatha. On the other hand, civility must compel him to behave well in her companion's presence. She was of the opinion he would not show his displeasure to any but herself, since his utter lack of consciousness appeared to permit him every sort of licence. She was ready to believe he would kiss her if she was wanton enough to permit him. Wretched man! He had turned her world upside-down in more ways than one.

She sent for Rowley to the book-room as soon as she had breakfasted. Miss Flook had gone upon her errand to find suitable entertainment for the invalid, and a breakfast tray had been taken upstairs. Lance's needs now met, she might turn her attention to the prospect of getting him out of her life.

CHAPTER SIX

Confident in having taken such measures as she could for the future eviction of Lord Pettipher from her home, Chloe took her turn at his bedside in the afternoon with a lighter heart.

He greeted her with a smile, and no immediate sign of his former ill temper. "In good time, Mrs Quilter. I have been beat all hollow by Miss Flook here, who has taken nearly all my geese."

Chloe was amused to see Agatha flush with pleasure.

"No, indeed, my dear lord, do not say so. Had you recalled the rules, I am sure you would have won too." She was collecting up the pieces as she spoke, stowing them neatly in the box.

Lance folded the board and handed it to her. "The wonder is I recalled it at all, for I have not played since childhood and my memory was rusty."

Interest stirred in Chloe. "You remember that?"

"Certainly. Should I not?"

She hesitated, a riffle of excitement shooting through her. Miss Flook forestalled her.

"Indeed it is not surprising you were rusty, and I have the advantage of you, my lord, having frequently played with my charges over the years."

Lance gave a crack of laughter. "How unfair of you to propose it then, Miss Flook. Next time we will play at this German Whist of yours. I have at least been used to indulge in Whist lately."

Agatha agreed to it and in a flurry of excuses, got herself out of the room. Chloe turned back to her patient to find him regarding her with a disturbing warmth lurking at the back of his eyes. She took Agatha's vacated chair by the bedside.

"You seem in good spirits."

"As good as they can be in your absence."

She chose to disregard this. "How is your head?"

"I don't feel it at all."

"Then I think we must ask the doctor if you may try getting up tomorrow."

Assuming all went well this night, but she refrained from saying as much.

Lance made no answer, settling back against his banked pillows and continuing to survey her in that disconcerting fashion he'd adopted from the start. He'd said he liked to look at her, but her consciousness of his confusion over her true identity caused her a good deal of discomfort. In a bid to divert him, she risked a tentative probe.

"Do you remember much of your childhood?"

His brows drew together. "Naturally. Why should I not?"

Heavens, had he now forgotten about his lost memory? Had it all come back to him without his recalling that it had vanished? Impossible to tell, and she dared not interfere with whatever process was causing the change. She tried for a casual approach. "Had you any siblings?"

The frown deepened. "Well, you know I had, Clarissa."

Shock ripped through her. What now? Oh, Lord, what would he now be at? For the life of her, she could not prevent the protest. "I am Chloe, sir."

"Chloe?" His brow cleared. "Of course you are! Did I call you Clarissa again?"

"Yes, you did. And you must be aware that I know nothing of your family."

He looked surprised. "You don't? Surely I told you? Besides, you have met my sister I don't know how many times."

"No, I have not, Lance." Steadfast, she held his gaze. "I am Mrs Chloe Quilter, a widow, of Derry Lodge in Staggesden, which is where you are now."

"Well, of course I know that! What are you talking of?"

Bewildered now, Chloe stared at him. "I thought — I thought you had forgotten."

He blinked as if equally puzzled. "Why in Hades should you think so? I am perfectly aware of your status. What I don't know is why you should have married this Mr Quilter, whoever the devil he may be, without a word to me. Nor why you did not at once send to tell me you had survived the accident. Didn't you suppose I should be grieved and distraught? Had you no pity for me, no faith in my loyalty?"

"Oh, dear God!"

Unable to remain still, Chloe leapt from the chair and paced about the room, her thoughts in chaos. Where was he now? Were his wits utterly overthrown? He believed she was indeed Clarissa! What in the world was she to say to this? She could not answer him in the character of the woman he supposed her to be. Yet she ought not to protest her real identity.

She was aware of his eyes following her, knew his puzzlement to be complete. He understood her as little as she him, but from a widely differing perspective.

No, this was not to be borne. She would not reject his words outright. But let her give him her truth and see if that might jog him out of his error. She returned to the chair and sat down, lifting her eyes to his.

"I will tell you why I married Mr Quilter." He did not speak, but his gaze narrowed, seeming to try to focus more closely on her face. "When my father died, I had neither means nor employment. Basil, who is now my butler but was then my father's henchman, you might say, determined to bring me back to England."

"You'd left England? But, why?"

The question gave her no clue to his understanding. Did he still suppose her to be Clarissa?

"My father plucked me from the safety of my grandparents' home when my mother died. She had left him years before. He chose to exercise his parental rights. I will not trouble you with the tale of my years on the Continent. Suffice to say they were wearisome and did nothing to improve my lot."

Lance was frowning. "I don't understand. Your parents are well. I saw your father only the other week."

She squashed this at once. "You are talking of Clarissa's parents. I am an orphan, sir."

"You changed your name?"

"I never bore the name of Clarissa. I have always been Chloe. Chloe Kittisford before I married Mr Quilter."

He put a hand to his head, rubbing at his temple. "Why are you making up such a tale? Is it to torture me?"

"I have no wish to torture you, but you are mistaken, Lance. I am not Clarissa. Clarissa is dead."

His other hand joined the first and he held his head as if he would stop it from bursting. Chloe wanted to jump up and run away. She'd blundered horribly. She should not have denied him. Now what was she to do?

All at once he dropped his hands, a disturbing expression of doubt creeping into his face. "I've lost my mind, haven't I?"

The pain of this utterance wrung Chloe's heart. She put out a hand and grasped one of his. "You are merely confused, Lance. It will settle, you'll see. Give it time."

He shook his head but his fingers clung to hers. "I don't know anything. I cannot rely on anything."

"Oh, you can! You are making progress. You have remembered more of your past, have you not?"

He sighed. "I remember snatches, like a patchwork of ill-collected pictures that will not fit together."

"Yes, I suppose it must be like pieces of a puzzle which you must slot into place."

"Exactly that." He smiled and released her hand. "I am giving you a deal of trouble. The sooner I go home, the better for you, I dare say."

She felt instantly ashamed, horribly conscious of the arrangements she had set in train. Should she mention them? "I have sent your groom to your home with a letter. He will tell them there what has happened. When you are well and able to travel, your people will come to fetch you."

His face clouded. "Then I must lose you too."

"No such thing. When you are fully recovered, I will be delighted to have a visit from you."

He sighed deeply. "No, you won't. You'll be glad to be rid of me and you won't think of me again."

She knew not how to answer this, believing it sprang from his disordered mind rather than considered thought. Best to ignore it, perhaps. She adopted a cheerful tone. "Come, tell me what you do remember."

He shrugged. "I am disinclined to examine the dregs of my life, I thank you." His voice changed. "Coffee! I should dearly love to have some, if it is not too much trouble."

"No trouble at all."

Rising, Chloe went to the bell-pull and tugged upon it. As she came back, she saw a couple of books on the bedside table and picked them up. "Did Agatha bring these for you? *Tristram*

Shandy and *Roderick Random*. An interesting choice. Shall I read to you?"

"If you like." He sounded listless, disinterested.

Chloe tried for a bracing note. "I have read *Roderick Random* and it is a stirring tale, if a trifle warm in places, but I shall not regard that. Let us essay."

She opened the book, but before she could begin, Little Tibby stumbled into the bedchamber, breathless as usual.

"Yes, mistress? Yes, mistress? What's to do?"

"Ah, there you are, dear." Chloe slowed her words, enunciating clearly for the girl's better understanding. "Ask Mrs Vaughan to send up a pot of coffee, please, dear."

Tibby bobbed once or twice, nodding her head. "A pot of coffee. Pot of coffee. Yes, mistress."

"That's right, dear. A pot of coffee to be sent to this room."

"Pot of coffee to be sent to this room, pot of coffee to be sent to this room…" The litany continued as the girl limped her way to the door and exited.

Chloe turned back to find Lance with raised brows. She felt warmth in her cheeks and laughed. "One has to treat her gently, but she is very willing, poor child."

His smile warmed her. "You have a kind heart, Chloe Quilter."

"Why, thank you. I do what I can. I know what it is to be isolated and something of an outcast."

A faint frown crossed his face. "That was not Clarissa. She was a flighty piece. Disobedient and thinking only of her own gratification."

Chloe dared not say a word. This was the first indication of his seeing any difference between her and the girl he'd lost. Indeed, the first words of criticism he had uttered of Clarissa. Was it possible he was coming out of his confusion?

Rather than refer to it, she chose to return to the volume on her lap and picked it up. "Shall we begin?"

He regarded the doctor's frowning features with a burgeoning feeling of trepidation as the silence lengthened. He'd asked to speak to him alone and had ignored Chloe's troubled look as she left them. He suspected she withheld what she knew of his condition and he would have the truth despite her caution.

"Well, sir?"

Doctor Goodleigh pursed his lips. "You ask me for assurances I cannot give, my lord. Each case is different."

Impatience gnawed at Lance. "But you must have some indications by which to judge. Give me a round tale, I beg of you. Have I lost my wits?"

A bark of laughter greeted this. "My dear sir, the very fact that you are able to ask proves the contrary. No, no. Your mind is sound enough, I believe."

A sigh escaped Lance and he relaxed a little. "Mrs Quilter told you of my wandering in the night, I presume? I did not remember it."

"That is but another instance of the memory betraying you. If I understand it correctly, you are having difficulty in distinguishing between past and present, yes?"

"Chloe told you so? Well, she has reason."

"But is it so?"

"Yes, if you must have it."

The doctor paid no heed to the begrudging note, but settled into the chair and leaned forward with his arms across his knees. "I realise it is difficult for you, but I believe it will be well to talk of what you remember. You may compare it to the present circumstances. Ask questions if you wish. I have no doubt Mrs Quilter will oblige you with truthful answers."

"She won't. She is wary with me."

The doctor smiled, peering over his pince-nez. "That is because I instructed her not to reject your association of her with the lady to whom you were once betrothed."

"Clarissa." Lance looked away. "The resemblance is uncanny."

The doctor's frown reappeared. "Can you descry no difference?"

Lance shrugged. "It was a long time ago. I daresay my image of her is a trifle blurred."

"Have you her likeness in a portrait somewhere?"

His mind jumped. "A miniature! I carry it with me always. In a fob. I suppose it must be among my belongings."

"Then we shall ask Mrs Quilter to search for it. Make a proper comparison, sir. See if you can find where their looks differ."

To his own surprise, Lance felt reluctance. He did not want to find Chloe markedly different from the Clarissa of his imaginings. Would he then lose his feeling towards her? She was the first woman to engender such feelings — except that now he could not be sure if he cared for her or the ghost of Clarissa.

"My advice to you, my lord…"

He started, hardly hearing the rest. "I beg your pardon? I was not attending."

"I am merely repeating my advice, my lord. Ask questions. Talk of your memories as they arise. I believe it will help you to sift out your present circumstances from your past."

"You think so?"

A smile came. "Well, we have tried reticence, which has resulted in confusion. Let us essay a different tack and see what comes. I will give Mrs Quilter permission to speak freely of her life as well as to enquire into your memories of your own."

Apprehension rose again. "And if I persist in this conjoining with Clarissa?"

"She may remind you of who she really is. Let us tear the barriers down, my lord, and hope for a positive outcome. Oh, and I think you may safely rise from your bed. Although, take it gently and rest the moment you feel tired."

A flash of amusement hit Lance. "Have no fear. Mrs Quilter will undoubtedly bundle me back to bed at the first hint of my weakening."

Doctor Goodleigh laughed. "A very capable female is Mrs Quilter. I gather she has had to be. As I understand it, her life has been unenviable in many ways."

Curiosity attacked Lance, laced with a good deal of dismay. To what additional trials had he subjected Chloe? It would not do. He must curb his urges in that direction — if he could.

He slept well, or so he believed, having drunk of the draught the doctor left.

"It will do you no harm, sir, and give you a restful night."

He woke to the sound of the little lame maid making up the fire, and there was no Chloe sleeping in the chair. He addressed the girl. "Good morning."

She started, turning her head and dropping the poker with a clatter. "Oh!"

"Don't be afraid!"

"But I weren't to wake you, sir!"

"Well, I won't tell on you, child. Will you open the shutters, if you please?"

She scrambled up, moving rather towards the bed than the window. "Shutters… What, them shutters?" She pointed.

Amused, Lance also pointed. "Yes, those shutters. Can you open them?"

She nodded fervently. "I can and all, sir."

"Then do so, if you please."

Nodding again, she scurried with her odd limp across to the window like a fierce little spider, muttering as she went. "Open the shutters … open the shutters."

He recalled how she had repeated her instructions when Chloe had sent her for coffee. It was both touching and irritating. How Chloe bore with it day in day out was a mystery. She must be patience itself. Well, she was, of course. Look how she bore with his megrims and changes of mood.

As he watched the girl struggle with the shutters, he realised he was thinking of Chloe as Chloe rather than Clarissa. A wave of warmth washed through him. His mind had survived the night intact. Then there was hope.

Light entered the room as the little maid succeeded in shifting one of the shutters back and grew brighter as she folded the other. She turned and scurried back to the bedside, bobbing like a cork on water.

"I done it. Opened the shutters like you said, sir."

Her eager little face under the maid's cap, dotted with patches of soot from her labours at the fireplace, was endearing and Lance wondered no longer at Chloe's patience with the child.

"Well done, indeed. Thank you. That is much better."

She beamed. "Got to finish the fire."

With which, she was off again, her motions quick and ungainly as she dropped down to resume poking and blowing at her coals. It proved one task at which she had evidently learned to be adept for presently a little flame flew up, grew and enveloped the smoke. The child pushed to her feet and picked up her bucket of coals.

Without thinking, Lance called to her. "Can you ask someone to bring me coffee?"

To his consternation, she dropped the bucket where she stood, regardless of any mess it might produce on the wooden floor. It landed with a thump and the maid came bobbing back to the bed, painful concentration in her face.

"Tell it again, sir."

He remembered Chloe speaking slow for the girl and mimicked her. "Can you ask someone to bring me coffee? Can you remember that?"

She nodded several times. "Ask someone to bring me coffee."

"No, the coffee is for me, the invalid, you know." He amended the instruction. "Ask someone to bring coffee for the invalid."

"Ask someone…" Her face fell. "Who be someone?"

Lance cast about in his mind for a name and found the one he knew best. "Jack. Ask Jack to bring coffee for the gentleman."

He repeated it and the child's eagerness revived.

"Ask Jack to bring coffee for the gentleman … ask Jack to bring coffee for the gentleman…" She had no further attention to spare for him, muttering the words as she trotted back to her coal bucket, picked it up and exited, pausing neither for permission to leave nor making a curtsey.

It occurred to Lance that she never had curtsied, unless the bobbing was meant to convey that obeisance. He was inclined to doubt whether any coffee would be forthcoming, but he'd had no time to do more than make use of the chamber pot before the footman entered, bearing a tray.

"Ah, Jack! In excellent time."

"Good morning, sir. Tibby said you wished for coffee."

"Indeed I do, but I confess I had little hope of her remembering to tell you."

Jack had set down the tray on the dresser and was busy pouring from the pot. "Oh, yes, sir. Tibby is perfectly able once she understands what is wanted. And you must have took care to say it slow." He came to the bed. "Allow me to bank the pillows for you, sir."

"Thank you."

The footman held out the saucer for him to take the cup and laid it on the bedside table. "I've ironed the clothes you picked out yesterday. I'm no valet, but I'll do my best to help you dress, sir."

Lance thanked him. "It will be a pleasure to wear anything other than a nightshirt."

Jack hesitated. "You look better this morning, sir. Not so pale, and them shadows in your face are less."

Putting up a hand, Lance ran his fingers under his eyes and laughed. "I dare say I must look a very scarecrow."

The footman did not deny it. "You'll gain your weight back once your appetite improves, sir. Now, I'll be off to fetch your hot water."

Lance nodded and resumed drinking, reflecting that he need not be surprised Chloe had refused him. He could hardly be a prepossessing sight. Small wonder he could not attract her. The coffee put heart into him. At least he now had a chance to meet her on equal terms. It was hard indeed to make a favourable impression lying on one's back and at the mercy of her ministrations. How might she react to his presence as more guest than invalid?

Chloe emerged from the book-room with Basil, with whom she'd been in conference about the day's requirements, just in time to see Lord Pettipher descending the stairs. He was supported by the bannister on one side and Jack on the other, his progress slow and careful.

Not wishing to distract him, Chloe stood and watched, struck by the elegance of his figure, his unexpected height and the difference made to his decidedly gaunt features by hair neatly combed and a pristine neck-cloth. In health, he must be singularly good-looking. That he had not been snapped up into marriage was a miracle. The power of Clarissa's memory must be great indeed.

He saw her as he took the last few steps and the smile that charmed her broke out. "See how effective has been your nursing, ma'am?"

Chloe moved forward. "I am very glad to see you up at last. Come into the dining parlour and we may all take breakfast together."

She led the way across the hall and entered to find Miss Flook already seated at the table. She looked up and exclaimed. "Gracious, you are up! How excellent." Rising from her seat, Agatha made haste to pull out the chair where an extra place had been laid. "Sit here, my dear lord. You cannot be too careful, and I dare say even the stairs may have tired you."

Chloe regarded the invalid with a critical eye and saw that he was indeed leaning heavily on Jack's arm. Had he been allowed up too soon? She made up her mind and turned to Basil, who had moved to the sideboard where the breakfast dishes were laid out.

"When you are done serving, Basil, please have Tibby make up the fire in the back parlour and move the daybed near it. His lordship may rest there after breakfast."

"And where will you be?"

She had spoken in a low voice, but Lance had evidently heard it over the business of being tenderly handed into his seat and fussed over by Agatha. She came to the table and waited for Basil to draw out her chair before sitting.

"I have work on hand, but I will sit with you for a space."

"Yes, indeed, my lord," chimed in Miss Flook, "and I may take a turn when Mrs Quilter has to leave you."

Lance did not look to be much satisfied with this programme, though he thanked her, remarking that he might have his revenge upon her for his geese. He accepted a cup of coffee from Chloe's hand and was persuaded to a plate of ham, though he rejected the eggs.

"I have not yet a strong enough stomach for baked eggs."

Miss Flook could not let this pass. "Oh, but eggs are more easily digested than ham, my dear lord."

"Let him be, Agatha. He knows best what he feels like eating." Chloe smiled across the table. "As long as he eats something, I am satisfied."

Lance returned the smile. "I will do my poor best. I am in general a very good trencherman, you must know."

"Are you? You remember being so?"

He frowned, seeming to look inward. "Yes, I think I do." A grin came. "Well, not as a rule the morning after a night of carousing."

Chloe lowered her cup, studying him over the rim. "Indeed? Do you make a habit of carousals then?"

"I did, when my friend Wintringham was in Town. A terrible influence he was used to be. Though he has become a very saint since his marriage."

Chloe began to butter a roll. "I believe you have mentioned his name before."

"I might well do so. We have been intimate since our days at the university." A mischievous look rippled across his face. "Whenever, that is, we were not being sent down for some misdemeanour or other. Not, I hasten to add, of my making. Wintringham was to blame."

"The more I hear of this Wintringham, the less I am disposed to approve of him."

Lance laughed. "No one did. Vince was always very wild."

Miss Flook, who had been consuming her portion of egg, now re-entered the conversation. "But did you not imply that marriage had tamed him?"

"Oh, Lily had him on a leading string in a matter of weeks. If he is not precisely a pattern card of virtue, he has settled down a good deal. He dotes on his wife so that it is quite a comedy to see how he lights up the moment she enters a room." His gaze slipped to Chloe's and he held her eyes briefly. "I envy him his luck."

She felt warmth rising in her cheeks and looked away, hunting the table for a distraction. The jam pot caught her eye and she seized it, taking refuge in dropping a dollop of the dark blackberry preserve onto her plate.

To her relief, Agatha took up the subject. "I believe it is often the case that a young man may be turned from a life of vice by a good woman. A good many tales have been written about that very thing."

Chloe could not let this pass. "Oh, you will be quoting your beloved romances, Agatha. I very much doubt of real life proving out your theory."

"Oh, but —"

"I fear Mrs Quilter is in the right of it. Besides, there was never any viciousness in Vince. He was merely a rebel and now has no reason to be kicking up his heels."

"And why was he a rebel?"

Lance frowned, seemingly concentrating and Chloe became conscious of feeling mildly apprehensive. She was not therefore much surprised at his disappointed look.

"That I can't remember. I recall that he was rebellious, but the reason for it escapes me."

She felt an irresistible urge to reassure him. "Perhaps because it is further in the past? I believe you said you were coming from a visit to your friend when your carriage foundered here."

His brow cleared. "Yes, you are right. I did say so, didn't I? I had been visiting at Wintringham Hall before Christmas. Is it nearly Christmas?"

"Why, yes. We are within a couple of weeks of that festival."

He took a draught of coffee and set down the cup. "Yes, Christmas." A frown came. "We talked of Nelson. Now why?"

Chloe exchanged a glance with Miss Flook, who looked dismayed. Well, why not say it? She assumed a light tone. "I expect because of the Admiral's untimely demise."

"England's hero!" Agatha whipped out a handkerchief, dabbing at her eyes. "Such a tragedy that he should lose his life while keeping the invaders from our shores."

A frown creased Lance's brow for a moment. Then it cleared. "Trafalgar! That was it."

"Indeed it was." Chloe gave Agatha a tiny shake of her head and made haste to direct the talk back to a less painful channel. His moods were difficult enough without adding the distresses of the wider world to the mix. "But that was in October and here we are approaching the season of goodwill. I wonder you did not remain at Wintringham Hall with your friends for the festivities."

Lance did not appear disturbed by the change of subject. "They urged me to remain for it, but I know I had reasons why

I must go home." He gave a sly grin. "Besides, I felt horribly *de trop*. I must fall in love and marry myself before I go again, I think."

The pointedness of this Chloe could not mistake. She busied herself with replenishing his coffee cup, and was glad when Agatha, resuming a cheerful mien, began to twitter in response.

"Oh, I am sure, my lord. A gentleman as prepossessing as yourself? There can be no difficulty. You have only to throw the handkerchief, I am persuaded."

Lance smiled, but made no answer, instead addressing himself to his plate.

Chloe seized on this. "Yes, sir, I wish you will cease talking and set yourself to do a little more justice to the ham, of which I note you have as yet partaken of no more than a bare slice. Agatha, say not one word more to him until he has eaten at least half of what he has before him."

"Oh, indeed, my dear lord, that will not keep a sparrow alive. Do, do take a little more."

Lance threw Chloe a glance brimful of amusement, but obediently ploughed his way in silence through another slice before pushing the plate away. "No more. I am done."

Chloe urged the basket of warm rolls upon him. "Try a sweet roll. They are very light."

The green eyes appraised her. "I will eat it, if you will butter it for me."

She paused, holding the basket aloft. "I am not convinced you are too weak to wield a butter knife, sir."

His lips twitched. "Perhaps not, but I plead weariness and may faint if I am obliged to do everything for myself."

She had to laugh. "Wretched creature! Very well then."

She set down the basket and became aware of Agatha's astonished gaze going from her to Lance and back again.

Feeling horribly conscious and convinced her colour must be heightened, she attempted to laugh it off.

"Would you have believed, Agatha, a day or so ago, that this wretch would begin funning in this abominable fashion? I declare, I am half inclined to refuse to do the deed at all, except that I dare say he is relying upon my anxiety to have him eat a little more."

The explanation did not appear entirely to allay whatever surmises had arisen in Miss Flook's head, but she readily took up the last. "Oh, indeed, so important, my dear Mrs Quilter, that he should recruit his strength. Would you wish me to do it in your stead?"

But Chloe had already taken one of the soft sweet rolls and was busily cutting it in half. "I shall indulge him this once, my dear Agatha, but must take leave to inform him —" turning a kindling eye upon the culprit — "that the trick will not work upon me a second time."

He had the grace to laugh. "I am all apology and gratitude, dear, kind and condescending Mrs Quilter."

She was in the act of buttering the roll, but at this the knife stilled and she cast him a darkling look. "Do you wish for this roll to be thrown at you, sir?"

He made his mouth prim, though the green eyes danced as he held out his plate. "By no means, ma'am."

She laid the roll upon it. "Do not imagine I am fooled by that meek tone. Agatha, you may stop laughing if you don't wish to join his lordship in my ill graces."

Miss Flook's hiccupping giggles, which had in fact relieved Chloe's burgeoning embarrassment, here redoubled for a moment. "F-forgive me, dear Mrs Q-Quilter! But if you will be so very… How very naughty of you, my lord, indeed."

"There, you see, sir, it is all your fault."

Lance shook his head in mock regret. "I am desolated. Pray do not throw me out into the snow, even though I deserve as much."

"You do, but it ceased snowing a day or so ago. There is very little left to show for the storm that preceded your accident."

He had been nibbling at the roll, but he set it down in a bang, slapping a hand on the tablecloth. "Accident! I remember! There was an obstruction, was there not? Rowley warned me of it a little too late. I lost control and we slid. My horses! Are they injured? Did they survive?"

The sudden change of mood was disconcerting, but Chloe hastened to deflect his concern. "No, they were lucky. A few grazes in the pair behind who became distressed. One caught his leg over the trace, but Rowley has been treating his wound daily and believes nothing serious will come of it."

A sigh escaped Lance. "Thank God! My prize team are those blacks. If they had taken any serious hurt, I could not forgive myself. I should have changed them at the first halt rather than pushing them on. Though they are excellent cattle and ought to be good for two stages."

"But perhaps not in the snow?"

He shook his head. "Decidedly not. If I'd had my wits about me, I would not have been travelling at all."

"You need not reproach yourself for that. There were few vehicles on the road that day, it is true, but I understand the mail coaches continued to run throughout."

He appeared dissatisfied, though he said no more. But his mood had darkened and he picked at the roll in a desultory fashion. Chloe found Agatha regarding her with a look compound of concern and question. She shook her head to indicate the need for silence and herself drank the last of her coffee.

At which point Basil, who had retired after seeing everyone served, re-entered the room. "The back parlour is warmed now, ma'am, if his lordship should care to rest there."

Chloe rose. "Come, my lord. If you are finished, let us repair to the parlour. Basil, pray take his lordship's arm, if you please."

Lance had risen, but he balked at the offer of assistance. "I am sure I can manage alone."

"I dare say you can. But Basil will remain at hand as we go."

She was dismayed to see that in fact his strength began to fail when he had barely entered the hall. But Basil was on the watch and moved into place, setting an arm about Lance's back. The motion was unobtrusive and accepted without comment. It did not take many minutes to reach the back parlour, and Chloe thought the invalid looked glad enough to sink down upon the daybed and rest against the cushions placed to receive him. Basil lifted his legs up for him, setting his feet upon a convenient cloth so that his shoes would not dirty the upholstery.

Chloe saw Lance's eyes close and took a seat on a chair opposite, watching him with a little concern. Was this mercurial temperament habitual or engendered by his injury? She wished she had known him before it so that she might judge. It was hard to know if she was drawn to the real man or to his puppet shadow.

CHAPTER SEVEN

The effort involved in rising, dressing and making his way to the breakfast table had taken its toll. Lance had felt revived by the coffee, enough to indulge in banter — the urge to tease Chloe was irresistible — but found eating almost too great a burden on his strength. And he was not really hungry. For a few moments, he took time to rest on the daybed, content with Chloe's presence in the parlour. His mind roved a little, details of the accident turning in his mind.

"I cannot understand how it happened."

"Of what are you talking?"

Her voice roused him and he opened his eyes. He had not been aware of speaking aloud. "The accident. The curricle slid in the snow, but I thought I had them well in hand."

"Your horses, you mean? You were not to blame."

Irritation flared. "I must have been. But for the life of me, I can't recall what error I made."

Chloe had been relaxed back into the chair, but at this she sat up. "You made no error, Lance. Your wheel hit a milestone concealed by the snow."

The memory of a sudden crunch leapt into his head. "So that was it! I recall the bang and the splinter of wood. The wheel must have broken."

"Yes, for I saw it all. Your carriage very nearly overturned with the impact and both you and your groom were thrown. He fell into the road and scrambled up at once, but you were less fortunate."

"I fell into the ditch?"

"Onto the verge. I have not had leisure since the thaw began to go and see what object your head may have struck, but I have no doubt it will be obvious enough. The roadside is pitted with rock from a small hill opposite."

Even as she spoke, an image of the snowy height at the right of him as he drove came to mind. "Yes, I can see it. I must have taken the curricle too close to the edge."

"The slippage did that, though I remember thinking at the time your vehicle was going a little too fast."

There was no reproach in her voice, but Lance felt the force of the accusation nevertheless. He sighed out an irritable breath. "I knew there had been a misjudgement of some kind. Well, I have come by my deserts."

"For heaven's sake, Lance!" Chloe's tone had sharpened, and she wagged a finger in his direction. "I wish you will not be so foolish. There is no occasion to be punishing yourself. Better men than you have come to grief while driving. It was an accident, that is all."

A wealth of feeling engulfed him and he had no control over his tongue. "Just as it was a mere accident that Clarissa chose to fly over thin ice? In the face of my prohibition and warning? Accident forsooth! There is no making nothing of one's culpability in such a case."

She was silent, eyeing him with a steady regard that did more to induce shame than anything she might have said.

Lance clenched his fists, forcing himself to calm. "I beg your pardon. I had no right to… Forget I said such a thing. It's been long. I should have mastered my resentment by this time."

Still she did not speak. The discomfiting constriction in his chest began to subside and he breathed more easily. With fastidious care, he forced his hands to relax.

Her voice came softly then, full of the gentleness he associated with her. "What more do you remember? Of Clarissa's death, I mean."

He winced at the word. The images ran in his head, just as they'd done in his dreams these few days. "I can see her skimming across the ice. I call out a warning, but she laughs and ignores me. She begins to spin. I shout and shout but she chooses not to hear. Then there is an almighty crack and she drops. She vanishes. Like a wraith. I hear screams, shouts, but I'm numb. I try to get to her, but they hold me back. Running, shouting somewhere behind me. I drop to the ice and crawl, dragging myself … slowly … too slow…" He stopped, balked by the hideous, beautiful image that ever haunted him. The face below the ice, eyes open, golden hair billowing about her exquisite, dead face. "Clarissa…"

He closed his eyes, willing the pain away as he'd done over and over again through the endless years. And he'd succeeded too. But the guilt! That he could never banish.

He heard a swish and a soft click. His eyes flew open. As of instinct, he looked across at the chair on the other side of the fireplace and his heart sank.

Clarissa — no, Chloe! — was gone.

Chloe stood outside the parlour door, leaning against it, one hand pressed below her bosom where her heartbeat thumped a painful tattoo. She'd heard the story from Rowley and been shocked. But to hear it from Lance, as if it were unfolding before his eyes, was more distressing than she could have believed. She wished she might weep for him, but she could not. Her escape was made lest he suspect the agitation under which she laboured.

She felt exposed, as if she, and not Clarissa, had been the subject of his discourse. She, whose likeness to the dead girl had revived all the associations of her demise. All unwitting, she'd taken him in and thrown her own heart into danger.

She drew a steadying breath. Well, she had not yet succumbed. And she would not. She was Chloe Quilter, née Kittisford, and it was scarcely her fault she happened to resemble the creature he recalled with such strength of feeling.

Turning, she opened the door and re-entered the room, adopting a cheerful mien that in no way mirrored the truth of her disordered bosom. "I am going to ring the bell and ask for a restorative. A glass of Madeira? It is early, but I think allowable to celebrate your emergence from the sickroom."

Chloe was aware of Lance regarding her in a puzzled way, but she would not allow it to deter her. Best to pretend she was not in the least troubled. Better for him too. Sympathy would only keep him locked in the memory. She tugged on the bell-pull and then returned to her chair, smiling at him as she took her seat.

"A rough beginning to your first day up, I fear. Let us talk of things less apt to distress you." She drew a steadying breath. "Tell me of your home. Ravensthorp, as I believe it is called?"

His brow creased. "I have no image of it. I know it to be a substantial property, but its look escapes me."

"Have you any remembrance of individual rooms, perhaps?"

His features lightened. "A vast hall, with a chequered floor. The staircase rises on two sides from the landing. As a boy, I never used the stairs if I could instead slide down the bannister."

Mischief shone briefly in his eye and Chloe laughed. "I can readily believe you were a handful for your nurses."

A shrug and a smile. "I dare say. My sisters would tell you I am that still."

"How many sisters do you have?"

"One now. My younger sister did not survive her first child."

A shadow crossed his face and Chloe was smitten with sympathy for yet another grief. She shifted her questions. "Your groom spoke of an elderly relative? An aunt, who lives in your house?"

"Great-aunt Adelaide. She is my mother's aunt and has lived with us forever. She suffers from an arthritic complaint." He frowned again, casting a puzzled glance at Chloe. "Now why do I remember that and not know how long she has been incapacitated? Or why she lived with us?"

"It is good that you recall as much. It shows your memory is returning."

"In fits and starts."

"Well, that is better than the blank you had at the outset."

The charming smile appeared. "What an ungrateful dog I am, Mrs Quilter. To have taken a fall and landed in such company should be enough to content me. What do I care for a past that did not include you?"

Warmth swept into Chloe's cheeks and her tone sharpened. "I wish you will not speak in that nonsensical style. It is perfectly absurd. You know nothing of me —"

"Then tell me."

Lance sat up, swinging his legs to the floor. The sudden movement was rash and instinct sent Chloe to her feet, rushing to his aid as he swayed, putting out a hand to grasp at the daybed's raised end against which he'd been lying.

"Foolish creature! Why will you not remain at rest like a sensible man?"

She seized his shoulders, holding him hard. His hand came up to grab her arm and she winced at the strength of his grip. He looked up into her face, but whatever he might have said was silenced by the opening of the door.

Chloe looked round. "Jack! Please assist his lordship to lie down again. He is unsteady."

The footman leapt to obey and she released Lance, who allowed himself to be returned to his former position. Jack, whose stature and burly form had gained him his place in Chloe's household, had no difficulty in lifting his limbs back onto the daybed.

"There, sir. Comfortable again?"

"Yes, I thank you, Jack."

Chloe detected irritation under the mild tone, but chose to ignore it. "Jack, will you bring Madeira to this room, if you please?"

"Right you are, mistress."

He left and Chloe turned to Lance, speaking on a scolding note. "It is of no use to grow impatient with yourself, sir. You must needs give your body time to recover."

A grin flashed. "Now you sound like my nurse again."

"Well, it is my role, though I must confess to being glad I had not the charge of the boy Lance. The man is troublesome enough."

His light laugh sounded. "Poor Chloe. I am a horrid imposition."

She threw up her eyes. "You are, but I ought to be used to members of the male sex imposing upon my charity."

Curiosity gleamed in his eye. "Ought you? Why?"

"Oh, because it is my invariable lot. My father began it, and I dare say it became a habit with me to allow myself to be ridden over roughshod." She recollected herself and gave an apologetic smile. "No, that is unfair. Mr Quilter never did so, and he deprecated the petty tyrannies of my stepchildren."

"You have stepchildren? Why do they not live with you?"

Chloe uttered a sputtering laugh. "They would die rather. So, I may add, would I. But the males of my household would not dream of distressing me. They ought rather to be praised for ensuring my security and comfort."

"It is an odd household, I'll say that much."

She had to laugh. "You may well. Basil scolds me for taking in every waif and stray who comes within my ken."

"Like the girl with the uneven gait. She is an original, I grant you. An amusing child."

"You've spoken with her?"

"This morning. But who is this Basil?"

Chloe was conscious of slight reluctance. How did one explain a special relationship with one's butler? "You will think it odder still, but he has been both friend and mentor to me since I was a girl, though you have seen him apparently in my service."

Light dawned in his face. "You mean the other fellow in the house? The elderly man?"

"Yes." He kept his eyes on her, seeming to wait for her to continue. Goaded, she almost threw it at him. "He may act like a butler, but he is more, much more. Without Basil Clinch, I should likely have sunk into penury."

"A woman as capable as you are? Surely not."

"I was not always so. I lacked the confidence instilled by Mr Quilter. To my disreputable father I was merely baggage and usefulness." The old resentment bubbled up and she could not keep her tongue. "As long as I sewed torn buttons, patched his shirts, brought a powder for his morning head and ran his errands, he was affectionate enough. But the moment I whined or refused to attend him — for I hated to be obliged to do so while he was at the tables in some gambling den or other — I became a nuisance he swore he would send back to England." She read shock and disbelief in Lance's face, but his words were mild enough.

"It sounds a most unwholesome life for a girl."

"You may well say so. I hated it."

"Perhaps it would have been better for you if your father had sent you back to England."

"To what end? My grandparents washed their hands of me when I elected to go with him in the first place, the more fool I. The threat was empty. I had nowhere to go and my father knew it."

"He used it to ensure your obedience?"

"Exactly so. If it had not been for Basil taking care of my interests…"

"He has been with you so long?"

"He was my father's servant and his boon companion, though he'd grown up in my paternal grandfather's service. When my father was ejected from the family home, Basil went with him."

"Did he never regret that choice?"

Chloe laughed. "Frequently. But he was fond of my father for all that and remained loyal to the end."

The door opened to admit Jack, armed with a tray upon which stood a decanter and two glasses. Chloe was not sorry to be interrupted. She had not meant to speak so freely. In general, she took care to conceal her ill beginnings. Why Lance should induce her confidence she did not know.

"Thank you, Jack. Set it down by me, if you please, and I will serve his lordship."

A side table was brought, the tray settled upon it and the footman withdrew.

Chloe lifted the decanter and smiled across at the patient. "I am persuaded I should not be encouraging you in dissolute habits, but we will refrain from telling Agatha and thus hope to escape censure."

Lance laughed as she poured. "Is she so severe upon you?"

"She would wish to be, but the poor creature flounders in recalling that she works for me. Her scolds are couched in affectionate terms." She rose and went to hand him a glass of the ruby liquid.

He took it with a word of thanks and sipped. "An excellent wine. You would appear to have a well-stocked cellar."

"For that you may thank Basil. He grew to know wines upon the Continent. Mr Quilter came to rely upon his recommendations absolutely."

Lance's brows flew up. "There seems no end to the fellow's usefulness."

"There isn't. I should not know how to go on without him."

The door opened again and Basil himself came into the room. He closed it behind him with an air of finality, and a horrid presentiment shot into Chloe's bosom. She knew that look.

"Basil! Is it ill news?"

He cast a brief glance at the invalid. "Not precisely, Miss Chloe. I regret to say Mrs Jolliffe is here."

Chloe's heart sank. "Oh, no! I did not hear any sound of an arrival."

"You will. Her carriage is coming up the lane from the village. I happened to be in the drawing-room and saw it from the window. I recognised her coachman."

Chloe was on her feet. "Dear God! Why must she come now?" She set down her glass and threw out a hand towards Lance. "What in the world shall we do with you? Basil, is there time to get him back upstairs?"

"Better if his lordship remains here. Mrs Jolliffe can have no occasion to enter this room."

She saw that Lance was looking both chagrined and bewildered. "I have not run mad, I assure you. Pray stay here and don't come out. The last thing we need is for Matilda to find you tête-à-tête with me in this cosy way."

"But who in the world is this Matilda?"

"My stepdaughter. She would be only too glad to find means to condemn me."

Her stepdaughter? Left alone, Lance could only wonder how Chloe's stepdaughter should be a married woman. It must mean her husband had been a deal older. The way she talked of him did not suggest a love match. Respect, yes. Duty perhaps. But not love.

A wash of warmth swept through him. Then he stood a chance. She was clearly out of mourning, but if she'd loved the man she would be yet unreachable. God knows he understood as much!

He sipped his Madeira, aware of the rising memories and the endless guilt. Was he a fool? Did he want Chloe because she reminded him so poignantly of Clarissa? It was madness. He ought to run, and fast. In her vicinity, he must be ever subject to the memories he had successfully subdued over the years. Chloe saw this more clearly than he. She thought his affection a false one, and she might have judged aright.

Yet the pull of this woman, alive and warm and gentle…

And he was nowhere near well enough to leave. This excursion from his room this morning had proved as much. He was as weak as a new-born kitten. Moreover, he had recovered snatches only of his past life. He had little choice but to remain here for the present — if Chloe would have him.

His thoughts were interrupted. The door opened and Miss Flook poked a head into the room. Her brow was furrowed but lightened as she caught his eye.

"Oh, excellent!" She tiptoed into the room, setting a finger to her lips. "Dear Chloe sent me to make sure you had not wandered. That woman's carriage swept into the back yard but a moment since, and we are convinced Mrs Quilter is also within for I happened to be in the back premises conferring with Mrs Vaughan and I had an excellent view from the scullery window. I caught a glimpse of a second person, and who could it be but Mrs Quilter?"

Bewildered, Lance broke in upon this hurried speech. "I beg your pardon, but I don't think I understand. Mrs Quilter left me but a moment ago."

Miss Flook threw up her hands. "Oh, how silly of me! Of course you would not know. I am talking of *young* Mrs Quilter. She is our Mrs Quilter's daughter-in-law. Though indeed that is quite as odd a circumstance as that Mrs Jolliffe is by law her daughter too, and it is ridiculous to be calling her young Mrs Quilter for both are years older than dear Chloe. And Bernard must be approaching forty, if he is a day."

Doing his best to unravel this, Lance was again thrown by the introduction of yet another name. "Bernard?"

"Mr Quilter."

"But I thought Mrs Quilter is a widow."

"Oh, yes, but Mr Bernard Quilter is the son."

"And he is near forty? Good God! Then how old could the father have been?"

Miss Flook had come to rest in Chloe's vacated chair, but this brought her half up again as she leaned towards Lance in an eager fashion, her voice dropped to a confidential murmur. "You may well be surprised, my dear lord, for I believe he was something older than I when they married, and I am turned fifty."

If Lance suspected this was paltering with the truth, he did not say so. Miss Flook's agility was surprising, but her withered features betrayed signs of more years than that. But his attention was securely caught by the realisation that Chloe's husband might well have been older than sixty at his death. A great age for any man, but his imagination balked at the implications. Such a disparity struck him as singularly unsavoury.

"How could Chloe bear it?" He was only half aware of speaking aloud, and was a little startled when Miss Flook answered him.

"Oh, you will never hear dear Chloe complain of her lot. She has spoken often to me of Mr Quilter, and in affectionate terms. 'Oswald', as she often speaks of him, was 'the kindest of men' or 'the most generous'. Indeed, she once confided to me that Mr Quilter was no less than her saviour. What is more, I understand she was in no way coerced to accept him. She told me she weighed the matter with care and chose to do so of her own free will."

This came as dismaying news to Lance, but he concealed his disapproval. What right had he to judge? From the little Chloe had let fall of her early life, such an opportunity to better her lot must have been tempting beyond her capacity to reject it on the grounds of her suitor's great age. He returned to the matter of the unwelcome visitors.

"It certainly explains the superior ages of her stepchildren. I gather they did not approve of their father's choice?"

"Quite the contrary!" Miss Flook's thin cheeks flew colour and her eyes sparkled with indignation. "If you could but hear the way Mrs Jolliffe speaks to her! She is insolent beyond bearing, and dear Chloe will never reprove her for it. It quite makes me burn when I am obliged to listen without a word of protest. And Harriet Quilter is quite as bad."

"The daughter-in-law?"

"Worse indeed," declared Miss Flook, warm in defence of her employer, "for she prefaces every nasty accusation with the remark that *Bernard says*, as if it is he and not she who thinks such and such or so and so. Dreadful woman!"

"Have you reason to suppose Bernard does not say or think these things?"

Miss Flook waved agitated hands. "There is no knowing if he does or not, for he would never say so before dear Chloe. He at least, to my observation, addresses her with the respect that is due to his stepmama. He is a little stiff in his manner, to be sure — quite unlike his father, so dear Chloe tells me — but I have never heard him talk to her in the rude fashion of his sister."

A burning curiosity urged Lance to probe, though he guessed Chloe would deprecate his pumping her paid companion. "What kind of a man was Mr Quilter, do you know? I mean her husband. Oswald, did you say?"

A shake of the head answered him. "I really cannot say, never having met the man. I go only by what dear Mrs Quilter has from time to time let fall."

Lance sipped the last of his Madeira and waited, not unhopeful.

A murmur of voices caught his attention. Miss Flook must have heard them too, for she glanced towards the door. "They are in the house. Chloe instructed Mr Basil to conduct them to the drawing-room, so we should not hear them from here."

She looked a trifle disappointed, and Lance suspected she would have much preferred to be one of the party receiving the guests rather than sitting on guard with him. Yet her disposition was as gossipy as any other old tabby, and he might with advantage learn yet more from her. Reprehensible it might be, but his desire to know outweighed the promptings of his conscience.

The elderly dame appeared to have fallen into reverie, sitting in a listening posture with her eyes on the carpet.

"You were speaking of Mr Oswald Quilter?"

She started, looking up as he set down his empty glass. Her eye fell on it. "Do you wish for another glass, my dear lord?"

"No, I thank you."

She was silent for a space. Then, with a guilty look towards the door, she lowered her voice again. "I fear I may have been indiscreet. I am sure dear Mrs Quilter can tell you far better than I."

Damnation! How was he to get her to open up? He changed tack. "I should not wish her to think me vulgarly inquisitive." He smiled with deliberate intent. "But I admit I am curious, Miss Flook. Will you not satisfy the whim of an invalid?"

To his intense satisfaction, she proved eminently susceptible. Her cheeks flew colour and she simpered. "You are being very naughty again, my dear lord. If Chloe could hear you!"

"But she can't. She is otherwise engaged and you have a duty to amuse me, do you not?"

She wagged a finger at him and tutted, but he grew confident she was not proof against the combination of his mischievous intent and her own long tongue. "Well, I suppose you will be answered willy-nilly."

He contented himself with a smile and was relieved when she crumbled.

"Oh, it is little enough that I can tell you, in any event. Chloe rarely speaks of him, but when she has fallen into reminiscent mood, it is always 'Oswald this' and 'Oswald that' until one is forced to believe him a very paragon."

"How so?"

"Well, she speaks of his humour and his bonhomie — so very unlike his children. He seems to have been an outgoing man, fond of company and good living. For his age, he was energetic. He rode until the end, Chloe says, and would keep up with her on a walk. She says he laughed a good deal, though she insists he had a shrewd head for business and would not suffer foolishness in his dealings."

"He sounds a remarkably good fellow." Though Lance was reluctant to admit as much. "Or is this Chloe's prejudice?"

"I cannot think it is, for she seems to feel she owes him more than mere gratitude. He was not one of these gentlemen who believe females to be mere ornaments in the home. Indeed, he insisted, she says, upon her learning how to keep accounts as well as running the household. He directed her reading and even taught her the rudiments of Latin and Greek as well as mathematics." She nodded. "You may well look surprised, sir. I found her as accomplished as I am myself, if not more so in certain areas, and I had to learn to be for I had been a governess for years."

"Are you speaking of those accomplishments a female generally acquires? What is it they all do? Drawing and painting, dancing, singing and playing an instrument?"

"Chloe does not play, and she declares she has no time for such pursuits as you mention. But I have no reason to suppose her deficient in these areas."

Lance at once countered the bridling note. "I had no intention of suggesting as much. I was merely clarifying it in my own mind."

The ruffled feathers subsided. "Of course, I perfectly understand. I do believe Mr Basil was responsible for her early education, but I do not know just what she was taught."

"Mr Basil? Ah, she said he had been more to her than his present position suggests."

"Yes, indeed. She makes no secret of her indebtedness to him, though it is not known to the servants, of course." She adopted that confiding air, leaning a little towards him. "If you wish to know, my dear sir, it is my belief that Mr Quilter was more a father to dear Chloe than a husband."

"You think that is how she thought of him?"

"Not she. I am certain she was a dutiful wife in every way."

Here a blush overspread her features, which Lance put down to consciousness of the implications. And indeed conjured images he preferred not to contemplate.

"But Mr Quilter did not think of her as a daughter, I'll warrant!"

"No, no, it is only a supposition of mine that comes about from the completeness of her education at his hands. I did not mean to imply…"

She faded out and Lance had no difficulty in interpreting what she was unable to put into words. The marriage bed was clearly very much a part of the bargain. The wonder was Chloe had not produced a child of her own.

The thought caught at him. But perhaps she had? Or had become pregnant and not been fortunate enough to carry the infant to term. Or was it her husband's great age that had rendered him less fertile? No matter. Bad enough she'd been subject to the needs of a man more than twice her age. He was persuaded it must have been a test of endurance. It could not have been a pleasure. No, for she had not loved the fellow. That much he would swear to.

Not, at least, in the way he had loved Clarissa, the way he loved Chloe now.

He caught the thought and threw it back to examine. Had he not already determined it to be a copy merely? An infatuation brought on by the confusion of his mind from the accident? After all, as she had pointed out, he barely knew Chloe.

"Though how much does one need to know a person?"

"I beg your pardon, sir?"

He'd forgotten Miss Flook. "Nothing. I was in a reverie and spoke without thinking."

She nodded in a sage manner. "It has been a feature of your condition, I notice. Is it hard to separate your thoughts? Or merely your memories?"

Surprised, he gazed at the woman. Hidden depths? Her manner was so fidgety he had taken her for something of a widgeon. Yet she'd been a governess. She could not be quite a fool. He found himself thinking seriously of her question. "I don't know. The memories slip into my head as thoughts. I do not always associate them with the past rather than the present."

"Most disconcerting for you, my dear lord."

"For Chloe too." It slipped out. He looked to see how Miss Flook took it and spied a tiny frown on her forehead.

"Yes, I suspect this habit of thinking her to be another has discomposed her a trifle. I have never seen her as flurried as when she determined to send to your people."

She stopped, a guilty expression overspreading her features. Clearly he should not have been told that. It hit hard. He'd playfully put it to Chloe that she'd be glad to be rid of him, but it was the bare truth. Or was it?

"Is she finding me a trial?"

Miss Flook at once began twittering. "Oh, no, no, my dear lord, I did not mean… There is no suggestion of… You must not take it amiss. Dear Mrs Quilter would never dream of sending you away until you are fully in your senses — or at least recovered enough to be able to travel."

The amendment pricked at him. Chloe did not wish him to remain, cluttering up her home while he pieced together the bits and pieces of his past to make a whole. Well, could he blame her? It might take months. Years perhaps, before he could depend upon recalling every little detail.

"That's why she sent to my home. She told me she had done so, but said nothing of her agitation." She would not, of course.

The companion twittered the more. "Oh, dear, I should not have said anything. My dear lord, I pray you do not dwell upon the matter. Dear Chloe will tell you herself you are welcome for as long as you need to stay. I know — I have every reason to know — she would never turn away a fellow creature in need of succour." The elderly dame began hunting in her sleeves and pockets, her voice thickening. "She is the kindest, the most compassionate being. A very angel! You must have observed it, sir."

He watched her drag out a pocket handkerchief and blow her nose, sniffing back the tears. Plain enough Miss Flook had every reason to speak as she did. "Yes, I have observed it, ma'am. I believe I took her for an angel in my half-dreaming state at the first."

The handkerchief was flourished in an impatient gesture. "Oh, a delusion! But Chloe is fit for heaven indeed. You might not think it to hear her, for I never knew anyone so capable, but she has a huge heart."

He smiled. "Big enough to encompass even these obnoxious relatives?"

"Them! Heaven knows they don't deserve as much. But Chloe will never retaliate. She preserves the strictest propriety in their presence and even says she understands Mrs Jolliffe's jealousies. The wretched woman thinks she should have this house, even though her father left it specifically to dear Mrs Quilter's use for her lifetime."

"Then she does not own it?"

"No, indeed. It is by way of a dower house, I understand, though it had never been designated as such. Mr Quilter was determined to ensure her future, and I am happy to say the lawyer in the case — Mr Sperring, that is, a very good sort of man — is scrupulous in seeing that his wishes are carried out."

"He was an executor of the will?"

"That I don't know, but I imagine so, for it is he who sees to the allowance and advances any monies for repairs and such. I know dear Mrs Quilter applies to him rather than to Mr Bernard Quilter, who has of course inherited the main house in Mortain. I have only been there once, for Chloe does not like to visit where she is not welcome, but it is a large establishment. I do not know how dear Mrs Quilter managed when she was obliged to run the place."

Lance heard this with an odd leap in his chest. The thought flitted through his mind that Chloe would not be dismayed by the task facing her at Ravensthorp. No, he was going too fast. There was scarcely a hope of persuading her to that future. He was far from succeeding even in attaching her, let alone persuading her to marriage. He'd offered several times already, but he knew not whether he was any more serious in his proposals than Chloe in hearing them.

"Shall we play at German Whist, my dear lord? It is a game suitable for two. I believe there is a pack of cards somewhere about in the desk."

Miss Flook was up and searching a small bureau parked against the wall. Along with the daybed, a small table or two and a couple of chairs, this seemed all the furniture the little room possessed. It was both cosy and odd. Was he unused to small rooms?

Lance pretended pleasure as the elderly dame triumphantly held up a pack of cards. He might as well play. Loath as he was to give up talking of Chloe, he recognised the danger of giving himself away. Unthinkable, when he did not yet know his own mind.

"My dear Matilda, I am persuaded you would not have had me refuse my help. Especially when I was a witness to the accident."

Mrs Jolliffe's disapproving mien did not abate. The strong jaw she'd inherited from Oswald had been attractive in him, but gave an unfortunate hardness to a womanly face, especially one broadened by the exigencies of childbearing, which had also thickened her figure. Chloe had long suspected Matilda's dislike to be rooted in envy of her stepmother's youthful form. Her face too, perhaps, for Oswald had not scrupled to remark favourably upon it in his daughter's presence. She pitied the woman, even while her spite rankled.

The two visitors had parked themselves on the long sofa in the drawing-room Chloe kept ready for visitors. It was more formally set out than most of the rooms in Derry Lodge, with the seating accommodation almost hugging the walls, which made it appear larger than it was. The white marble mantel set off the thin-striped wallpaper and gilded matching sofas and chairs. Its elegance was especially valuable to Chloe when her stepdaughter chose to come, since she was aware Matilda envied her taste — which afforded a measure of satisfaction since she was predictably critical of Chloe's charity towards Lance.

"I fail to see why you should have housed the fellow. He could very well have been suitably attended at the inn in the village."

"Well, no, he would not have been suitably attended, I'm afraid, Matilda. Perhaps you are little acquainted with Mrs Buller, the landlord's wife? She is utterly unsuitable to be nursing an invalid."

"But a nurse might have attended him," chimed in Harriet, as spare as her sister-in-law was ample, and setting her head sideways in the birdlike way she had. "Bernard said he was persuaded you must have brought in a nurse, and Mrs Buller could well have done the same."

"True, but I fear she would have balked at having an invalid in the house. Besides which, I told Doctor Goodleigh I would not entrust the delicate task of nursing a man with a concussion to Mrs Prettejohn. Her style of nursing is a deal too rough and ready for my taste."

A spasm which might have been a smile crossed Matilda's face. "I did say, Harriet, did I not, that it would be found to be typical of Chloe to be taking in any unfortunate who came in her way?" She added on a waspish note, "I dare say you set that glumping child you insist upon keeping here to look after the man."

Setting her teeth, Chloe fought down a hot protest. "No, Matilda, I have more sense than to be setting Little Tibby to a task beyond her powers. She does very well if one is careful to speak slow and repeat one's orders a time or two. But you know very well she is incapable of caring for an invalid."

Harriet tittered. "So I should suppose. Indeed, Bernard says he is astonished the child is capable of anything."

Perfectly aware that Harriet's more damaging statements were attributed to her husband as a matter of course, Chloe ignored this. "You will both no doubt be relieved to know that Lord Pettipher has today been able to leave his bed for the first time."

The effect of this announcement could not have been more startling. Matilda's jaw dropped and Harriet's rather protuberant eyes, which always seemed too big for her head, seemed in danger of springing from their sockets.

Before either could recover, the door opened to admit Basil, laden with a tray, and with Jemima behind him, similarly burdened.

"Ah, excellent. You'll take a glass of something, I hope?" Chloe waited while the trays were set down upon the table at one end of the room. "Wine? Or is it Ratafia, Basil?"

The butler inclined his head and looked pointedly at Matilda. "Ratafia or claret, madam?"

Chloe eyed her goggling relatives. "I think it had better be the claret for both, Basil. And if those are Mrs Vaughan's jumbles, Jemima, hand them around, if you please." Then to the visitors, "You will find them exceedingly tasty."

The business of supplying both ladies with a glass and a little plate set on an occasional table convenient to each elbow gave time enough for each to recover from stupefaction. Indeed, Harriet, having taken a gulp of the fortifying liquid, barely waited for the servants to leave the room before leaning towards Chloe, her tone awed.

"Is that who he is? A lord?"

Concealing a guilty triumph, Chloe raised her brows. "My visitor, you mean? Did you not know? I had supposed your informant must have told you."

"Indeed, no. I mean — well, it was only a rumour when all is said, and of course we had to come and verify it."

"Of course."

The dry note was lost on Harriet, but her sister-in-law, setting down the glass at which she had been sipping, frowned her down. "Hush, my dear." And turning to Chloe, "I should not wish you to think we had come here on a mission of mischief. Concern for your reputation was all that brought us."

"Why, thank you." Chloe gave a smile as false as the other's unctuous tone. "There was no need, however. It is not as if I live alone. Miss Flook has shared the nursing of his lordship, and —"

"What kind of a lord is he?"

"Harriet!"

Chloe ignored Matilda. "He is the Earl of Pettipher."

"Great heavens!"

"For pity's sake, Harriet! It makes no matter which lord he is, and if he is an earl, it is worse than ever." Matilda turned her disapproving gaze on Chloe. "How could you be so indiscreet? If it should become known you have an earl in one of your spare bedchambers!"

"He's not in one of the spare bedchambers at this moment. He's in the back parlour with Miss Flook keeping him company."

Matilda's already high colour deepened. "That is nothing to the purpose. It is scandalous for him to be here at all."

"How so? It is not as if I am unchaperoned. The house is full of servants besides."

"Servants!" The scoffing note became pronounced. "Servants are no protection. And you said yourself you have been nursing him. You must have been in his bedchamber."

"I could scarcely nurse him from the corridor."

Harriet had subsided into her claret, but at this she tittered. "How true. A task even beyond your capabilities, and Bernard says his papa had made you all too capable."

Matilda brushed this aside. "The point, Chloe, is that you have been frequenting the man's chamber, and I have little doubt you sat with him at night, alone, and in your night attire."

Warmth rose in Chloe's cheeks and her bosom was hot with indignation to which she might not give way. She could not deny the accusation, but she evaded it. "I don't know why you should assume as much, Matilda. But I should certainly not scruple to do so if it were necessary in the course of tending to his lordship."

"And set the world talking! Oh, I know you think your servants are loyal, but they must have talked or the news would not have got about."

Bridling, Chloe fought back. "You think so? Then you make no allowance for the tongues of the villagers, several of whom were necessarily privy to the news of the invasion. There was a curricle and four horses to be rescued too, besides the groom.

I expect the whole event gave rise to a good deal of speculation."

"Well, that must be so," said Harriet in a judicious tone, breaking off a portion of the jumble biscuit on her plate in an absent way. "And Bernard has always done you the justice, Chloe, to believe your actions in taking in these oddities of yours to spring from disinterest. He would not suspect you of trying to entrap this earl as you entrapped —" She broke off, dropping the biscuit in her lap and throwing a hand to her mouth, her prominent eyes showing consternation, her thin cheeks taking on a touch of colour.

Chloe remained unmoved. It was not news to her that she was held by her stepchildren to have bewitched Oswald for her own ends. "Since I had no notion of his identity when I took in Lord Pettipher, I must hope to escape that particular accusation."

"It is immaterial what we think." Matilda's hard eyes challenged Chloe. "The world and his wife will not be so forgiving."

Chloe was within an ace of saying that the world and his wife could go hang, but she held her tongue. Instead, she adopted a placating note. "If it comforts you, I have sent to Lord Pettipher's people. I don't doubt some responsible party will be along to fetch him home at an early date."

"The sooner the better. You cannot be too careful, Chloe. A widow is particularly vulnerable."

"True, Matilda, which is why I hired Miss Flook for my companion."

Harriet, apparently recovered from her embarrassment and with the bit of jumble once more in hand, piped up again. "Will we meet him? This lord, I mean? What was his name again?"

"Lord Pettipher. You will certainly meet him, if you intend to remain here for any length of time. Did you come prepared to stay?"

Matilda's gaze narrowed. "Naturally not."

"I am disappointed. I thought you might have determined to lend me countenance." Both women flushed and Chloe hid a smile. "But I am being selfish. Of course your two households will not run without you, and you have children and husbands to care for. I suppose it will make you too late home if you were to remain for dinner, but you'll take a luncheon?"

The offer was graciously accepted and Chloe left them to wine and jumbles with the excuse of making arrangements, aware both tongues would be busy the moment the door closed behind her. She headed for the book-room, intending to send for Mrs Vaughan to come to her there, but an intrusive thought made her halt. Best to warn Lance. He might prefer not to meet them, and who could blame him? He might be exhausted by this time in any event.

Shifting direction, she hurried to the back parlour and opened the door upon a cosy scene. Agatha had pulled up her chair to the sofa and, with the little table between them, the two were engaged in a game of cards.

Lance looked up as she entered, and Chloe felt a flutter in her bosom as his eyes lit and his handsome features broke into a smile.

"Here she is!"

This brought Miss Flook's head round. "Dear me, is it you, Mrs Quilter? Have your visitors gone?"

"By no means. I came to warn you they will be here for luncheon. They are agog to meet you, my lord, but if you are too tired to go into company, I will make your excuses."

He frowned. "Why in Hades should they wish to meet me?"

"I told them who you were. Few earls come in their way, you know, and your situation here is of avid interest."

He did not look to be much gratified, but Agatha forestalled anything he might have said, jumping up from her place. "Was Mrs Jolliffe severe upon you, my poor dear Mrs Quilter? Did she give you a scold?"

"She tried her best, but I was proof against her. And Harriet all but accused me of —" She broke off, realising where her words were tending. The last thing she must do was to give Lance the notion he had compromised her, which he would take if she mentioned anything of entrapment. He would use such ammunition to the full if he had it, she was persuaded.

Fortunately, Miss Flook's indignation glossed over her slip. "How they should dare! It is too bad. As if you had our dear lordship here by design."

Lance's eyes danced. "Ah, I begin to understand. My presence had been thoroughly objectionable had I not been of the peerage. Well, I suppose I must satisfy their curiosity."

"Not if you don't feel up to it," Chloe insisted. "They have no rights in the matter and I am the more inclined to deny them, to be frank with you."

His eyes quizzed her. "But I have the liveliest curiosity to meet them, Mrs Quilter. And I have been resting all morning on this daybed, have I not?"

"Well, on your own head be it." Chloe turned for the door. "I must see my cook. Agatha, will you slip into the drawing-room and play hostess until I return? I dare say his lordship will survive a few minutes alone."

On her return to the drawing-room, Chloe guessed at once that the visitors had been pumping her companion for information. Miss Flook's spare cheeks were flying colour and she was looking indignant, sitting very straight in her chair with her eyes snapping.

She looked up in obvious relief as Chloe entered. "Oh, there you are, dear Mrs Quilter! I have been telling Mrs Jolliffe and young Mrs Quilter how poor Lord Pettipher has little recollection of his past life."

Chloe took it up at once. "Very true. Indeed, he does not recall the accident very well either."

"No, and as I have been saying, we have no information about his situation in life beyond his rank and the name of his home. Is that not so?"

The pointedness of this was unmistakeable. Matilda and Harriet had clearly been attempting to discover the extent and value of Lance's estate. It struck Chloe for the first time that she'd had no interest in either. Her sympathies were caught by the man rather than his status. But of course her relatives were bound to suppose she would take the first opportunity to acquaint herself with all the details of his lordship's possible wealth, considering their opinion of her character. Naturally she would be ready to take advantage of the ripe plum that had fallen into her lap!

She retook her seat, forcing a smile. "It is hard indeed for his lordship, since he has only snatches of memory, rather like a patchwork, you know."

Harriet's stance became more intense, her nose thrusting forward like a beak. "But he did know who he was?"

"By no means. At first he had no memory at all. And Doctor Goodleigh would not permit us to tell him anything."

Matilda sniffed. "That seems an odd proceeding. Surely you could have helped him remember by giving him his own history."

"Gracious, no," chimed in Agatha. "The doctor specifically instructed us to refrain. It was most important that his lordship should remember by himself."

Chloe took it up. "But when his memory began to return, it became frustrating for him not to receive answers to his questions and Doctor Goodleigh then changed his tactic. However, as we know nothing of his lordship's life, we have not been particularly helpful."

Both parties looked dissatisfied and Chloe could only be glad she had not engaged in extensive discussions with Rowley, though indeed a groom's knowledge was necessarily limited.

"Well, and how is his memory now?"

"Really, Matilda, we have had small opportunity to find out. As I told you, today is the first day his lordship has been well enough to rise from his bed."

No sooner had she spoken than the door opened and Lance appeared in the aperture. He remained in the open doorway for a space, holding on to both the door and the jamb, his eyes sweeping the room.

Both Matilda and Harriet were riveted, and Chloe had no difficulty in realising why. Lance's height and handsome features, despite the gaunt shadows in his face, were striking. She could well imagine what thoughts were passing through their minds.

Rising, she went towards him. "My lord, is this prudent? You should not be standing about in this way. I wish you will sit down."

He stared at her. "Clarissa, who are these people?"

Shock swept through her. He had not mistaken her for some hours. Must he lose control of his mind just at this moment? She met his eyes. A spark within them alerted her suspicions. He was faking!

She gave him a minatory frown and took his arm. "I think you had better sit down, my dear sir. And you have forgotten again, I fear. I am Chloe, not Clarissa, remember?"

He allowed her to take his arm and lead him to a seat beside Agatha, who was occupying the sofa opposite the one where the visitors were perched.

Chloe turned back to the ladies. "You will forgive my lord Pettipher, I know. He is not well enough to be performing the normal courtesies. My lord, allow me to present my stepdaughter, Mrs Jolliffe, and my daughter-in-law, Mrs Quilter."

Lance was leaning back in the sofa, gripping one arm for support. He set the other to his brow as he inclined his head. "Forgive me. I am a little confused. My late accident…"

"Yes, they know, my lord," Chloe cut in, moving to retake her chair, which she had brought forward and set at a slight remove from the sofas. Conveniently, the position enabled her to see everyone without being obliged to keep turning her head from one side to the other.

Harriet lowered her voice, casting an admiring glance at Lance as she turned to her hostess. "Why did he call you Clarissa?"

Chloe saw a quiver at Lance's lip, but he did not look at her. Was the wretch amused? He had done it on purpose, then. What in the world would he be at?

"It seems I resemble a lady in his lordship's distant past. In his delirium — you do not object to my mentioning it, I hope, my lord?" Lance wafted a couple of fingers, his hand still at his brow. Permission? Very well then. "In his delirium, he very naturally thought I was indeed Clarissa. Occasionally, he slips into using the name still."

Lance lowered his hand and gazed across at the avid interest in the faces of the visitors. He produced a sigh. "It is an unfortunate resemblance. I have given Mrs Quilter a deal of trouble upon the matter, I fear. I had no memory other than that at the outset."

The bracket-faced creature Chloe had introduced as her stepdaughter looked decidedly sceptical. "Indeed? But I gather you have recovered more by this time?"

"Snatches only. I regret to say I am weak in mind as well as body. I fear I may be a charge on Mrs Quilter for some time to come."

The other, skinny Mrs Quilter chose to seize on this. "Until you are able to travel, we understood?"

Damn the woman! Was she intent upon queering his pitch? What was it with the two of them? Jealousy? Or did they suppose Chloe compromised by his presence? He'd meant to spy out the land and anchor himself in the place at need. Or at least make it clear he was as yet unable to leave — which was not to be laid at Chloe's door. But if they cherished the notion he endangered her reputation, he must squash it. Nothing could more surely prejudice his chances than for Chloe to believe he offered for such a reason as that.

"I believe Mrs Quilter has sent my groom to Ravensthorp. He will make all possible arrangements. I have to thank her for such a mark of thoughtfulness." He flicked a look at Chloe as he spoke and found her tight-lipped. He dared not smile his reassurance, but added, "There are those at home who will be anxious for my safety."

Let them make what they chose of that.

Mrs Jolliffe proved equal to the challenge. "I make no doubt of it. And with Christmas on the horizon, I am sure they will be anticipating your early return."

The other turned her avid bug-like eyes upon him. "Or one may come to you here, perhaps? Anyone close to you must wish to be personally assured of your safety, my lord."

Fishing, eh? He could afford to take the bait, could he not? "I believe I do have memory of one such. It is not very clear. No doubt an arrival will help to banish any such obscurity."

The skinny creature appeared convinced by his act, but he was by no means certain of the stepdaughter. Was there a sceptical gleam in her eye? Lance set himself to charm.

"I do not know this country. Beyond that I am presently in a village." He looked to Chloe. "What was the name again?"

"Staggesden. But you need not trouble yourself with such details, my lord."

Lance ignored the minatory note. "But I wish to know." He threw a smile over the two visitors. "Have you come far? Is this an obscure place?"

The stepdaughter — Mrs Jolliffe, was it? — bridled. "Scarcely obscure when I understand your carriage came to grief in the main road below us here. This house lies between Bedford and Northampton. A quieter spot, I grant you, than my village of Goldington. We are just outside Bedford. It has its conveniences, but I venture to say Chloe is more pleasantly placed here."

There was a suggestion of venom in the tone. Had not Chloe said the creature coveted this house? He was not obliged to answer as the other Mrs Quilter leapt in, head on one side.

"It is a pretty establishment, and Chloe does not mind the change, do you? Though I must suppose you miss the spaciousness of Mortain." She tittered. "I have supplanted her as mistress there, you must know, and I do feel for you, Chloe."

"You need not, Harriet. I am perfectly content." Chloe turned on Lance, as it seemed to him. "If you wish for a map to guide you, sir, I can supply you with one in my book-room. But I dare say you would be better employed in re-acquainting yourself with your own country."

He gave an elaborate sigh. "So I should, if I could only remember its location."

"Ravensthorp lies beyond Northampton, as I understood from your groom. Beyond that, I can tell you nothing."

The woman Harriet's eyes lit. "A Peerage! Have you one, Chloe? There will be detail in there of your estates, my lord. And indeed of your family connections too."

True enough. A real curiosity attacked Lance and he looked to Chloe for the answer. She shook her head, looking regretful.

"I don't have one, I'm afraid. No doubt Oswald kept one at Mortain, but I never had occasion to use it."

The woman Harriet's triumph was palpable. "I will hunt for it upon my return." An eager look came Lance's way. "I may copy it out for you, my lord, and send it."

"Why, thank you, ma'am. How extremely kind."

She beamed, positively basking in his gratitude, Lance thought. Not so Mrs Jolliffe.

"Good heavens, Harriet, I should think you have something better to do than to be spending hours copying from the Peerage! Someone roundabout must have one. Let Chloe borrow one instead."

"Oh, it will be no trouble to me, Matilda. I enjoy copying. And if it may help Lord Pettipher…"

"It would indeed, but I should not wish to put you to any inconvenience."

Her protestations were voluble and Lance was satisfied with the change. The more she concerned herself with his needs, the less she would think of Chloe's situation. It was in his head to draw her out on her home, since that was where Chloe had evidently lived with her elderly husband, but a wave of real tiredness hit him.

He reeled slightly and caught at the arm of the sofa, putting a hand to his head in a genuine gesture this time. His voice all but failed him. "Forgive me … been up too long…"

Chloe was by his side in an instant, catching him by the shoulders to hold him steady. "Agatha, ring the bell! Or no, go into the hall and call for Jack. It will be quicker."

He heard her through a daze, aware of the rustle of skirts and a distant murmuring.

"Head down, between your knees! You mustn't swoon!"

He did as the voice bade him, recognising Chloe's nursing tone. The position was uncomfortable, but presently the faintness began to recede. He sat up slowly and found Jack in Chloe's place.

"That's it, sir. Up you get! I've got you. Lean on me, sir."

"The back parlour, Jack," came Chloe's voice a little ahead of them. "Let him lie on the daybed until he is well enough to take the stairs."

Recalling the ladies, Lance tried to turn. "Must say farewell. Excuse myself."

"You have already done so, and no farewell is necessary. I will say all that is needful."

It was the soothing Chloe he knew well, and he allowed himself to abandon effort, moving as Jack directed until he settled, with some relief, on the daybed, closing his eyes.

"Give him a little of that Madeira, Jack. Or better yet, get him a drop of brandy. I will stay until you get back."

A cool hand was laid upon his brow and he gave a sigh of contentment, only half aware of murmuring aloud. "So good … have my nurse back."

Her tone changed. "Well for you it was real this time. For an instant, I thought you were play-acting again."

"Wasn't…"

"Yes, I knew that when your face drained of colour." The hand left his forehead, but he felt her take up his wrist and feel for his pulse. "You should have stayed put, foolish creature!"

He blinked his eyes open and found her regarding him with concern, and a trifle of exasperation. "Wanted to protect you…"

"I know. Quixotic of you, but quite unnecessary. I am well able to handle those two."

He grimaced. "I know what they think. She does. Matilda? The other —"

"If you suppose you have charmed Harriet into taking my part, I am sorry to disappoint you. She always follows Matilda's lead."

He was chagrined, but as Jack returned at this moment, he said no more. The brandy, which he threw down his throat in one burning swallow, revived him. Within a few minutes, his senses were back under his control and he was able to sit up.

"Back to bed for you, my lord Pettipher."

"I'd like to protest, but I am obliged to admit to a longing for it. And I'm hungry."

"Jack will bring you a tray. I'll tell Jemima to prepare it."

She took his empty glass and nodded at the footman. With a regretful sigh, Lance gave himself up to Jack's assistance, glad of the man's strong arm as he negotiated the stairs. The effort was enough to make him lose interest in what might be going forward in the drawing-room below. He was relieved to resume the irresponsibility he'd enjoyed these few days, letting the future take care of itself.

The bed was inexpressibly comforting, and a stray thought floated into his mind as he drifted into sleep. All that was wanting was the warmth of Chloe's body laid against his own.

CHAPTER EIGHT

The visitors did not depart until the early afternoon, keeping Chloe too engaged to attend to her patient. She was obliged to content herself with sending Miss Flook to check upon him just before luncheon was served.

"He has been asleep, but he woke just now when Jack brought him a tray," Agatha reported on her arrival in the dining room where the ladies were just taking their seats.

Harriet laid her napkin across her lap. "Is he better? I declare, he went perfectly white. It gave me a quite a turn." Since she had already expressed herself several times in much the same terms, no one but Agatha paid attention to this speech.

"His colour is indeed returned. He says he still feels tired."

"No wonder. How long has he been abed did you say, Chloe?"

"I did not, but it has been four days only."

"Four days! Goodness, why in the world did you let him up?"

The disapproval rankled, pricking at a guilty feeling Chloe had not before recognised. She nodded to Basil to begin serving the meats and patties, augmented by some pickled beans and a hastily thrown together fricassee of mushrooms. Mrs Vaughan was clearly on her mettle.

"You are right, I fear, Harriet. His lordship was insistent, however, and the doctor had sanctioned it."

"Well, I am astonished. I cannot think —"

She was interrupted by an impatient Matilda. "If the man was wishful of getting up, Chloe could hardly stop him. I am no believer in coddling. It does no good to languish in bed, growing weaker by the day." She helped herself as she spoke from the platter of cold sliced beef Basil was offering. "I applaud him for making the effort. And his injuries, I gather, are not extensive."

Chloe took the questioning look to herself. "A few bruises, other than the wound to his head, which is healing well."

"But if it has been the cause of his losing his memory," Harriet began, in an argumentative tone, but was at once crushed by her sister-in-law.

"That is nothing to the purpose."

Chloe could not let this pass. "I beg your pardon, Matilda, but it is everything to the purpose. The wound may be superficial, but it is evident there has been some internal injury. A concussion cannot be considered a small thing, and I blame myself very much for leaving him alone in the back parlour. He would not then have ventured to wander, which I must suppose was the cause of his collapse."

Silenced, Matilda pursed her lips and addressed herself to her meal. But Harriet positively glowed. Triumph? Perhaps Lance had indeed charmed her. Though it was doubtful she would long hold out against Matilda's obvious disapproval. It manifested again once she had partaken of a fair portion of beef.

"How long do you suppose you may be obliged to house him?"

"I have no notion. It is early days, and you can see how he is. I shall certainly not turn him out until he is ready to go."

Harriet looked eager. "His lordship himself said he might be here for some time."

"Of course he did," snapped Matilda. "An invalid is ill qualified to judge, since he is no doubt feeling incapable at this moment. I dare say he will be itching to be off as soon as his strength permits him." She cast Chloe one of her venomous glances. "Unless you are foolish enough to insist upon his remaining."

Defiance rode Chloe. "I shall, if I judge him unfit."

Matilda's narrowed gaze flicked to the butler and Jemima, standing by to whip away the plates as soon as they were empty, and replace them with smaller ones for the fruit waiting upon the sideboard. Chloe guessed she was chagrined at being unable to utter her warnings in their presence. Relieved, she turned the subject.

"You have not yet given me your news, either of you. I trust your children are all well? And what of Mr Jolliffe and Bernard?"

Harriet at once launched into a recital of the successes of her two little ones and Bernard's pride in their achievements. Matilda was more reserved, confining herself to speaking of the good health of all, while her expression showed her mind was still centred upon Chloe's situation.

Preferring to meet Matilda head on, Chloe signed to the servants to retire once the fruit was set on the table and the coffee served. "Now, Matilda, you may have your say. I can see you are bursting with it."

The direct attack disconcerted her stepdaughter, just as she'd hoped.

"Nothing of the kind. I hope I am charitable enough to realise you had little choice in taking in Lord Pettipher. However, I cannot deny my concern, which increased as soon as you mentioned his status. It is bound to get about, and I fear for your reputation, Chloe, I really do."

Suppressing a sigh, Chloe was about to respond when Miss Flook, quivering with indignation, leapt to her defence.

"Quite unnecessary, my dear Mrs Jolliffe. You need have no apprehension while I am in residence. It cannot be thought improper for a widow, accompanied by a woman of my age, to be attending his lordship."

"If that is what you think, Miss Flook, you do not know *our* world." Though Agatha bridled at the emphasis, Matilda paid no heed. "The presence of an unmarried gentleman, and an earl at that, must always be damaging in the eyes of our acquaintance."

"I fear that is true," mourned Harriet, adding her mite. "There is no persuading people of innocence if they choose to believe otherwise."

Seeing Agatha about to burst out again, Chloe gestured to her for silence. "I am obliged to you both for your concern, but there is nothing to be done about it, I'm afraid. As you have seen, his lordship is unequal to be sent on his way and I refuse to trouble myself about what cannot be helped. People may say what they choose." She smiled upon them both. "Happily, you are both now in a position to set them right if anyone should place a false construction upon Lord Pettipher's presence in the house."

Effectively silenced, Matilda sniffed and drank her coffee. Harriet, to Chloe's amusement, began to nod like a bird pecking at the ground.

"Very true indeed, is it not, Matilda? I shall certainly testify that his lordship is far too weak to be capable of dalliance — I mean…" She broke off, reddened and coughed, resuming in an unctuous tone. "Bernard I know will be happy to hear it."

"Yes, do assure him that I have not been tempted to join Lord Pettipher in his bed."

The gasps that greeted this would have amused Chloe had she not been so irritated. Even Miss Flook failed to hear the dry note.

"My dear Mrs Quilter, I beg of you," came in a frantic whisper.

Matilda recovered first. "I have always deprecated your levity, Chloe, though no doubt Papa would have found it matter for laughter. A most unbecoming remark."

"Bernard always says you are a deal too outspoken, my dear Chloe. I shall certainly not distress him by relaying your words."

Oh, would she not indeed? It was likely the very first thing she would tell her husband. But Chloe was obliged to acknowledge it was foolish to have set up Harriet's back at least. She had no doubt undone all the goodwill engendered by Lance's charm. She perforce must backtrack.

"Forgive my little spurt of temper. I'm afraid I find it trying to be pilloried for what is in effect a good deed. It has not been easy to have my household turned upside down to accommodate his lordship's needs. Jack, for instance, has been obliged to neglect his duties to valet the invalid, and both Miss Flook and myself have been almost constantly in attendance, besides losing a great deal of sleep. I trust you will make allowances."

To her relief, Agatha at once came to her aid. "Oh, it is very true, upon my word. Everyone in the place has had to assist in one way or another."

Matilda chose to be gracious. "I can well imagine it. I am sure I am the last person to take unnecessary offence."

An outright falsehood. Chloe hid her true feelings, however. "Thank you. I felt sure you would understand."

"Well, of course," said Harriet, entering the lists. "Besides, having met his lordship, it is clear he has every idea of how indebted he is to you, dear Chloe. Bernard will perfectly understand the circumstances."

Within an ace of saying she had no interest in courting her stepson's approval, Chloe bit her tongue on the words and substituted what she knew must please. "I beg you will do all you can to reassure him, Harriet. And if you do have the time to seek out Lord Pettipher in the Peerage, I shall be eternally grateful."

Soothed, Harriet reiterated her intention of doing the necessary copying. Luncheon over, it was not long before the two ladies were ready to depart, having been escorted upstairs to Chloe's bedchamber to make whatever preparations seemed good to them.

She saw them off with unalloyed relief and went back into the house with Agatha as Basil shut the door upon the sound of the rumbling coach. "All things considered, I think we brushed through that pretty well."

Miss Flook tutted. "If only they won't turn upon you now they are out of earshot."

"I am perfectly content for them to do so, as long as I am not obliged to hear it." Chloe turned to her butler. "Basil, would you bring wine to the drawing-room, if you please? I'm sadly in need of a restorative."

He bowed and departed to the nether regions. Agatha took instant advantage of their privacy. "I have a horrid fear Mrs Jolliffe and young Mrs Quilter will not do what they may to scotch the rumours, my dear Chloe."

Chloe laughed as she headed for the drawing-room. "I fear Matilda is more likely to blast my reputation if she can. Though I was surprised at Harriet, were not you?"

"Oh, she was bowled over by our dear lordship, did you not observe it?"

"Indeed I did and must be thankful for his charming her as he did."

Agatha had taken her usual seat on the sofa, but at this she sat up. "Do you suppose he meant to do so?"

"Undoubtedly. Did you not notice that he was pretending to be disorientated when he first entered the room?"

"No! Was he indeed? How very naughty of him! Now, why?"

Chloe plonked into her chair, letting out a sigh. "A misplaced notion of chivalry, I fear. He guessed I might be under attack for his being here and meant, I believe, to demonstrate the need for it." She laughed. "But he was hoist with his own petard, the wretch."

Surprise swept into Miss Flook's face. "His collapse was then genuine? I must say I had thought so at the time, for he did indeed pale dreadfully, did he not?"

"Oh, yes. He was taken at fault for abandoning the daybed. If he gets up tomorrow, it had better be for a short period only."

But when the morrow came, there was no question of Lance rising from his bed. Jack, the first to tend him, came to the door of Chloe's bedchamber where Jemima, who maided her, met him.

"Mistress is dressing. What's to do?"

"Please tell the mistress his lordship is not well this morning."

Overhearing, Chloe came to the door in her dressing-gown, attacked by apprehension. "What is the matter with his lordship, Jack?"

The footman's features were creased in concern. "He's weak, mistress. I think it was too much for him, getting up yesterday."

"But you said he was ill!"

"A bit feverish, as it seems to me, though he's not hot."

Chloe opened the door fully and moved into the corridor. "Feverish how?"

"I'm not sure, mistress. Just in his manner."

"Oh, no, is it his memory again?" She was heading towards Lance's room, Jack keeping up beside her.

"No, he knows where he is and all. Only he's a bit agitated. He tried to get up, but he couldn't stand and I had to help him with the … well, I had to help him."

Chloe needed no further urging. Her heart in her mouth, she hurried through Lance's door, her eyes flying to the bed. It was empty.

Alarm gripped her and she turned to the footman. "Where is he, Jack?"

Three strides took Jack to the bedside. "I left him right there!"

Chloe advanced into the room, her gaze whipping from place to place. A thought seized her. "Has he fallen out?"

She ran to the foot of the bed even as Jack leaned across it. Chloe looked along the floor on the far side. Nothing. She turned to Jack. "We must search the house! He cannot have got far if he is as weak as you say."

Jack was out of the door before she had finished speaking. Chloe followed in a bang and heard the footman shout.

"He's here, mistress!"

She looked towards the stairs. Jack was a couple of steps down, leaning over something that she could not see. She hurried across. By this time, Jemima had joined them, and

Jack's shout had brought Miss Flook hurrying out of her chamber. Chloe took them in only in the periphery of her mind as she discovered Lance was sitting on the stairs in his night attire, grasping at the bannisters with both hands, his head bowed upon them. Chloe's instinct was to yell at him, but she repressed it, moving down to his level. Jack made room for her, standing below Lance in a stance ready to catch him if he should fall.

Chloe spoke gently. "Lance?" He did not move, but an indistinguishable mutter reached her. "Lance, this won't do. You must let Jack help you back to bed."

He lifted his head and his eyes seemed to focus on the footman.

Jack leaned down, hands at the ready. "That's right, sir. Let me help you up the stairs."

The invalid did not move. Chloe's heart sank. She tried again. "Lance, look at me!"

He veered his head round and blinked at her, his eyes narrowed as if in pain. He looked dreadful. Apart from the stubble at his chin, shadows marked his face under the eyes and from nose to mouth. Still he did not speak.

"Please will you allow Jack to help you back to bed? You will take cold sitting here on the stairs."

A frown creased his brow. "You're sitting here."

"Yes, but only for the purpose of urging you to return to bed. I have no wish to take cold either."

A stubborn look entered in. "I like it here."

Nonplussed, Chloe hesitated. On instinct, she did not argue. "What do you like about it?"

He regarded her steadily. "I want to stay. I don't want them to take me away in the coach."

Chloe's alarm quickened. He was not himself at all. She tried for a soothing note. "I will allow no one to take you away. But I desire you will go back to bed."

"No." He grasped the bannisters more firmly. "I won't go. You can't make me."

"Then I suppose I must sit here with you. Jack, you should sit as well. We will keep his lordship company."

Lance frowned as he watched Jack take a seat on the stairs below him, though the footman sat sideways so he could continue to keep an eye on the patient.

"There, now," Chloe said with a smile. "We may all be comfortable here on the stairs. Will that content you?"

A little sigh escaped Lance and his hold on the bannisters relaxed a little. "I don't want to be a lordship. I don't like it. They'll take me away from here."

Dear Lord, he was perfectly out of his mind again! Chloe felt far from cheerful, but she adopted a tone as close to it as she could. "Now, you know that is nonsense. This is my house and no one can take you from it if I refuse to allow it."

"Even a lordship?"

"Yes, even an earl. You are my patient, are you not?"

"Am I?"

"Yes. And do you know, it will be much easier to stop anyone from taking you away if you are safe in your bed."

"Not the stairs?"

"No, the stairs are not at all safe."

She was aware of Jemima goggling from above and Agatha leaning over a little way along the balustrade. Thank heaven neither sought to intervene!

Lance seemed to be considering her words, looking down the stairs and up them. At length, his eyes returned to her. "You are afraid I will fall if I stay here."

Chloe seized on this. "Yes, I am afraid of that. You are not yet strong. You will be much safer and more comfortable if you return to your bed."

He blinked several times, put a hand to his head and groaned. His voice changed and he glanced from one to the other of the persons gathered around him. "What the deuce am I doing here?"

"Oh, thank the Lord," uttered Chloe before she could stop herself.

Lance did not pick it up. Instead, he looked round at her with a frown. "Chloe? Why are we all sitting on the stairs like this?"

"I have not the remotest conjecture. Shall we get up?"

He made to rise and sank down again. "I will, if Jack will help me."

"Right you are, sir. I'm at your service."

He was, as Jack had said, excessively weak. Chloe got out of the way as the footman heaved Lance to his feet and turned him towards the upper floor, where Jemima and Agatha hastened to get out of the way. Jack half carried his burden up the remaining stairs and supported his tottering steps into the bedroom, letting him down onto the bed.

Lance sat there unmoving, getting his breath while Chloe watched, anxiety uppermost.

What had sent him out of his own control again? He had been doing so well. The change distressed her. He had slipped back in a heartbeat, but that he wavered at all was troubling.

"I will leave you to see to him, Jack, while I dress. Call me if you need me." She came to the bedside and gently stroked Lance's hair. "I will come back presently. All will be well, you'll see."

He gave a wan smile, but did not speak.

Her eyes pricked and she hurried from the room, dismayed to find herself close to tears.

He struggled with recollection as he toyed with the baked egg, staring absently at the bedpost and the footman seated in the chair by the door. Why Jack had been detailed to watch over him escaped Lance. He felt ridiculously weak today and had only a vague notion of washing and being dressed in a fresh nightgown. He'd obeyed when the maid appeared with a tray and Jack urged him to sit up and banked the pillows behind him. But he truly had no appetite, although the coffee was welcome.

He was troubled by the odd notion of having been sitting on the stairs in his night attire, Chloe beside him. Was it a dream? And there was something about the ladies who had been here. A couple of days ago. Or no, was it only yesterday?

Time had little meaning. He could not even remember how long he had been here. His life before was a blank, beyond a few flashes of unrelated pictures, merging without sense one into the other. Yet underneath it all was the conviction something menaced him. Some factor from the unknown past? Or an individual? He felt unsafe.

"More coffee, sir?"

He had not noticed Jack coming up to the bed. The big man loomed over him, the coffee pot held ready.

Lance looked up. "Am I safe here?"

The fellow frowned, and then smiled. "Safe as houses, my lord. Mistress will see to that. Don't you worry none, sir."

All very well to say, but he could not help it. He consented to have his cup refilled, but pushed the plate to the back of the tray. "I'm not hungry."

"Right you are, my lord. I'll take that away, if you wish, though you've only had a bite when all's said."

"It's all I want."

The footman sighed and picked up the plate. "Well, if you get peckish later, I can bring you up a snack."

Lance thanked him, and watched him set the plate on the dresser and retake his seat. "Aren't you going to take it downstairs?"

"No need, sir. Jemima will be in for the tray presently."

Lance eyed him for a moment. "She's told you not to leave me alone, hasn't she?"

The footman hesitated, and then nodded, looking sheepish. "Only as you're feeling weak today, my lord. Mistress is afraid you might fall if you get up by yourself."

A wash of indignation rose in Lance. "Or I might lose my mind again and go wandering, is that it?"

"That is it exactly."

Chloe's voice! He had not seen her enter the room, but there she was, coming towards the bed from the doorway. She paused and turned her head. "Thank you, Jack. You may go now. And take the tray, if you please."

Lance held up his cup. "Not the coffee!"

Chloe took the cup. "You want more? Ask Jemima to bring it up fresh, if you please, Jack."

The footman had already taken the tray and Chloe set the empty cup upon it. Lance watched her every motion. She did not speak again until Jack had departed and then she perched on the edge of the bed and reached for his hand. Lance allowed her to take it, curling his fingers about hers. The spurt of irritation drained away and a glow of warmth crept in.

"How do you manage to calm my senses with your very presence? Are you a magician?"

Her smile embraced him. "Well, you mistook me for an angel at the outset, remember?"

Darkness flooded him and he released her hand, withdrawing a little. "I don't remember. I don't even remember what made me go and sit on the stairs." Her smile had gone, leaving solemnity in her face. Was that his fault? Yes, of course it was. "I've upset you."

She made a negative motion. "I am only troubled for you, Lance. I too would like to know what made you do so." He saw her hesitate and then her chin lifted. "You spoke of fearing to be taken away in a coach."

It rolled back in a bang. "I had a dream! It must have been a dream. I was in a coach with those women. They took me away from you." He eyed her in some anxiety. "That can't be real, can it?"

Her smile came. "By no means, if you mean our visitors from yesterday."

"Was it only yesterday? I've lost track of time."

"That does not surprise me. To tell you the truth, I am a little confused about it myself. When I counted I realised you have only been here a matter of days. We have been premature in expecting too rapid a recovery."

Lance felt cheered. "Then you don't anticipate being rid of me too soon?"

Chloe hesitated, regarding him with an unreadable expression in her eyes. "Is that what troubles you?"

The urge to tell her he never wanted to leave was strong. Lance withheld it, prevaricating. "I don't want to go back to my responsibilities." The moment he said it, he realised it was true. His gaze shifted from Chloe's face and he stared across at the window. The square of sky was all he knew of the world outside. Somewhere out there he had a life, one filled with persons who owed their very livelihood to his position — if he was indeed an earl. That much he understood, without knowing why. "I can't go back."

He expected to hear from Chloe that he must, that he had a duty to fulfil. In the back of his mind floated the conviction he would be forced to return to the life he'd known before the accident, if not by others by his own sense of what was fitting. The notion was anathema.

Chloe said nothing of the kind, to his surprise. Instead she got up from her perch on the bed. "Here is your fresh coffee."

He had not seen the maid enter. Chloe directed her to set the tray on the dresser and Lance watched the girl set it down. This was the capable maid — Jemima? One of these unobtrusive girls who remained unnoticed. There was a plethora of them at Ravensthorp, going about their various tasks with an efficiency that made them almost invisible. No footman would dare address him with the familiarity Jack used. Even his valet Finch was always deferent. Where the devil was Finch?

"Why isn't my valet with me?"

Chloe was pouring from the pot. She set it down and looked across. "I believe you had sent him on ahead in your coach, along with most of your luggage."

"I should have travelled in the coach."

She had returned to her task, now adding cream and sugar to the coffee. "Perhaps."

"There is no perhaps about it. I can't think what possessed me to take the curricle on such a day."

Chloe came to the bed and handed him a cup and saucer. "As I understand it, you directed your coachman to drive direct to Ravensthorp while you stopped off to spend a night or two with your friend Wintringham. That would explain why you were in the curricle, would it not?"

He sipped the coffee and felt his spirits revive. "This is excellent. What kind of coffee do you use?"

Chloe was fetching the chair by the door. She set it down near the bed as she spoke. "I really have no idea. Mrs Vaughan does the buying."

"I must ask her. We use the Arabic variety, but this is better."

He watched Chloe settle in her chair, her own cup and saucer in hand. She drank as he did and smiled. "You're right. It is good."

He frowned. "What the devil are you talking about?"

"The coffee? You spoke of its merits just now."

"Did I?" Confusion wreathed his brain. "I don't remember."

"Well, it makes no matter."

But it did. He was aware in a vague sort of way that his mind jumped from one thing to another. He could not always grasp a thought before it floated away.

"I've lost control of my mind."

Her eyes registered dismay, then veiled quickly. She set her cup down in the saucer. "It will pass, Lance. Yesterday, you were perfectly lucid. This is a small setback, I am persuaded. Doctor Goodleigh advised rest, and I think we allowed you to overdo it too soon, that is all."

A flash of amusement struck him. "At least I managed to follow that."

She laughed. "Well done. Now drink your coffee. It might help."

Obediently, he drank, enjoying the rich flavour. His wayward thoughts strayed again and the menace returned. "I don't want to go back, Chloe."

"Yes, I can understand that."

"You can?"

She smiled again, warming him. "It is not so surprising. Your body is weak and your memory is erratic. I can well imagine how much of a burden your life as an earl must appear to you at this moment."

He sighed. "I hate it."

"Now, perhaps. However, as you gain strength and recover more of your life's memories, it may not seem quite so burdensome."

"You think so?"

"I am certain of it. Shall I tell you why?"

He finished the last of his coffee and leaned back against his pillows, content to hear her talk. "Yes, do."

"Because I think your condition is akin to that of grief. Your memory has betrayed you and it is a loss. One tends to feel exhausted and incapable when one is grieving, and I suspect this is the same."

Her words made sense to him, but he was caught by the hint of sorrow in her own life. "When were you grieving? Was it for your husband?"

A shadow crossed Chloe's face. "Yes, I did grieve for him. We were fond. But also for my mother." A grimace crossed her face. "I was too deeply grieved to choose wisely when my father came for me. Had I opted to remain with my grandparents, my life would have been markedly different."

"Who are your grandparents?"

"I doubt you would know of them."

"But they are of the gentry?"

"Yes, but like my late husband, of no particular note. Although Oswald's family includes one minor peer." She smiled. "Which is why Matilda gives herself airs and is so concerned for my reputation."

A ripple of dismay attacked him. "That's my fault."

"Don't be nonsensical. You were unconscious when I took you in. How could it be your fault?"

Urgency engulfed him. "If you marry me, they can't take me away!"

A faint flush mantled her cheeks, but she smiled, her tone soothing. "No one is going to take you away, Lance. Not until you are willing."

"I shan't ever be willing. I want to stay with you forever."

There, he'd said it. Anxiety rode him as he watched the fleeting expressions that crossed her face. They were too quick to read, but he guessed she did not know how to answer him.

He set down his cup on the bedside table and sat up, leaning towards her. "You don't take me seriously. You think I am speaking out of my illness, my condition as you call it. But I'm not, I promise you. I've loved you, wanted you from the moment I first saw you."

Her face changed. He saw a leap of anger in her eyes. Her fingers gripped the sides of her saucer and the kindness was gone from her voice. "No, you haven't! You took me for Clarissa. It isn't me you love, if indeed you love anyone. You're infatuated, Lance. With a memory. Not with me."

She got up, setting down the cup on the dresser. In the silence of despair, he saw her set her hands on the edge of the veneered surface and bow her head over them, her shoulders moving with the rise and fall of her chest.

He'd distressed her, the last thing he wished. Yet he knew not how to make an impression on her, to convince her. He wanted to override her disbelief, force her somehow to believe. If only there was not a niggle of suspicion in the back of his mind that she might be right.

She turned at last, wearing a smile he was sure was forced. "I'm sorry. I should not have ripped up at you like that."

He shifted his shoulders. "You can say what you like to me. You've earned the right."

Her hand brushed the air. "Nothing of the kind."

"Then know I don't mind it. I would willingly hear whatever you chose to say to me, Chloe. You're my lifeline, my connection to the world. Without you, I'd have nothing, can't you understand?"

She was still breathing as if her feelings threatened to overcome her. She retook her seat and he noticed the quiver at her fingers.

"You're trembling."

She met his eyes and a faint smile crossed her mouth. "Yes. I'm a trifle overset."

"A trifle!"

A tiny laugh escaped. "Very well, a great deal, if you must have it." Then she sighed. "Oh, Lance, what a pickle we are in!"

He was relieved to see a measure of relaxation entering in. "How so?"

"How so? How can you ask? Is it not obvious?"

"Not to me."

She sighed again. "No, I suppose it would not be. Well, never mind."

She reached out and he took her hand and brought it to his lips. Then he laid it down and held it within his own. Her warm smile embraced him.

"Let us get you well. That is our priority. All these matters can wait."

The shadows crept back into Lance's mind and he could not help himself. "Only tell me that you care a little."

Her fingers moved within his and she did not flinch from his gaze, instead holding his eyes. "I care a great deal, that is the difficulty."

CHAPTER NINE

The letter arrived in the middle of breakfast. For the third day running, Lance was well enough to join them downstairs. Chloe had permitted his venturing forth, provided he rested quietly in the back parlour afterwards.

Rather to her surprise, he'd been content to do so, playing at Fox and Geese or cards with Miss Flook or reading if he was left alone for a space. There had been no further recurrences of wandering or complete confusion since the last. Chloe could not avoid setting it down to what she must call her confession.

It cost her a good many anxieties on her own account, but the moment she'd told Lance she cared, his seemed to vanish. He did not again press her to the idea of marriage, nor mention his fears of being removed from Derry Lodge. Keeping her doubts and difficulties to herself, Chloe refrained from reminding him and was led to hope his mind was settling.

Doctor Goodleigh, when the episode was reported to him, took a light view. "I think we must expect a few such setbacks."

"That was my own opinion, though I admit to some qualms. He was so very fearful. And his mind jumps with bewildering speed."

The doctor took off his spectacles and gave them a polish with his pocket handkerchief. "A lack of concentration is a verified symptom of such injuries. Our minds are inclined to throw a great deal of information at us from all directions. Under normal circumstances, we are capable of setting these in compartments, as it were, holding only to what is of interest at the moment. With his lordship's memory suppressed as it is, the slippage of information will be out of his control."

"Then you suppose it will settle as his memory returns?"

"That is the documented prognosis. We have no reason to believe otherwise. The less excitement, the more quiet you can keep him, the likelier he is to remain in his senses."

Which suggested the episode could be set down to the disturbance of the intrusion of Matilda and Harriet. Doctor Goodleigh, when she put this to him, agreed. "I am of your opinion, Mrs Quilter. Especially if, as you say, he had a dream of their taking him away."

Considerably relieved, Chloe brushed her personal feelings aside and set herself to the task of keeping Lance sufficiently entertained to be content with his situation. She talked of indifferent things or read to him while Agatha in her turn engaged in the diversion of games. Chloe took care to ensure she was not at Lance's beck and call. Better for her, since she could envisage no future in which she might figure. Better for him too. The sooner he was weaned from his dependence upon her, the sooner he would recover. She could not avoid the suspicion, painful though it might be, that her presence, with its inevitable pairing to his past loss, kept him chained. To some degree at least. Who was to say whether, freed from the disturbance of that particular confusion, Lance might not snap back to a present he could remember?

Meanwhile, his needs must be met. Though she and Agatha shared the duty of keeping him quietly engaged, Jack tended him morning and night and at mealtimes, remaining with him while he ate and, at her instructions, speaking cheerfully of whatever was going forward in the house at the time. The footman had a knack of telling a good story, and often made Lance laugh.

His physical progress was observably swift. He began with excursions in his dressing-gown, Jack in attendance as he walked the upper corridors and at length took the stairs.

One morning, after a few days of this mild exercise, Lance declared his wish of dressing before making his appearance. A flurry of concern attacked Chloe, mingled with a trifle of dismay at the onset of an inevitable end. She quashed it, concentrating on Lance as her patient rather than anything else.

"Will it not tire him to go through all that preparation, Jack?"

"He's a deal stronger, mistress. I think he'll do."

"Well, have him rest once he's dressed before he comes down. We'll wait breakfast."

Chloe found she need not have been apprehensive. Lance was clearly a good deal better than when he'd ventured down on the fateful day of her stepdaughter's arrival. He ate well, smiling and chatting in a manner that could not but charm her the more. His face had filled out and the shadows were nearly gone. Apart from the odd lapse in attention, he appeared perfectly normal. Or as normal as Chloe could suppose, since she had never known him prior to the accident.

As to his memory, there were glimpses of its return. He'd been helped a little by Harriet's promised copy of the entry concerning his estate in the Peerage, which arrived while he was yet keeping his room. Chloe had gone over the contents with him and Lance had been able to corroborate some of the facts, though he'd felt divorced from them.

"It sounds like a catalogue of someone else's life, not mine. I can't own it."

Chloe did her best to counter this attitude. "Well, it helps me, I must say. At least I know a little more about the man with whom I have to deal."

He frowned. "You don't need all that. You know me as the man I am. I'm me, Chloe, not the Earl of Pettipher."

"You are both."

"Yes, but this is me. That earl is someone I no longer know myself."

She'd said no more, fearing to drive him into disquiet. Nor did she wish to engage in a discussion which would assuredly lead to entering into her feelings. Difficult enough to keep them buried as it was.

Instead, she'd put the papers into the drawer of his bedside cabinet. "You may read them at your leisure. Perhaps it will trigger something."

But as far as she knew, Lance had not even taken the papers out. He might do so in the night hours, she supposed, but if he did he never spoke of them. Nor did he talk of his home or the people in his household. Was he bent upon ignoring his past? God help her if he persisted in this obstinacy! The longer she was obliged to house him, the more tender she became.

The past was thrust upon his notice this morning, however, when a letter arrived addressed to *The Right Hon. The Earl of Pettipher.* Basil had set it beside his place at the breakfast table, following his habit of setting Chloe's by hers.

Miss Flook, who was down before her, immediately drew her attention to it, speaking in a lowered tone of suspenseful mystery. "He has a letter!"

"Who has?"

"His lordship. Look there, beside his place. It is addressed to the Earl of Pettipher. Do you suppose it comes from his people?"

Chloe stopped by Lance's place and picked up the letter, which was folded into an envelope, both sealed and franked. A ripple of alarm went through her. On his account and on her own. "I should think undoubtedly it is from his people. Who else knows he is here?" She examined the signature on the frank. "I can't make this out."

"Oh, but it must be a peer, must it not?"

"No doubt." She laid the letter down, apprehension rising, though she kept her voice even. "I must say I expected to hear sooner. Rowley must have reached Ravensthorp days ago."

"You would suppose someone would come rushing to his rescue, would you not?"

The indignation under Agatha's tone echoed in Chloe's breast. "Very true. Though as I understand it, there is only an elderly aunt who is incapacitated. Perhaps it has taken a little while to locate a suitable person who could take appropriate action."

Which satisfied Miss Flook. "That must be it. We know he has one sister living from the details the other Mrs Quilter sent."

"Yes, he mentioned her once."

"Do you suppose it is she who has written to him? Why did she not come?"

Chloe took her seat. "It is useless to conjecture, Agatha. We will know more when his lordship opens the letter."

But his lordship, when he arrived in the breakfast parlour, still leaning a little on Jack's arm, was not in the least inclined to do so.

The exertion of dressing still took more of a toll on Lance than he was prepared to admit. He was relieved to sit down in the chair the butler had pulled out for him, looking up at the footman.

"Thank you, Jack. I will do now."

"Right you are, sir. Ring if you need me to help you to the parlour."

He smiled at the man. "I don't know what I should do without you."

Jack reddened. "It's no trouble, my lord."

With a small bow, he left the dining room and Lance glanced around the table. "In fact, I am a great deal of trouble to the fellow, I've no doubt." The very sight of Chloe warmed him, together with the cosy atmosphere, which put him so much at ease. For Chloe's sake, he gave no sign of his partiality in company. "Good morning, ladies. I trust you both slept well?"

The elderly dame gushed with reassurance as she always did, but Chloe brushed it aside. "More to the point, did you? Was it a peaceful night?"

He nodded to the butler, who had the coffee pot poised. "I slept like a babe." The maid Jemima was hovering and he turned to her. "What have you today?"

"Baked eggs, ham, beef and rolls, sir — my lord."

"I will have beef, if you please. I'm hungry."

The maid scurried to the sideboard and he had leisure to return his attention to the women, half expecting Chloe to comment upon his appetite. She did not, and Lance became aware of her serious mien. About to question it, he was arrested by Miss Flook, who cleared her throat in a marked manner.

Lance looked over and it became obvious the woman was labouring under suppressed excitement. "What in the world is to do?"

Miss Flook nodded towards his place and he looked down as Chloe spoke. "There is a letter for you."

For a moment it did not register. Then he saw the envelope lying on the cloth beside his place. He read the superscription without touching it, dismay threading through him. Was this the summons he'd dreaded? The demand to return to that life he could no longer call his own? His heart thrummed in his breast.

Jemima's hand crossed his vision of the letter, setting a plate down before him. He looked at the beef and his stomach urged a protest. But it offered a respite. Reaching out, he shoved the letter away from him, snatching his fingers back as if it burned them.

"I'll read it later."

He took up a fork and shovelled a portion of beef into his mouth. Without raising his eyes from his plate, he chewed, horribly aware of the silence around the table. No one spoke to relieve him. He heard a clink of a cup in a saucer, the scrape of a knife and the pour of liquid. Then Chloe's voice broke the quiet.

"Thank you, Basil. Will you pass the jam, Agatha?"

"Oh, of course. It is the raspberry, Mrs Vaughan's best."

"A little sharp perhaps, but I prefer it."

The discussion moved to the merits of the seeded bread against the soft rolls and Lance breathed more easily. But the food stuck in his throat. He could still see the letter in the periphery of his vision. He pushed the beef around his plate.

"Is the beef not to your liking, Lance? Would you prefer an egg? Or a roll, perhaps?" Chloe knew. She saw his dread.

Lance seized an excuse from the air. "My eyes were bigger than my stomach, I fear."

"Jemima, take it away, if you please. Set a clean plate before his lordship." The maid whipped the offending beef away. "Pass his lordship the bread basket, Agatha. Where is the butter? Ah, here it is."

A clean plate appeared before him and Lance took the first roll to hand from the proffered basket. He busied himself in cutting it in half and applying butter.

"Jam, my lord?"

Miss Flook urged the pot in his direction. Lance shook his head. He picked up the roll and stared at it.

"Thank you, Basil. We can manage ourselves now."

The butler set the coffee pot on the table and signed to the maid to leave the room. With a small bow, he followed and Lance looked up at Chloe as the door closed.

She gave him that warm smile. "Drink your coffee, Lance. It always revives you."

Miss Flook half rose from her seat. "Do you wish me to…?"

"Stay, Agatha. You are privy to everything and you have not finished your breakfast."

Lance could well have dispensed with the companion's presence, but he was in no condition to object. The letter menaced him. Even Chloe could not halt the inevitable. He had obeyed her without thought, drinking of the bitter liquid. He'd forgotten to put sugar in, but he did not care. The taste suited well with his mood. Indeed, it felt more natural to his palate. Had he taken it unsweetened before?

"Lance?"

He looked up. Chloe's soothing tone, low and gentle. Her smile was reassuring.

"It will not serve to put it off. Anticipation will only make it worse."

He let his breath go in a whoosh. "I don't want to read it."

"I know. Do you recognise the hand?"

He eyed the envelope. From here he could not see well enough to judge. "You are forcing me to pick the thing up."

Miss Flook, who was seated between them, set her hand near the letter. "Shall I put it nearer to you, my dear lord?"

Her voice dripped with sympathy, but Lance was quick to note the rampant curiosity underneath. A flare of irritation won out. "Damnation take it!" He set down his cup, reached across and snatched up the envelope. He studied the writing. "It seems familiar, but I can't recall whose hand it is."

"What about the frank? I could not make it out."

He examined the signature. Once again, it had a flourish he would swear he recognised, but the name, whatever it was, did not register. "No, I can't read it either." A suspenseful pause ensued. He could almost hear Miss Flook willing him to take the plunge and open it. He raised his eyes from the envelope and looked across at Chloe. "I feel like I'm standing on the brink of a precipice."

Her regard did not waver. "You'll have to jump."

"You are a hard taskmaster, Chloe Quilter."

"Just open it, Lance. It won't bite."

"How do you know? There may be crocodile teeth in here."

Her stern look vanished in a laugh. Lance immediately felt lighter. He broke the seal. Spidery writing covered the entirety of the sheet and the lines were crossed. The interior of the envelope was likewise decorated in the same fashion.

Lance held it away from him. "I can't read this! Good God, I'll need a magnifying glass!"

Chloe's calm tones came. "Do you not have a quizzing glass among your belongings? Or no, I have a glass in my desk. Agatha?"

The companion instantly rose. "I will fetch it."

She hurried out and Lance let the letter fall, anguish in his heart as he stared across at Chloe. "I can't bear it! I don't want to read it. It's Rosaline, I know it is. She'll say I must go back. Chloe, I don't want to go back!"

Concern was in her face, but she spoke in that nurse voice of hers. "Rosaline? That is your sister, if I remember from the Peerage notes."

"My elder sister. Aunt Adelaide must have sent to her."

"Well, can you blame her? She must be frantic with worry about you. No doubt your sister will be too. They care about you, Lance. They are your people."

The dread rose up. "But I don't know them. I don't want them!"

"You knew the writing, did you not?"

He wanted to repudiate it. Foolish of course. "Yes. I wish I didn't."

"Come, now, Lance, you are putting the cart before the horse. Let us see what she says before you —"

"I don't need to see it. I know how it will be. It's the beginning of the end, and I'll be forced to leave you."

"You don't know that."

Her tone had changed, a hint of something in it that drove him into panic. "You want to be rid of me!"

"That's not true!"

"Clarissa…" His voice broke and he bowed his head over his plate, struggling with the rise of confusion. In a moment he felt a hand on his shoulder. He had not heard movement, his head too full of demons.

"Hush now, hush! Don't let it win. You can control this now. Come, you are here with me in the dining parlour, partaking of breakfast. All is well. There is nothing to fear."

The soothe of her voice penetrated the maelstrom and a sliver of common sense began to tap on the walls of his mind.

What was he doing? Yes, he was letting it take him again. He drew harsh breaths, trying for calm.

"Well done. That's better. Look at me, Lance!"

Pulling his head up, he opened his eyes and found her face — the angel features he knew and loved. It smiled and warmth swept into him again. He groped for her hand and it closed about his. "What happened? Why did I lose it all again?"

She was stroking his hair. It felt intimate and right. His hold tightened on her other hand. "It was the letter, Lance. Do you remember?"

His mind was a blank. "Letter?"

Her fingers left his hair and she picked up a sheaf of paper from the table. "From your sister. She is concerned to hear of your accident, I've no doubt. Shall I read it to you? Or would you like to read it yourself? Here is Agatha with the magnifying glass."

Miss Flook came into his line of vision, holding up a gold-edged glass with a handle. "I'm sorry I was so long, my dear lord. It took me a while to find it."

He looked at the glass and back to the papers in Chloe's hand. A vague recollection surfaced. "Rosaline? Is it she who has written to me?"

"You said it was her hand, yes."

She held out the letter. Spidery writing covered it. He'd seen it before, he was sure. He knew the hand. "Yes, I think it is my sister's writing. Shall I read it?"

"If you wish."

Chloe held the paper in front of him and Miss Flook set the magnifying glass down within his reach. Lance hesitated. A riffle went through him and he remembered he'd been upset. Was it because of the letter? He did not take it, instead looking at Chloe again. "This set me off? I lost control of my mind again?"

"Correct. You see, you do remember. That's very good, Lance."

The congratulatory tone made him laugh. "I'm improving, then."

"Here, take it."

He accepted the sheaf, though gingerly. The moment he tried to read the crossed lines, however, he balked. "Illegible as ever. She never could learn to write a decent hand, my sister. She should have left it to Jasper. Though that would ensure a dry piece. This will be full of comment and question, you may be sure."

Chloe picked up the magnifying glass. "Use this."

He took it and applied it to the letter, which immediately became clearer. Half aware that Chloe was returning to her place, he began to read.

"*Dearest brother*, she begins. She always did so." Words expressing her shock, her horror — all to be expected, yes. He laughed out. "Palpitations! I dare say she was prostrate, silly creature." He glanced at his audience. "This is typical, you know. Here she wastes half a page telling me of her symptoms." He read on, finding without surprise that Rosaline had supposed him to be merely dallying as he always did when Aunt Adelaide sent to her. "My aunt was alarmed by my absence, it seems."

"Well, one can scarcely be surprised at that," came Chloe's matter-of-fact comment.

He tapped the letter. "Yes, but Rosaline pooh-poohed her fears. She was taken at fault when she heard what had happened."

"Did your aunt write again?"

"No, she sent Rowley to tell it in person."

"Ah, that may explain the delay."

Lance was still perusing the letter, shifting the magnifying glass down the page, and he replied absently. "Yes, for my sister's home is at some distance from Ravensthorp… There is little here but comment and question. She does not seem to understand that my memory is affected. I don't know who these people are she talks of — *Lavinia, Beatrice and Felix*. Who the devil are they? And why should she write to me about them?" He lowered the letter, directing his question to Chloe.

She smiled. "Let me hazard a guess. Your nieces and nephew, perhaps?"

Light dawned. "Of course, yes. Three of them?" He checked the letter. "That's it. There were two girls before at last she produced the boy she wanted. Genius, Chloe! Ah, you see, she says she cannot leave them… One is unwell, I cannot make out which because now these damned lines are badly crossed."

He turned the letter and had to hold the magnifying glass close to decipher the words running counter across the page. "If I am reading this aright, Aunt Adelaide wants her to rush hotfoot to the rescue. There is a great deal of nonsense here about her regret that she can't do so." He was conscious of relief lifting his spirits. If his sister could not come, he was safe here for a while longer. He pressed on and the blow fell. "Oh, dear God! She is sending Jasper instead!"

"Jasper?"

"My brother-in-law. Enderby."

Here Miss Flook cut in, awe in her voice. "Would that be the Marquis of Enderby?"

Lance regarded her with interest. "You know him?"

Miss Flook waved agitated hands. "Gracious, no, my dear lord. But I had occasion to write to her ladyship when I heard she was looking for a governess. A few years ago it was. Dear me, I had no notion your sister was the marchioness."

"No more did I until this moment." He struggled with an elusive thread. "Jasper married her when Rosaline was barely eighteen. I remember using the fact when arguing my case for Clarissa with her parents. They would not permit a betrothal. They pointed out, quite rightly, that Jasper had been more than thirty at the time, while I was only a year older than my intended bride."

Silence greeted this and he wondered at it. Instinct sent his gaze to Chloe and he found her white of face, a withdrawn look in her eyes.

"What is it? What have I said?"

Her lips quivered, but no smile appeared. "Nothing at all. It is good to find you have memories slipping into sight."

He felt dissatisfied with her response, but the words distracted him. "I have remembered more? You think so?"

She set her hands on the table. They looked oddly stiff. "I think your sister's letter has triggered a series of memories, which is an excellent thing. You have talked very naturally of her character and of your brother-in-law."

His mind jumped again. "He's coming here, did I say?" He bent his eyes once more upon the letter. "Rosaline says she will send him with all manner of comforts she mentions here, in hopes I will be able to sustain the journey home. He is coming to fetch me." Realisation hit and his heart dropped. He let the letter fall and stared across at Chloe. "I said so, did I not? I said they would take me away in a coach. How can I stop them? What am I to do?"

While her voice soothed, Chloe's mind seethed. So comfortable had she allowed herself to become with Lance, she'd almost forgotten the wretched Clarissa. Until he said her name again. Until his erratic memory presented him with yet another little piece of the puzzle.

"Nothing is to be gained by panic." How was she able to say it when her own panic jumped in her bosom like a rebellious snake? "All must depend upon your brother-in-law's coming. Does she say when?"

Lance bent his eyes to the letter again, but her heart clenched as she saw the tremor in his fingers. The temptation to tell him she would send this marquis packing flowered dangerously. If she was able to believe in his affection, in its truth towards her real self, she would do so. But she could not, because the ghost of Clarissa would not permit so reckless a proceeding.

"I can't tell. She writes only of Jasper's coming. Thank heavens! It may be weeks." Lance dropped the letter again and slammed the magnifying glass to the table. It landed on the sheet that had enveloped the letter and Chloe pointed.

"You've not read the writing on the inside fold of the sheet, Lance. Does the letter not continue there?"

He pushed aside the glass and picked it up, the gesture impatient. "It's a postscript." A crease appeared between his brows. "This is not the same hand."

"Perhaps it was penned by your brother-in-law?"

An eager look leapt into Agatha's face. "Oh, then I may recognise it, my dear lord, if you do not. He it was who wrote to me." Then her face fell. "Or, no, perhaps he only signed it. Has he not a secretary? These great men usually do, I believe."

An explosive sound came from Lance. "Well, I wish he'd had him write this then, for it's a worse hand than Rosaline's."

"But is it Lord Enderby's?"

Lance threw the letter in Chloe's direction. "It's no use asking me, is it? See if you can make it out."

She reached out to take the paper, eyeing him meanwhile. His temper was rising. A different manifestation of his fear? There was rebellion in the green gaze, which went from the paper to her and back again. She dropped her eyes to the sheet. It was legible enough. Clearly, Lance did not wish to know the contents. Had he a healthy respect for his brother-in-law's mental capacity? Unlike his dismissal of his sister's sentiment. She read the lines through, her disquiet a little allayed by their content. Looking up, she found Lance's gaze still fixed upon her. Likewise Agatha's, with avid curiosity.

"It is signed Enderby, so I think we may safely assume it was written by him. In essence, he says he will not set forward until he hears either from you or *this Mrs Quilter* that you are in a condition to travel." She had to smile at Lance's instant glowing look. "It's only a respite, I'm afraid. He desires me to send an express at once. I must do so, of course."

"No! You can't, Chloe! You need not write to him at all. I shall write and tell him I am far too ill to be making a journey."

"Then you would be far too ill to write as much." Chloe gave him back the envelope. "Don't fret. I will tell him to come in a week."

"A week! Say rather a month!"

Good heavens, no! A month would see her heart so entangled she would never get free. The sooner he was removed from her vicinity, the better for her. Before she could form acceptable words to deny him, Agatha intervened.

"You should go, my dear lord, as soon as you can. Do but consider your dependents. How must they feel without your hand at the helm? I declare, I should be lost if dear Mrs Quilter were to be too long absent, as would her servants. There must be a hundred things they cannot do without your sanction. And you have a great estate. There is nothing so injurious as an absentee landlord."

Impressed by Agatha's common sense, too often overborne by consciousness of her inferior status, Chloe watched to see how Lance would take this. His look of pain was not encouraging. He sighed.

"Perhaps I too have a secretary."

Chloe embraced the notion for his sake. "Or a steward. An agent at least. But Agatha is right. There is a limit to how long they may be able to hold the fort without you."

"But I don't know anything! Even were I there, I could not advise them."

"There is every reason to hope it will come back to you once you are in your proper milieu."

Agatha added her persuasions. "That is very true, my dear lord. You cannot hope to remember everything, isolated as you are in this place."

Chloe could see him struggling. She was glad of Agatha's presence, which kept him from saying what she knew he wanted to say. Lord knew she'd give anything to be able to give in to him! Yet she knew it would be madness. Even were her own doubts and feelings not in question, Lance must have the opportunity to recognise his own reality. How dreadful if he were to recall his entire past only to find himself shackled to a widow with a shady background whose only claim to his affection was a passing resemblance to his dead affianced bride. The possibility was anathema, not to be endured. She wanted him out of her house, out of her life. Only then might she hope to regain the contentment she'd cherished before the intrusion of a personable injured earl who greeted her with a mention of mistletoe and a clandestine kiss.

Lost in her thoughts, she was startled when Lance spoke.

"Then if you insist upon sending me home, Chloe Quilter, you must come with me."

CHAPTER TEN

Too startled to respond at first, Chloe bought time by seizing the hand bell. The jangling note chimed with the echo of his words in her head while her tongue threw out platitudes.

"You've been sitting too long. We'll talk of it presently. Agatha will join you in the back parlour for a space."

She was aware of Lance's frowning regard as she rose, glad of her companion immediately following suit. Gathering up the separated parts of the letter, she handed them to Lance.

"Take this. You may wish to peruse it again at your leisure. Perhaps it will trigger more memories. Agatha, take the magnifying glass with you, if you please." She was almost at the door when it opened and she nearly collided with the butler. "Basil! Where's Jack? Or perhaps you could help his lordship instead? He is removing to the back parlour. Oh, and take fresh coffee there, if you please. I will take a cup in my book-room."

Without waiting for an answer, she passed him and crossed the hall to her refuge. Closing the door, she leaned against it, feeling her legs begin to wilt beneath her, the thrum mounting in her chest.

You must come with me… You must come with me…

His voice in her head, the words a command. If she'd obeyed her instinct, she would have said it on the instant.

Yes, of course I will go with you, my dearest dear.

Lord help her! She'd bitten on the words, refusing to let them out. What a tribute to the lesson learned long ago to keep her tongue between her teeth though everything in her urged her to scream at her father whenever his excesses exposed him for a feckless, irresponsible reprobate. She'd used the habit to good effect in her marriage, never allowing her temper to get the better of her with Matilda or Harriet.

At first Oswald had taken it for serenity, but he'd seen through it. "You need not refrain from speaking out, Chloe. Not on my account."

But she rarely had, beyond an occasional ironic remark. Which, in the present instance, was a blessing.

Her reflections had carried her to the desk. She pulled out her chair and sat, resting clasped hands on the surface and gazing unseeingly out of the window beyond.

Was she a fool? How long had she known him, for heaven's sake? Ten days, if that. Did she truly know him? She knew a man scathed, lost in a limbo of unrelated time. Was it the Lance of years, or a shadow created out of the present? Like the shadow he had built in her likeness in his head.

The remembrance of Clarissa settled her unquiet nerves a little, forced her to recognition of the present reality. He was a man in chaos. How could he know his own heart? He called upon her presence from dependency. Understandable. She'd become his rock in the disturbing waves in which he knew not where to turn. Could she then in conscience abandon him? The instant rise of anticipation gave her the lie. She was seeking justifications to do what her heart desired. A mistaken heart, if it cried out for a man who was not who he truly was. Or might not be. Truth was she did not know, could not know until he recovered himself. At which time…

Let her not again go over the probable consequence of a mistaken union. It was impossible on all counts. Until Lancelot Ravensthorp was himself again, there could be no question of the future upon which he was insisting. Chloe was certain he would marry her tomorrow if she agreed. Just because of that, she could not, must not surrender. It went against every precept of right.

He was going to plague her with this new demand, was he not? Of course he was. He would play upon her senses like a virtuoso, because he was afraid. She could not blame him. But neither could she risk her heart further by acceding. If he left now, she would be heart-sore for a time, true. But one survived these losses. She would rally and find again the contentment of her careful construction, surrounded by the friends she'd made of her true dependents. She did not need this complication.

Thus determined, she opened a drawer and extracted a sheet from her sheaf of fresh paper and laid it on the writing pad. Picking up a pen from the china standish with its little figurine of a milkmaid, she checked its point and then dipped it into the inkpot.

Derry Lodge, Staggesden. My lord…

Lance pretended to doze, unwilling to engage in the usual pastimes with his substitute companion. He wanted to be alone with his thoughts, at least until the coffee came. He had begun to crave it, finding his lacerated feelings soothed by its heat, his mind revived and stimulated to better effect. Had it been so before? He had no way of knowing.

The idle thought dissipated as the menace seeped back. It had come as he'd known it would: the summons.

Instinct had spoken when he said Chloe must accompany him. She had not answered. A dismissal? Or was she playing for time? She did that when she disliked his utterances. She was good at evasion. Secretive? Yes, secretive. A flare of feeling tightened his breath. Cruel — to deny herself when he needed her most. Was she not his salvation? She knew it. Yet she fled his presence, refusing even to acknowledge his plea.

His words slid back into his mind. Had it been a plea? No, more a command. Was that his mistake? She did not like to be commanded. Why must his chosen women be so independent? Clarissa! Just such another, disobedient to a fault. Spinning on the ice, spinning on the ice…

"Ah, here is Jemima with the coffee."

The image broke in his head, splintering, fading away. Lance opened his eyes to an alien scene. Disoriented, he watched the girl set down a tray beside the elderly woman who sat by the fire. Aunt Adelaide? No, it was another. What had she said? Jemima? He knew no Jemima. He watched her leave the room and returned his gaze to the old woman, who was pouring coffee.

"There now, my dear lord. Do you wish for cream? I noticed you did not take sugar at breakfast."

Irritation caught him. "I never take sugar. Nor cream."

She looked a trifle surprised, but rose, picked up the cup and saucer and approached the daybed.

Lance took it from her, puzzling at her presence. "Why are you here? Who are you?"

Dismay flickered in her eyes. "Oh, dear, have you forgotten again?"

"Forgot?"

She hesitated, a frown creasing her brow. She gave a smile, clearly false since her voice was fluttery. "Well, it makes no matter. I dare say it will come back to you presently."

What the deuce was the woman talking of? He watched her retake her seat and return to her task with the coffee pot. He found a cup and saucer in his hands. "What is this?"

She looked up. "Your coffee, my lord."

My lord? Was she a servant then? Detailed to do what? Pour him coffee? The whole thing was extremely odd. He lifted the cup to his lips and sipped. Bitter! "There's no sugar in this."

The creature sprang up, seizing a silver bowl from the tray. She came to the daybed and presented it.

He stared at it and then looked up into her face. "Do you expect me to do it myself?"

Without a word, she took up the tongs and dropped a lump into his cup.

He tutted. "Well, stir it."

Her frown deepened and she pursed her lips. But she collected a spoon and did as he asked. "Is it to your liking?"

A trifle curt, but he would overlook it this time. He tasted the brew and nodded, relaxing back against the rolled end of the daybed. Why he was lounging here he had no notion. It must be a whim of his mother's. He dared say this woman was one of her numerous distant relatives in need of a refuge like Aunt Adelaide. Though Aunt Adelaide had always lived with them. But this was not Aunt Adelaide.

He looked at the woman again. Her features became abruptly familiar. Likewise the room, the tray at her side and the maid who had brought the coffee.

His fingers froze, the cup halfway to his mouth. Dear Lord, he had drifted off again! Panic took him. "Where's Chloe? Tell her I need her! Tell her she must come!"

"Have a care, my lord! The coffee!"

He looked at the cup. It was dangerously tilted. He righted it before the hot liquid could spill. But a rustle beside him brought Miss Flook to the daybed. She took charge of the saucer and put a couple of fingers under the cup, raising it.

"Drink, my dear lord. It will revive you."

He sipped and grimaced. "I don't like it. Too bitter."

"Let me put cream in." She took it away.

He felt plaintive and weak. "Where is Chloe? Why is she not here?"

"She will come presently. Here, my dear lord, drink this. See, I have put cream in. It will taste better now."

"But I want Chloe."

"Drink and I will fetch her. Or no, I will ring for someone to call her. I dare not leave you in this state."

She flitted away and he sipped at the brew. It tasted good and he began to feel a little calmer. He was unsure why he had become alarmed. Had his mind been jumping again? The letter! Yes, Jasper had written, had he not? Chloe meant to send to him. What had she said? A week? A week! No, no, he could not. He must persuade her to postpone. She could not be so cruel as to send him away. Or if she did, she must come with him.

His mind buzzed. Had he not already spoken of it? Heaven help him, he had come full circle! "It is of no use. I cannot do without her. I shall go mad!"

The door opened to admit the butler. "You rang, ma'am?"

"Oh, Mr Basil! Yes, I did. Pray will you request Mrs Quilter to come. As quickly as she can, if you please."

Relief swept through him. Chloe would come. Chloe would bring balm and comfort. He would not have to struggle alone.

With all her careful reasoning awry, Chloe had no choice but to plan anew. Agatha's report troubled her, quite aside from Lance's moving plea.

"Let me stay or come with me, Chloe. Either will do. I can't cope without you. Who will bear with these strange excursions of my mind? None but you can understand. I swear I will be lost without you."

She had to give him more time. Her feelings aside, it would be cruel to abandon him. She could not do it, any more than she could dismiss Little Tibby or reject Agatha's companionship.

"We are too close to Christmas," she reasoned. "Let us get through the festivities and then your brother-in-law may fetch you in the New Year. I dare say it will be more convenient for him too."

Lance remained dissatisfied. "But you'll come with me? You must, Chloe. Consider! I know no one there and if I drift they will think I have gone off my head. They will have me confined or carried off to Bedlam."

She laughed at that. "Don't be ridiculous."

His alarm had not abated. "I'm serious." He gestured with impatience. "Well, not Bedlam perhaps if I'm an earl. But that alone will put me at risk. They will think me incompetent to rule and keep me locked up like our poor old King."

"Who are *they*? Who has authority to do such a thing, Lance? You are your own master."

"Is the King? When he goes through these periods of derangement? Jasper will tell Potticary to do it."

"Potticary?"

"My steward. Or is he my secretary? Something like. He will be running things in my absence. He always does so. I dare say he can manage for years, or until Hargrave is induced to take the reins."

Loath though she was to interrupt these clear recollections, Chloe was becoming confused. She chose her words with care. "Why should Hargrave take the reins at all?"

"He's my present heir. He does not expect to inherit. Nor wish to." His mood relaxed slightly as a smile curved his lip. "Indeed, Hargrave is assiduous in urging me to marry and beget sons to keep him out. He's a crazy young rascal, if you want the truth. Sporting mad and will likely break his neck over a rasper or come to grief in a racing curricle. And then there'll be two of us without a working mind between us."

"In that case, I dare say the earldom is safer in your hands."

He laughed at that. "Much. That wretched youth has no notion of land management. He'd hate it too. I like him, though. He's an amusing rattle and deuced light-hearted. I don't think he takes anything seriously."

To keep the memories flying, Chloe held to the subject. "How is he able to afford this obsession with sports? Has he a profession?"

"He's in the Life Guards. As far as I can tell, they have few duties and far too much time to get into mischief."

"How is he your heir?"

"Oh, a remote cousin. He's a Ravensthorp."

"Have you other cousins?"

"Too many to count, but none close. My father had no brothers who lived to adulthood, so we are obliged to go back a generation for Hargrave. I must marry to continue the line."

And if Clarissa had lived, he would have done so long since. But she was dead, and he ought to have picked one of the many debutantes no doubt thrown in his way season after season. He had not. In how many years — nine? Ten? Which told its own tale. No substitute would do. Until now. But Chloe could not live a surrogate life. She was not, never would be, Clarissa. Yet who she was made it impossible to refuse him.

"Very well, I will accompany you to Ravensthorp." His face lit, but she continued in a resolute tone. "And Agatha will be with us to lend me countenance. Also Jemima to see to our personal needs. We will travel separately and your people will know that I am there as your nurse companion to guide you through the first weeks of your rehabilitation."

Radiant, Lance waved dismissive hands. "I care not what arrangements you make, as long as you are with me."

But Agatha, when she heard of the scheme, entered a caveat. "My dear Mrs Quilter, what of Little Tibby? To be left with no female to guide her! She will never cope."

"Lord, I had not thought of Tibby."

"Yes, and you know Mrs Vaughan has little patience with the child. One fool is enough, she says, when I remonstrate with her."

"Well, I dare say Ned is trying for her," said Chloe excusingly.

"Nevertheless, I had best remain here. Or Jemima must do so."

"No. We will have to take Tibby along with us."

"What, to such a place as Ravensthorp? She would be overawed. And how do we know what reception she may receive there?"

"Jemima will take care of her."

"But surely there must be maids enough at Ravensthorp?"

"I dare say, but I am anxious to avoid particularity. To arrive with my own maids will ensure my status. And a chaperon is indispensable, Agatha, if I am to retain a shred of reputation. You must see that."

Miss Flook coloured slightly and consternation leapt in her eyes. "Yes, yes, of course. How silly of me. We must not forget how ready were Mrs Jolliffe and the other Mrs Quilter to insinuate a stain on your reputation. If you are determined on this course, then I quite see I must go with you."

Chloe sighed. "I had determined otherwise, but I can't in conscience leave his lordship to his own devices."

"No, indeed. He is far from recovery in his own mind. Such a pity he might not remain here until he is better."

"Yes, but that won't do either, will it? He ought to be where his surroundings are familiar enough to stimulate his memory to better effect."

Agatha was fervently nodding. "You are right, of course. Oh dear, how difficult it is. And to think but a week or so ago, we were living so very comfortably."

The mournful note struck at Chloe. Had Agatha divined the closeness between her and Lance? Was she thinking of a possible future that might not include her? Dear Lord, what a tangle! It had not before occurred to her that there were consequences other than the workings of her own heart, should she be foolish enough to accede to Lance's repeated requests for her to marry him. She was not so foolish, but she'd not considered how many persons would be affected besides herself.

Agatha, to be obliged to find a new situation at her time of life. She had likely supposed herself secure and might well be troubled by such a suspicion. And Basil? After all he'd done? He meant too much to her to be cast aside. As for Little Tibby, there could be no question of leaving her to some other mentor. Who would take her on? Treat her with kindness and understanding?

Jemima too, though she was competent enough to find another post. And Jack! Such a good, willing lad, but a clumsy footman. As for Mrs Vaughan and her boy Ned, either might manage elsewhere, though Ned was undoubtedly slow and there was no saying another household would be willing to take on the cook's son as well as the cook.

On all counts, it could not be done. A riffle of feeling crept through her. Relief? Or was it rather disappointment? At least she was armed. She had a mountain of reasons to refuse him. Though he had not mentioned marriage for several days. The realisation gave her pause. Had he abandoned the notion? Forgotten it? Had it indeed been a whim of the moment, brought on by his confusion? She'd suspected as much. Well for her then. She need have no qualm in taking this step. She might hope for Lance's recovery to make him lose all thought of matrimony.

The smart that accompanied this wish was swiftly crushed. The more he withdrew from her, the easier she would bear the inevitable end.

CHAPTER ELEVEN

With Lance up and about and able to participate more in the life of Derry Lodge, the days seemed to wing away. Immersed in preparations for Christmas in addition to keeping him cheerful and entertained, Chloe scarcely had time to think of the coming trip to Ravensthorp.

She had thrown her half-finished letter to Lord Enderby to the flames in the book-room fireplace and despatched a freshly written sheet outlining his present condition and the agreed plan. She took care to assign her involvement to Lance's specific request, which availed her little. Lord Enderby's response, brought by fast courier, was both curt and formal. He thanked her for the information and declared his intention of arriving to collect Lord Pettipher early in the New Year, when he would require his lordship to be speedily prepared to travel.

Chloe's feathers were considerably ruffled. What, no word of thanks for her care? No apology for her household having been turned upside down? Common courtesy alone dictated at least an acknowledgement of all she had done for his dratted lordship. To whom, however, she refrained from speaking her mind. With difficulty. Her opinion of the marquis dropped significantly and Chloe was moved to congratulate Agatha on a narrow escape.

"Well for you the position was already filled. This brother-in-law of Lord Pettipher's would have been a tartar of an employer, I suspect."

Miss Flook, who had been shown the letter under promise of saying nothing about it to Lance, took a different view. "Oh, but these great men have little regard for the sensibilities of their inferiors, you must know. I have remarked it often."

"Then you've been unfortunate in your previous employers, my dear Agatha. High rank is no excuse for bad manners. Mr Quilter was firm on that point."

"But I wonder, dear Mrs Quilter…"

She hesitated, her cheeks flying colour and her eyes registering that look of doubt Chloe knew well. "You wonder…?"

Hesitance. Then, "I wonder did you tell Lord Enderby of your scheme to go with our lordship?"

"I did, yes."

"Well, in that case…"

"What is it? What have you in mind? Be plain with me."

Agatha set a hand to Chloe's arm, leaning in and dropping her voice to a confidential whisper. "Is it possible Lord Enderby suspects you have a … a different design?" Shock swept into Chloe's bosom, depriving her momentarily of speech. But Agatha was not done. "Do you suppose he believes you to be an *adventuress*?"

A disbelieving laugh escaped Chloe. "An adventuress? No, I do not suppose any such thing. I dare say he might take me for a designing hussy, just as my stepchildren did when I married their father."

Agatha's colour fluctuated. "Well, that is what I meant. Of course I know it is utterly untrue, but —"

"But this marquis knows nothing of me, and why in the world should I choose to accompany the earl on his return to his home merely because I have been instrumental in his recovery?"

"Yes, that is it exactly."

The apologetic note did nothing to assuage the swamping fury. It could not be directed at Agatha, who was merely voicing what Chloe ought to have thought of for herself. She drew a steadying breath, but her voice was shaky. "You may depend upon it that if it is so, the idea came not out of the marquis's own head, but out of his wife's. Women, sisters in particular, are more prone to suspect their own sex than are men."

"You are thinking of Mrs Jolliffe."

"She was quick enough to pour poison on the situation. She and Harriet both. No doubt this Rosaline is of much the same cut."

Here Miss Flook took issue. "Not from what his lordship said of her. She seems to be quite scatter-brained and suffering from a good deal of sensibility. Which, as you know, is not at all like Mrs Jolliffe."

Chloe's lacerated feelings were beginning to settle. "No, and if I won't allow Matilda to outface me, I shall certainly not permit these unknown relatives of Lance's to deter me from what I conceive to be my duty. Let them think me what they choose. They have not been here to witness his bouts of distress and the odd conduct we have seen. If anything, this bolsters my determination."

Agatha patted her arm. "Well spoken, my dearest Mrs Quilter. And you were perfectly right to demand my presence. None can accuse you if it is seen you are well chaperoned."

Yet as Chloe went about her duties and preparations, the niggle of Lord Enderby's dismissive treatment remained. Until Lance received a second letter from his sister. Chloe saw it at once when she entered the dining room. It did not need Agatha's pointing chin and cleared throat to draw her attention to the sealed missive lying beside Lance's place. He was not yet down, and Chloe read the superscription with a sinking heart.

"His sister again," she said as she took her seat. "I hope to heaven she has not written anything to upset him this time."

With a few exceptions when his mind wandered out of the present and confused him, Lance had been calm and collected for the better part of a week. He had become engrossed with his steadily improving physical strength, refusing to rest as much and appearing unexpectedly all over the house. Jack took him out walking each day and he was even talking of going for a ride. He had been to the village, choosing to reverse the regime, now very much reduced, of Doctor Goodleigh's visits on a couple of occasions. Chloe was cheered by the doctor's report of Lance having conversed upon a number of topics without reserve, hitting a barrier only once or twice when his memory failed.

From Jack she learned, without surprise, that Lord Pettipher had caused a sensation among the villagers. "Gawped like they were seeing a freak at a fair, mistress. Such a bowing and scraping I never did see, and the wenches all blushing and whispering, be they fifteen or fifty."

Chloe laughed, reflecting on the increasingly personable features of her patient as his health returned. "They will be envying Jemima."

"You needn't tell me, mistress. Tossing her head already, she is, flighty piece."

Aware of Jack's secret hopes in that direction, Chloe made haste to soothe. "Well, she must be allowed a little moment of triumph over her rivals, don't you think?"

"If she had any sense, she'd know as she don't have any rivals," said Jack on a gloomy note.

Chloe hid a smile. "Christmas is nearly upon us, Jack. There is always the mistletoe."

The footman brightened. "I'd best remind Ned to cut a few sprigs."

With which, he went off, full of determination, leaving Chloe's thoughts to return to Lance. Inevitably, they strayed to the warmth in his eyes whenever they rested upon her. He had not renewed his persuasions, nor spoken of his affections, but his manner towards her was wholly possessive. In private at least.

He had taken to seeking her out in the book-room if she was too long absent from his side. She'd thought he was becoming restless, but he denied it.

"Not at all. I like to be near you." He waved a hand at her desk. "Carry on with your work. I will not disturb you, but only sit where I can see you."

Nothing could be more disconcerting than to have him plant himself in a chair at a short distance from her desk, his eyes fixed upon her as she tried to concentrate on accounts or a letter of business. Invariably, she ended by closing her books.

"That is enough for now. Let us go to the back parlour. I'll order coffee."

She was growing all too used to being in his company, that was the trouble. If there had only been a significant return of his departed memory, she would have been less anxious on that account. She was in no way sanguine that when reality struck, as surely it must at last, Lance's affections would remain steady. "Clarissa" slipped out every now and then. A pinprick reminder each time he said it. She did not draw his attention to it, but it rankled, causing her to keep a tight rein on her feelings. She could not afford to let go. As long as she did not allow herself to become too fond, nor dwell on the future, she could control the level of agony she anticipated in the loss at the end.

But the letter this morning gave her a jolt. Lance did not belong here. Lady Enderby was a symbol of his proper milieu. All too soon Chloe must take him back and ease him into his natural sphere. She'd taken that as her task, though Lance thought only of her keeping him from startling his relatives. She signified security. But as he regained confidence in himself, he would cease to need her. At least, so she hoped.

But what if this Rosaline had other ideas? Chloe had a horrid presentiment that the letter would outline the suspicions she no doubt held of the designing creature who meant to return with her brother to Ravensthorp. What effect might that have upon Lance's frail state of mind?

Pleased with his new ability to run lightly down the stairs, Lance came through the open door of the dining parlour, his eyes seeking Chloe. "I ran down. Oh, not with speed, so you need not look severe upon me, nurse of mine. But only see how my legs obey me now."

A smile flickered. "That is excellent, sir."

"Oh, but do take care, my dear lord! What if you should fall?"

Lance tugged his chair out, throwing the elderly dame a mischievous glance. "Then I would rely on you to pick me up again, dear Agatha."

She blushed, disclaimed and tutted as he took his seat. He loved to tease her for she was an easy prey and he'd grown fond of the creature. She'd become like an aunt to him, a pleasanter companion than Aunt Adelaide with her megrims and complaints. Though he should be more patient, for she had enough to plague her. He knew now how debilitating to the spirits it was to be at constant war with unwilling limbs.

The butler was hovering with the coffee pot. "Yes, if you please. You know my addiction, Basil."

He glanced at his cup as the fellow poured the dark liquid and his eye discovered a sealed letter bearing his name. His breath caught, his heart flooding with dismay.

"No! Not again!"

Chloe's calm voice came. "There is no need to be alarmed, Lance. We must rather be glad your sister does not neglect you."

He eyed the thing with loathing. "I wish she would. Why can't she leave me alone?"

"She is worried about you, and so she should be."

He left the letter lying where it was and picked up his cup, taking an unwary gulp. The hot liquid burned and he hastily set the cup down. "Damnation!" Glancing at Agatha, who was flushing again, he gave a deprecating smile. "Forgive my language, I beg. That was hot."

Basil hastened over with the jug. "Cream, my lord?"

"Yes, if you please."

Miss Flook began to fuss. "If you would only make up your mind as to how you wish to take it, my dear lord, you would avoid such accidents."

He was glad when Chloe intervened. "Now, you know he does not recall how he likes it, Agatha. Basil is quite right to begin with the coffee on its own. We've had too many rejections when it has been already larded with cream and sugar."

The dry note induced Lance to throw her a mischievous look, but he smiled at the butler. "I'm a trouble to you, I know."

"It's no trouble, my lord. You are at liberty to change your mind whenever you wish."

"You're a good fellow, Basil. May I have whatever is under that silver dish? I'm hungry today." The letter impinged again, quenching the spurt of good humour. He pushed it away. "This is too provoking. I'll eat first."

"An excellent decision."

"I am glad you approve, Mrs Quilter."

His heart lightened a little as Chloe laughed. "Well, I can't think the contents will be any more welcome for waiting to be read. You might as well enjoy your breakfast beforehand."

A full platter appeared before him, piled with bacon and scrambled eggs. His appetite quickened and he picked up his knife and fork.

"It is such a relief to see you eating well, my dear lord. You are beginning to fill out a little, which is an excellent thing."

His mouth full, Lance was unable to answer. He waved a fork in acknowledgement instead. But the gentle chatter served to make him feel aggrieved about the waiting letter. Why could he not be allowed to continue in this cosy way? The comfortable pace of life in Derry Lodge suited him. He was upon terms with the servants, even Little Tibby with whom he had several times chatted in the early hours. It pleased him to draw the child out. She was a confiding little thing in her own way. And then there was Jemima. He'd flirted a little with the girl until he noticed Jack's ill-concealed jealousy. It did not take much to get the fellow to open up and Lance, beset by his own desires, could not but be sympathetic.

He had his sights on Basil, hoping he might discover more of Chloe's early life. She kept it close, evading his questions. Her speciality, evasion. He did not think Basil would prove an easy target. But when opportunity offered, he fully intended to find out all he could prise out of the man. He was at home here, that was the trouble. The only home he knew, if the truth be told. He had no desire in the world to return to the alien place of which he could still remember only snatches. He'd been elated by the reprieve. January had seemed an age away. And now this.

He eyed the letter as he ate, beset by the onset of that feeling of menace. He knew it to be ridiculous. And now that Chloe had promised to return with him to Ravensthorp, his dread had diminished. But he hated the reminder he was to be torn from all he knew.

He was aware of Chloe covertly watching him, though she kept up a spurious discussion with Miss Flook about her endless Christmas preparations. Why she had so much to do when she kept saying they were to have a quiet time was a mystery. Those women were coming, she said. With husbands, evidently. He would not mind that if he was a husband too. Chloe's husband.

He glanced across at her and found she had finished her repast and was reading her correspondence. Dared he bring the matter up again? No, she would evade him as she always did. Well, she would not evade him forever. His determination was set. Marry him she would in the end. He could not imagine a life without her. Could not endure one. After all these years, she had come back to him. He was never going to let her go.

He speared another piece of bacon and lifted it to his mouth. His stomach revolted. "Why am I eating this?"

He laid down the fork and lifted the plate, holding it up as Basil came to the table. The man took it from him without a word and disposed of it somewhere. Lance did not care where, as long as he had not got to eat it.

"Where is the coffee?"

"Your cup is half-full, Lance."

The minatory note in Chloe's voice checked his irritation. He looked at the cup and frowned. "But it's got cream in it."

He blinked as the cup was whisked away. Jemima? The girl was like a wraith. He hadn't even known she was in the room.

Basil set a fresh cup and saucer down and poured liquid into it. A satisfying black. Lance reached for it and drank, sighing with satisfaction.

He became aware of silence around the table. "Why, what?"

Chloe smiled, but he could see effort in it. "Why, nothing. What should there be?"

"You look disapproving. And Agatha's got her Friday face on. What have I done?"

Twittering broke out from Miss Flook, to which he paid no heed. She was always quick to disclaim. Yet he knew something was wrong. He eyed Clarissa's lovely features. She looked drawn.

"What is the matter, Clarissa? Are you tired? Have I tired you out? Is it all this Christmas preparation you insist on setting up? I wish you would not. Why do we need all these people coming here?"

She rose from her place and came to his side. "Lance, you need to rest. Come to the back parlour. We will take this with us."

Bewildered, he watched her pick up a sealed package from beside his place. Annoyance gripped him. "What is that? Give it to me! Is it a letter?"

He made a snatch at it, but Chloe held it out of his way. "You may read it presently. Come!"

He stayed where he was. "I want to read it now! Is it from Aunt Adelaide?"

"It is from your sister. And you will read it when you are in a better frame of mind."

The nurse voice. She was angry with him. He looked at the letter in her hand. It became abruptly familiar. The letter! Dear God, it had made him lose his wits again! He groaned, setting his elbows on the table and clutching his head. "I shall never recover! Never! I wish I was dead!"

"That will do! I will not have you talk in that fashion, Lance! Now, get up and come with me. Jack, if you please."

"Come, my lord, here I am. Let me help you up, eh?"

He dropped his hands. Where had the footman come from? "I didn't see you, Jack."

"No, sir, I've only just come in. Now then, up you get."

He allowed the man to help him to his feet. They felt unsteady beneath him. He grabbed for Jack's arm. "Don't let go, Jack, or I'll fall."

"I've got you, sir. You won't fall. Lean on me, that's it. Now then, easy does it."

Somehow he negotiated the corridor, despair in his heart as the memory of running down the stairs came into his head. How was he reduced like this? He'd been doing so well.

He sank gratefully onto the daybed, letting his head fall back as the footman lifted his legs up. Really, he ought to be able to do that himself. Why was he suddenly so weak? He lay quiet, half dozing for a space. The rattle of the tray made him open his eyes. Jemima was setting it down by Chloe's chair. He looked at her.

"What, coffee again?"

"It's fresh. What would you like? Black? Or shall I put cream in?"

He did not hesitate. "Black, of course, with a little sugar."

She busied herself with the pot and he watched her pick up the tongs and drop in one lump. She stirred the coffee, rose and brought it across. Her smile calmed him as always.

"Thank you, Chloe. I'm sorry I angered you."

"I wasn't angry. I had to speak sharply to make you attend, that is all."

He sighed. "I'm sinking."

"Drink your coffee. It always revives you."

He obeyed, feeling the heat of it spreading through him. "You're right. I do feel better. And more capable."

She had re-seated herself and was sipping at her own cup. She set it down and picked up the ubiquitous letter. Damnation. She'd brought it with her.

"I believe this is what set you off, Lance. Do you feel equal to reading it now?"

Chloe saw his expression change and held her breath. Was he was going to slip away again? She still found it disconcerting. Perhaps because it happened less now.

A sigh came. "I suppose I must."

She got up and gave it to him, but remained by the daybed, alert to any change. He broke the seal and unfolded the missive, at once making a disgusted face.

"What a scrawl!"

"Use your quizzing glass."

He had taken to wearing it, along with fobs, seals and a ring he found among his effects — although Chloe noticed he wore no fob fashioned with Clarissa's image. He had said he did not recall having any of them, but he set them about his person in a practised manner nevertheless. Just as he now groped for the quizzing glass without taking his eyes from the letter.

"Two whole sheets of it! What in the world can Rosaline have to say to me to make her go to such expense?"

"Read it and you will find out."

His mischievous look appeared. "You have always a sensible answer, nurse of mine."

Satisfied he was stable, Chloe returned to her seat and picked up her own cup of coffee. Really, she was becoming quite as addicted as Lance.

He read in silence for a moment or two, shaking his head once or twice. Chloe's nerves felt strung. She'd been itching to open the dratted letter from the first and was quite as anxious to know what caused his sister to write at such length.

"Well, about time!" Lance looked up from the letter. "She wishes me to convey her thanks for your care of me, Chloe. But only, mark you, after a plethora of unnecessary detail about Christmas. Typical. Rosaline never could stop rambling. How Jasper bears with her I cannot imagine."

Conscious only of resentment at the casual mention of all she had done, Chloe strove to keep her tone even. "Well, that is good of her. Is it all she says?"

Lance was once more scrutinising the pages. "I wish it were. This is all nonsensical. She says much about regretting I am not to be at Ravensthorp for the festivities and wonders how the household will go on. I can't imagine why they should miss my presence. It's not as if the family gathers there."

"Don't they?"

The letter dropped. "Of course they don't. Who is there? It is Jasper who has a vast plague of relatives."

"What will happen to your Aunt Adelaide?"

"Oh, she will have Hargrave. And his mother, I dare say. She is bound to take her brood with her."

"It appears you do have a family gathering after all."

"Nothing of the kind. Hargrave's mother remarried and produced a string of half-brothers and sisters for him. They are not Ravensthorps."

"I see."

He resumed reading and Chloe felt, for the first time, a degree alienated. Lance had never before exhibited that sort of dismissive attitude. Was it pride in his lineage? Was he recovering the arrogance of rank along with the memories?

"Damnation!"

A whisper of alarm attacked Chloe. What now? "What's to do?"

He dropped his quizzing glass, striking the sheet with the back of his hand. "Impertinence! Rosaline is asking all manner of questions. About you, of all things. Listen: *Who is this Mrs Quilter? What is she?* What the deuce does she mean, what is she? What are you? Why should Rosaline care?"

Why indeed! But Chloe kept her reflections to herself, holding to a neutral tone. "Perhaps she is interested because I am to come with you to Ravensthorp."

"But that is not all. Here she wants to know who are your family, and thinks Mr Quilter was in trade. Was he? How in the world does she suppose I would know these things?"

"I expect she is hoping you will question me and tell her."

"Well, I shan't. How dare she make assumptions about you?"

An uncomfortable feeling attacked Chloe's stomach. "Does she? What assumptions?"

"You may read it for yourself. I don't care to."

Lance threw the letter in her direction and the leaves fluttered to the floor. Chloe bent to pick them up. She spread open the two sheets and cast her eyes swiftly down the opening lines, hunting for the reference to herself. There it was.

Chloe read no further. It was as she had guessed. Lady Enderby feared her motives. She could have dismissed the unspoken suspicion, if the question of marriage had not lain between herself and Lance. Despite her misgivings, her feelings were too much involved and a thread of guilt made this Rosaline's hints prick deep.

He was an earl. His sister a marchioness. Was it not natural she must question the advent of the nobody of a female who proposed to insinuate herself into his life at Ravensthorp? Innocent of any such design she might be. Her motives, on the surface, were pure. It had not been her wish to go. Or had it? Had she allowed Lance's condition to over-persuade her into doing what she secretly wished? What if she refused to accompany him when it came to the point? Wouldn't he recover anyway? Familiarity must do the trick eventually. On impulse, she tested the ground.

"Your sister says she will be with you at Ravensthorp. Perhaps she means to remain until you are fully recovered."

Lance had been drinking his coffee in a leisurely way, leaning against the upholstered end of the daybed, apparently gazing into space. He looked sharply round. "She won't. How should she when she doesn't know how long it may be before my memory returns? Besides, I don't want her. She fidgets me at the best of times."

This was news to Chloe. Yes, her letters threw him back into confusion, but that must be set down to the reminder he must return to a life he no longer understood.

"Has it always been so?"

"From childhood up. A more dithery creature I have yet to meet. Jasper pays no heed to it. I dare say he had no notion what he was taking on, for they were barely acquainted when he married her. It had been a long-standing arrangement."

One of these unions for the sake of rank and status, no doubt. Oswald had been scathing of the aristocracy on that account. Which had amused Chloe since their marriage had been a convenience. But this begged a question.

"Why then did your parents not arrange a suitable match for you?"

Lance gave her a puzzled look. "They did. You know they did."

She did not make the mistake of refuting this. But if he was again muddling her up with his dratted ghost… "You mean Clarissa?"

Lance stared at her for a moment. Then his frown cleared and he set down his cup. A sigh escaped him. "Clarissa. Not Chloe, but Clarissa."

"Exactly so. Was it not then a love match, Lance?"

He had put a hand to his brow and did not look round. "Both. We were near neighbours. I knew her from my boyhood. Clarissa was forever saying we were destined for one another. I thought she was being romantic until my father instructed me to offer for her. I was only too happy to do so."

"You loved her." The words grated on Chloe's heart as she said them.

"She was the world to me. Beautiful, desirable and a baggage. She would have driven me insane." His hand dropped. He turned, a ravaged look on his face. "You can't imagine the depths to which I sunk when I realised…"

Chloe's breath caught in her throat as a premonition leapt in her mind. "Realised what?"

"I felt relief. How cruel was that? How callous! Oh, I grieved. Truly, I grieved. I still do. It was not that I did not care, for I did love her. I missed her presence. She was vital and so alive. To have her gone left a hollow I couldn't fill. But…"

The but resonated in Chloe's bosom. She understood that but only too well. "I felt that with my father. Worse, perhaps. Overwhelming relief that he could no longer drag me where he chose or gamble away every penny he made. Yet I missed him terribly." Lost in remembrance, she said more than she intended. "Sometimes I think it's why I agreed to marry Oswald."

"Why, Chloe? A man old enough to be your grandfather, never mind your father."

She looked across and found disapproval etched in Lance's face. Her bosom flared with wrath. "You dare to judge me too? You are as bad as your sister! Or my stepchildren. Oh, I saw their point. A penniless upstart arrived from nowhere with a gambler for a father and an unsettled life behind me. They supposed me to be no better than I should be, as the saying goes. A gold-digger of dubious morals who turned their father's head with my wiles." She drew an unsteady breath and flourished the objectionable letter. "And here is your sister thinking the exact same thing. Well, I am not to be condemned, Lance. I bought my respectability at a price. It was hard won and I will give it up for no one."

She stopped, breathing hard. Lance had made no attempt to interrupt her. She'd hardly been aware of anything save his intent stare. Duty tapped remindingly at her conscience. Dear Lord, what had she done? What had she said? And he so vulnerable. She'd never before lost control so completely in his presence. She strove for calm.

"I'm sorry. I should not have… I did not mean to say as much."

He sat up, swinging his legs to the floor and leaned forward, setting his arms across his knees. "Is that why you married him? To gain respectability?"

Disconcerted, Chloe did not answer for a moment. Of all the things he might have said, this was the least expected. She found she did not wish to lie to him. "No, not directly. I had no thought of marriage at the time. Basil brought me back to England. He sought Oswald's help because there was no one else. At least, there were my grandparents but I dared not approach them."

"What did you expect from him, then?"

"Nothing, to tell the truth. Basil hoped for pecuniary assistance at least. At best, he thought Mr Quilter might have a cottage on his lands where I could live with Basil and a maid to look after me. Basil never dreamed of a bridal any more than I did."

Lance's intent stare did not abate. "Then this Oswald must have been besotted. Why else would he marry you?"

Heat swept into her face and Chloe knew she was flushing. Resentment revived. "Assumptions again, Lance? Yes, it is true Oswald doted on me, but he was not the besotted old fool everyone supposed. When he had heard all my story, he offered me marriage as a refuge. Because he did not think a lady of my standing should be eking out an existence in a cottage. Because he needed a mistress for his home and because he was a kind and benevolent man.”

She was answered with a curling lip and a disbelieving eye, but Lance’s words were mild. “He sounds too good to be true.”

“He wasn’t a paragon, if that is what you mean to imply. He was a busy man and his demands on me were plentiful.” She threw up a hand. “Not in the way you are no doubt imagining. But he made me learn to hold household and educate myself where I was lacking. I had to keep up. He was a strict and energetic taskmaster, but he was equally generous in rewarding me for a task well done. It wasn’t easy by any means. I was used to a beggarly existence, trailing about the continent, making do as we roamed from lodging to lodging, oftentimes having to leave in the night to escape creditors. Instead, I found myself mistress of a vast estate with no notion of how to manage it. I learned the hard way. And while I learned, I was the object of curiosity and speculation and the target of endless insults. That was the price I paid, for five years. And you can sit there and condemn me for bettering my life!” Again she stopped, shocked at how the words had tumbled out.

Lance threw out a hand. “I didn’t condemn you, Chloe.”

“You thought little of me for marrying Oswald.”

He spread his hands. “I didn’t understand. I’m glad you told me all this. You’re so close and evasive usually.” His mischievous look appeared. “Now I know I have only to enrage you if I want you to tell me anything.”

Her heart lightened as a laugh escaped. “I thank you, but I would prefer it if you did not take pains to make me lose my temper again. I hate it. One should not allow one’s feelings to run away with one.”

“Is that Oswald’s dictum?”

"Yes, drat you! Though I learned to keep my mouth shut with my father. He was not above slapping me if I dared to berate him."

"I trust your husband did not do as much."

"Good heavens, no! Oswald was first, last and always, a gentleman. He would not dream of offering violence to a lady. Or indeed anyone. It was not his way."

Lance held out his hand. "Give me that letter. And you need not fear my sister. She will have me to reckon with if she dares to disparage you."

Chloe could not but be gratified. "Thank you. I shall rely on your good offices." Assuming he remained in his right mind. But that thought she kept to herself. She got up. "I must get on."

His face fell. "Must you go?"

"This may be a much smaller establishment than yours, but it won't run itself. I'll send Agatha to entertain you."

Chloe's revelations stayed with him, fuelling both curiosity and a nagging ache of jealousy. Why he should resent Chloe's having enjoyed years of marital felicity with the wretched *Oswald* Lance did not know. Yet it irked him, and he tried in vain to crush the feeling of satisfaction it gave him to know she had paid in the discomfort of a general disapproval. That would teach her to disobey him and condemn him to years of loneliness.

The straying thought held in his mind. No, that could not be right. It was not Chloe who had gone through the ice. Clarissa. Clarissa, the light of his life, blinked out like a guttering candle before his very eyes.

The memory played in his head. Clarissa, skimming across the ice, spinning, laughing at his shouted protests. And the vanishment. There … gone. In an instant. Snuffed out.

Images began to tumble. The aftermath. Her frozen body laid on the bed, white-faced and beautiful, covered with her flowered shawl, a bier for a princess, golden hair spread and curling as it dried. The impossible meeting with Lord and Lady Cunningsby, she a pale echo of her daughter, tortured with grief, himself a bluff pretence with hollowed eyes that he knew gave him away. *The guilt.* Oh, lord, the guilt. He could wish that particular memory unremembered.

But they were coming fast now. Weeping on his mother's bosom. The only time he'd given way in the presence of anyone else. His father's tight embrace, too tight. And then the funeral, the public spectacle, he flanking Lord Cunningsby as the chief of the mourners. No women, thank heaven. If the women had been there, he could not have held himself in hand. His mother, already talking of a replacement. Within weeks, God help him! As if he could replace Clarissa.

Chloe's image leapt into his head and he started out of the reverie. He looked round, expecting to find her in the chair.

"Agatha?"

She jerked up, her eyelids fluttering. "Oh dear, I fear I had dozed off, my dear lord. Did you want me? You were so quiet, I did not wish to disturb you."

"You don't disturb me." An automatic response. He was disturbed, but not by Miss Flook. "I was remembering."

Her face lit up. "Oh, excellent! I'm so glad."

"It's not excellent. I wish such memories had remained buried. Now they're alive again and I won't be able to rid myself of them."

Agatha's expression changed. "Oh, dear. But have you no pleasant ones at all?"

He had to laugh. "I dare say. But not these."

She looked as if she would ask more. He had no wish to talk of them and seized a subject from the air. "Are we yet ready for this infernal Christmas?"

Agatha brightened again. "Indeed, I think so. The butcher's delivery arrived this morning and Ned is out cutting holly boughs for the dining parlour and the drawing-room."

"Holly boughs?"

"For decoration, you know. Dear Mrs Quilter likes to have the place looking cheerful. You can help to set them out, if you wish."

If it meant he could be in Chloe's company, Lance was only too ready to fall in with this suggestion. Besides, he needed occupation. Anything to distract him from the springing images of the past. He recalled his earlier thoughts of the ubiquitous Oswald and the question escaped before he could examine its wisdom. "Is there any portrait of Mr Quilter, do you know?"

A startled look came into Agatha's expressive face. "Mr Quilter?"

"Chloe's husband."

"Oh, I see. I have not seen one. She could not have brought the family portrait here. The one at Mortain, I mean."

"That's her former home?"

"Yes, where the other, young Mrs Quilter now lives, along with Mr Bernard Quilter."

"You've seen this portrait?"

"Oh, yes. A most distinguished looking man, I thought."

Curse the fellow! Must he have been so very universally approved? Could he not have been a hunchback or grizzled and ugly? Chloe might then have been relieved to be courted by himself. Nine years. Or was it ten? Whichever it was, they'd been long years during which he'd tried to like even one among the annual crop of fresh debutantes who might come close to making him forget. None had. A sea of faces swept through his head. Pretty girls. Simpering little misses and bold flirtatious creatures. None could hold a candle to his Clarissa. Except Chloe, who resembled her too closely so that he became confused and hurt her with his errors.

He knew she loathed it when he did so. He could see it in her eyes, though she tried to hide it. She never said it, but he knew when he'd done it because she was prone to find an excuse to leave him. She thought he did not notice, but he was all too attuned to her changing moods.

Where had she gone now? He'd provoked her into revealing more than she ever had about her life with this Oswald of hers. He was tempted to go and seek her out. But the well of memories was still flowing and his mind jumped away from the intention, presenting him with flashes of interaction. With Hargrave, with his friend Wintringham, with Jasper and Rosaline.

The letter! He looked about for it and found it on the nearby table, neatly folded once again. He picked it up and opened it. He might as well read it through. What else had his sister to say?

The pile of holly boughs was growing scanty. Jack, who usually worked alongside Chloe in the task, had instead taken half into the hall, leaving Lance to take his place in the garlanding of the drawing-room.

Chloe worried the exertion might prove too much for him, but instead he seemed to revel in it. He placed a full-berried branch along the mantel, which had been swept bare of ornaments except for the carved wood case clock Oswald had left her.

"There. How does that match the other side?"

Chloe stood back and regarded the effect with critical eyes. "It's well chosen, but move it a little further towards the edge. Yes, perfect."

Lance grinned as he turned. "I am becoming adept, am I not? For one who never did such things before, I believe I have an unerring eye."

She regarded him curiously. "You've never done it? Even as a child?"

A cynical look came into his eyes. "An earl's heir? Use your wits, Chloe. Is it likely I would be permitted to disport myself in such a fashion? That was for the servants."

"Was it indeed? Did you do nothing for yourself?"

He shrugged. "Very little, that I can recall. Oh, except for what was considered suitable to my station." The mischievous twinkle came. "Or when I managed to escape."

"Did you do so often?"

"I can't remember. I know that I did, but if you ask me for specific instances, I can't give them to you."

Afraid of his falling into melancholy again, Chloe adopted a cheerful tone, looking about the room. "Well now, where else? What have we missed?"

Lance looked about, the frown still there. He'd been brooding since yesterday. Agatha said he'd been having disturbing memories, but he'd said nothing of them to Chloe. She had seized on the suggestion to have him help with the decorations.

"For I said he might do so, dear Mrs Quilter, and perhaps it will distract him."

It had, until this moment. Chloe regretted probing, but it was her habit whenever he seemed to be grasping at the past, in hopes the memories would build.

He pointed. "One more in the corner there, do you not think?"

He sounded more himself, and Chloe at once moved to survey the corner nearest the door. She turned to smile at him. "You're right, Lance, you have an eye for it. Can you pick a suitable piece?"

He bent to the remains of holly and selected a bough laden with berries. "This is pretty."

Chloe crossed to the small table by the sofa and picked up the ball of string and the scissors. "You may secure it to the candle sconce, don't you think?"

"This one?" He was at the corner, testing the bough in different positions, but he looked up at the wall sconce set nearby.

Chloe came to his side. "Is it too far from the spot?"

"Not if you cut the string long enough."

"Well, I will trust your judgement." She measured out a length of string, drawing it longer at his request as he grasped the end.

"That's enough. Cut it." She snipped the string through. "Hold this for me."

Chloe took the branch, reflecting that he was evidently accustomed to command. She watched him secure the string to the candle sconce. He was deft and efficient. If his childhood had been restrictive, he'd learned somehow to be capable.

"How is it you are so handy if you were not allowed to do anything for yourself?"

One eyebrow lifted as he looked round. "Even an earl must learn to manage some things for himself. You can't handle a gun without knowing how to clean and load it. Nor a horse without understanding his needs. I might not shoe him, but I'm as knowledgeable as any stable lad when it comes to grooming and saddling. And I'm perfectly well able to cope without my valet, I thank you."

The haughty note was pronounced. Chloe stilled her inward stiffening and refrained from answering in kind. The more he came the earl, the more his memory shifted into view. She ought to welcome it.

"I'm relieved to hear it," she said on a mild note. "I see I need have no qualms in leaving you to complete this task."

Eyeing her askance, he took the holly from her. "Is that supposed to be sarcastic?"

"Not in the least. I am honoured by your lordship's condescension."

She dropped a curtsey and he had the grace to flush a little, though he laughed too. "I ought to give you pepper, but I'm too much indebted. Though I think you deserve a punishment, you wretch!"

She had to smile. "Do your allotted task, Lord Pettipher."

The mischief flared. "As you command, nurse of mine." He threaded the string and slung the bough, becoming absorbed in the necessity to create an artistic effect. He stepped back with a flourish. "*Voilà!*"

She regarded his work in a measured fashion, keeping him waiting. At last she inclined her head. "I'm suitably impressed, sir."

He threw up his eyes. "Tell me we're done with this room."

She glanced around and nodded again. "We're done with this room."

"Thank the Lord! Now what?"

"Let us go and see how Jack is faring in the hall."

The door was half open. Chloe pulled it fully back and walked through. There was no sign of the footman, but the hall was replete with holly boughs in all the spots she and Jack were used to place it, garlanding the wall sconces and with ivy threaded through the banisters.

A gleeful note sounded in Lance's voice. "Aha! The very thing I need."

She turned and found him pointing up to the arch that led through to the back of the house. Chloe followed his finger and her pulse riffled as she saw it. Jack's effort to entice his Jemima was in plain view.

"Mistletoe?"

"Indeed. And you know what that means, don't you?"

Before she could object, an arm came about her and she was danced to the spot directly underneath the large holly bough itself adorned with interwoven sprigs bearing the distinctive white berries. Her heart thumped as Lance lifted her chin, a burn at his eyes. Chloe could not say a word, though protests leapt in her head, reasons why this was madness.

Then his lips met hers. Soft and warm and paralysing. His mouth moved, persuasive. Heat engulfed her, shocking her into pushing him away.

"No, you must not!"

"Yes, I must. I said you deserved punishment, did I not?"

His face. So close. Too close. Those green eyes alight. Her tongue tied itself in knots. "That's not — it shouldn't — you can't… I don't call that punishment!"

A throaty laugh escaped him. And then his mouth was again on hers, the kiss intense, fervent with desire. Recognition sent streaks of fire down Chloe's veins. She could no more keep from responding than she could hold herself upright, her knees threatening to give way beneath her.

As the kiss ended, Chloe staggered. Lance caught her close. "Steady, my love."

Shock, consciousness and dismay combined to spring a thrust of fury into her breast. Chloe pulled away, looking frantically towards the back premises. "Don't call me that! Oh, dear God, the servants! If anyone should see!"

"Let them see!"

Lance made to snatch her back into his arms, but she evaded him, throwing out her hands. "Don't! Lance, stop! You go too fast for me. You should not have —! Oh, dear heaven, what have you done? How dared you kiss me?"

His brows snapped together. "Why wouldn't I dare? I love you. I've said it enough. You're going to marry me."

Still weak, Chloe grasped at the bannister, utterly disoriented. "Assumptions… Don't say that!" This was impossible. At any moment, Agatha would appear. Or one of the servants. She must have a moment to compose herself. "I can't stay here."

He made a move towards her, but she threw out a hand to stop him and headed for her study, half running. Reaching her refuge, she flung through the door and collapsed into her chair before the desk, setting her elbows down and dropping her face into her hands.

What had he done to her? How could a mere kiss do so much? Such a kiss! Wholly outside her experience. How was she to know it could turn her insides out and upside down?

The door latch clicked.

"Chloe?"

She straightened in the chair and glared at Lance. "Go away!"

He was walking towards her. "I won't."

She rose, backing away. "Don't come near me!"

He followed, the frown in his face intense. "Why, Chloe? Why did you run away from me?"

Fright claimed her. She thrust out shaking hands. "Stop! If you truly love me, stop this!"

He did, stopping short a few steps away. The frown did not abate. "I frightened you!"

"Yes." She pressed her hands against her bosom, feeling as if the palpitations there would choke her. He did not speak, only eyeing her now with concern. Chloe blew breath slowly in and out, trying for the calm which had ever been her armour. It eluded her. Instead, remorse cascaded into her bosom, loosening her tongue. "I've never felt like that, Lance. You unleashed something within me that I can't — I can't control. I hate that. To be at the mercy of — of — well, I dare say you know what I mean."

"The mercy of your desire, is that it?" His voice was harsh. "Or will you pretend you did not feel it? It's of no use, Chloe. You were as inflamed as I, and you know it."

She shivered. "I don't attempt to deny it. But you go too fast, Lance, with this talk of marriage. It won't do."

"Why won't it do?" There was pain in his features now. "You are everything I need. You are all I need. You know I can't live without you."

"Now, yes, perhaps."

She came back to her chair and sat down, waving him to another. With impatience, he seized one and brought it near, throwing himself into the seat. "I don't understand you."

She set her fingers on the desk in a precise fashion that helped concentration, forcing the unleashed wildness inside to settle. It was time for truth. She looked at him, taking in the mingled hurt and bewilderment. With deliberation, she gentled her tone. "I know you think you care for me —"

"I don't think! *I know.*"

She swallowed. "Very well, but let me say what I must."

Belligerence entered both face and voice. "I don't want to hear it! You mean to put me at a distance and I can't bear that."

"Lance, listen to me! For once, think of my needs, my wishes rather than your own."

He flinched as if she had slapped him. "Am I so selfish?"

She sighed. "I dare say you can't help it. I hope it is so. I hope it is a symptom of your condition and not one of who you really are."

He said not a word, his eyes turning cold, the green like chips of stone. Chloe's heart jangled. She'd gone too far. Been too bold with her truth. How to mitigate it? Unthinkingly, she put out a hand. He ignored it. Her bosom swelled with wrath.

"Oh, I've hit the mark, have I not? Now you will punish me indeed. Well, then, let me say what I have to say and to the devil with the consequences."

For a moment he stared at her with that cold, hard gaze. Then his eyes changed. His gaze dropped. His hands came up to seize his head, elbows on his knees as he kneaded at his forehead, guttural in response. "You're right, of course you are. Oh, Chloe, what manner of beast am I? I wanted to throttle you then!"

Her fury melted. Without thought she rose and went to him, setting her arms about him and drawing him close. In an instant Lance gripped her to him, burying his head in her bosom like the lost boy she'd first known. Just as she'd done in those early days, she soothed with gentleness. "Hush now, hush. All will be well. Come now, you are better than this." She urged him away and he raised his head, the ravaged look back in his face.

"It's Clarissa, isn't it? She's why you won't give in to me. My God, must she haunt me still?"

Chloe drew her chair forward, sat down and grasped his hands, holding them in a firm grasp. "Lance, it will resolve, but you must give it time."

He let out a ragged breath. "I don't have time. Jasper is coming to get me. And after this, you'll refuse to accompany me. I can't blame you for it."

"I won't renege on my promise, Lance. I've said I will go with you. But you must promise me something in return."

His hands lay slack in hers and his tone was listless. "You want me to keep my distance."

His perspicacity startled Chloe. But she had to say it nonetheless. "I must have your word you will not kiss me again, nor claim me for your future wife."

"And if I won't give it?" A trifle of bitterness sounded and he withdrew his fingers from hers. "You'll go back on your promise?"

Chloe gave an exasperated sigh. "For heaven's sake! Don't you see that is just what your sister fears? Already she thinks I am hankering for the role of countess. What do you suppose she will say of me if we are caught in a compromising embrace?"

"But what has it to do with Rosaline?" He was recovering fast, a frown stirring. "She has no say in whom I choose to marry."

"She will be there, Lance. I am supposed to be your nurse, not your affianced wife."

"It will be a deal easier if you will marry me now, before we go."

"Don't be ridiculous!"

"What is ridiculous about it? It seems to me the most sensible solution."

"Sensible! Dear Lord!" Unable to be still, Chloe rose and crossed to the window that overlooked the gardens to the side of the house, speaking as she went. "Even could I consent to marry you, I could not do so at once. There is far too much to be thought of. What of my household? My servants? And the legalities of my widowhood must be taken into account."

He threw up his hands. "All these matters can be resolved once we are married."

"No, they can't, Lance. And there is no use in thinking of them because I will not marry you."

He was on his feet. "Now we come to it. Why won't you? It is not because you don't care for me, for I won't believe that."

Goaded, Chloe flung the truth at him. "No, it's because I don't know if you care for me. Me, Lance. *Me*. Chloe. And I don't believe you know either."

He looked taken aback for an instant. Was there doubt in his face? The frown intensified. Had she got through? Slowly he sank back into the chair, no longer looking at her, his thoughts turning inward, she was certain.

"I see." He nodded, spreading long fingers and studying them in a meditative fashion. "Yes, I see."

Chloe held her tongue, unwilling to probe. Had he truly understood? Or was she going to be treated to some new manifestation?

He set his hands on his knees and looked up. "We'll play it your way, nurse of mine. I must prove myself to you and for that I need time."

No, he had not seen it at all. She took a couple of steps towards him. "You must prove it to yourself, not to me. Let us be clear once and for all. Clarissa is in your mind and heart. I am not Clarissa. I can never take her place. Until you know me for Chloe through and through, I cannot marry you. There, it is said."

His sweet smile appeared. "You need not have spelled it out. Do you think me a fool? Do you think I have not thought the same?"

"Then you should understand my hesitation, Lance."

"I hate it, but I understand it." He rose. "I've said we will play it your way. You will be with me, and that is all I ask." He crossed to the door and looked back, mischief at last making a return. "The kiss was everything I hoped it would be."

Chloe was left with a pattering heart and a fleeting regret for the vision of an impromptu bridal.

CHAPTER TWELVE

The house was all bustle and activity. Lance found it oppressive. It was worse than the few days of Christmas festivities, overshadowed with the fell purpose in these new preparations.

It had come as a shock to him to learn Chloe intended to bring a retinue to Ravensthorp.

"I told you I must do so," she said when he protested. "Agatha will ensure propriety and to bring maids with us is a matter of status."

"What, with Little Tibby?"

He had been ashamed of his scorn the next instant, but it was too late. Chloe flew up into the boughs. "The child is my responsibility. I can't leave her without guidance. It doesn't matter if she's incapable of proper maiding. And Jemima will see she behaves, if that troubles your lordship."

Her mockery riled him. "It doesn't trouble me in the least. I like the chit, as it happens."

"She'll be invisible in your vast mansion, in any event."

"Chloe, I wish you will hold your tongue. Is it my fault I'm an earl?"

She'd calmed at once, the spurt of temper over as quickly as it had arisen. Her apology had been swift, but she'd escaped on some excuse. It was not by any means the only disagreement between them. Chloe had been on edge ever since that ill-fated kiss. Lance had wished it undone a dozen times, except that the wish of kissing her again attacked him every time he passed under that afflictive bough, the white berries taunting him. He dared not give in to it, fearing she might indeed refuse to come to Ravensthorp — and that he could not endure.

Only the knowledge she would be with him enabled him to cope with the dread. It had marred Christmas, as did the arrival of Chloe's stepchildren, their respective spouses and a horde of infants, rendering the house hideous after an enjoyable couple of days of quiet. After the splendid dinner on the eve of Christmas, Lance found it pleasant to picnic and make shift for themselves once breakfast was over on the day itself, while the servants enjoyed their own noisy celebrations in the kitchen premises.

"It was Oswald's habit to ensure the servants were also able to enjoy the festivities," Chloe explained upon enquiry. "I've merely employed his method. Tomorrow, the locals will call and I have duty visits, so this, I'm afraid, is our only peaceful day."

In the event, the morning callers proved to be those with whom Lance was already acquainted: the doctor and the vicar whom he'd met at church once he started attending. But Chloe was in and out all afternoon, accompanied by Miss Flook several times. Lance took refuge in the back parlour with a book, but isolation rendered him vulnerable to disturbing thoughts and remembrance of the dreams that came to haunt him.

Clarissa was there too often, youthful and ripe for any mischief. But worse were the dreams peopled with alien faces from his past. In sleep, he knew them, knew how they fit into the puzzle of the life he could not piece together waking. Vivid in dreams, they drifted out of reach when he opened his eyes. The effort to recall them made him fretful and uneasy.

He had only vague notions: of striding across a field with a set of men, or riding, his horse leaping ditches. A hunt? Or was he crossing his acres? There'd been a ball once. A horrid realisation gripped him when he woke, of an entire swathe of persons of rank with whom he was acquainted. Would he recognise even one of them? Wintringham! Yes, one at least. His closest friend. But the others? He could visualise his deceased mother only in particular images. His father too. And Rosaline he could see in his mind's eye. But further than his immediate circle? God knew who else he had in his family. The snippet from the Peerage had told him only of close connections. There might be a plethora of relatives for all he knew.

Oh, yes, there was Aunt Adelaide. He could conjure her readily. Yet it was knowledge rather than images. When he tried to envision her features in any detail, the effort defeated him. She was an elderly woman sunken in a comfortable chair, especially adapted with wheels by the estate carpenter. He remembered that.

The instant of self-congratulation was short-lived as he reflected on how much he did not remember. He dreaded re-entering that life when he must confront faces he ought to know, people who depended upon him as her people depended upon Chloe. He'd thought since of her protests against marriage. But she hadn't understood. She thought he wanted to pluck her from all she knew and have her abandon her home and her entourage. But the bleak truth had hit him the moment he recalled her words. He wanted to marry her here and remain part of this household. This was where he belonged, where he felt safe, where he was understood and where no one expected of him what he could not perform. He never wanted to leave this place.

He'd thought of telling Chloe, but the opportunity did not arise. With the coming of her family hordes, she became lost to him for three hideous days. He'd have preferred to hide away in his retreat, but the ladies Harriet and Matilda sought him at every opportunity. The males of the party, too, could not be avoided. In particular, he was obliged to do the pretty over the port when Chloe took the ladies away after dinner.

Bernard Quilter interested Lance only in a possible reference to his father. According to report, he did not resemble the ubiquitous Oswald, in character at least. He was a man precise in both manner and speech, his every utterance measured. His attitude towards his stepmother was polite to a fault, but Lance bristled, detecting a degree of irony in his address.

Jolliffe, on the other hand, was a man as spare as his wife was full-bodied. Matilda clearly had the mastery over him, for he was largely silent and only became loquacious over the port when his spouse was absent. Lance both pitied and despised the fellow, cordially disliked Quilter, and was almost glad of his condition since both men appeared to find the extent and worth of his estates of inordinate interest.

"I must beg you to excuse me, gentlemen, for my own knowledge is lacking. I do not scruple to mention it, as I know you are familiar with the story of my unfortunate accident."

By dint of dwelling upon this circumstance, he was able to evade all such impertinent enquiries. Instead, he directed the talk into safer channels by asking what sport the country hereabouts afforded. Thereafter he was battered with talk of coverts, stone walls and ditches, which lasted until the port decanter failed.

The departure of the party ought to have afforded relief. The house had been full to bursting, every bedchamber occupied, truckle beds put up for the children, their attendants stuffed into the overcrowded attics.

"Usually I go with Agatha to Mortain," Chloe had explained, "but I excused myself on this occasion."

"Because of me?"

"Yes, and I felt obliged to ask them to come here instead. I confess I had no real expectation that they would. I don't know how we are to manage."

But manage they had somehow. It was a tight squeeze. It had occurred to Lance that such invasions had never felt burdensome at Ravensthorp. He had a sudden vision of the vastness of the place and was rendered acutely apprehensive. His fears increased when Chloe began immediate arrangements for a prolonged absence from her home. Lance had hoped for a revival of the former peace when the relatives left. Instead, the spectre of his return to his ancestral home loomed.

He objected in vain. "Surely there is no occasion for all this hurry. It is not yet January."

"Your brother-in-law gave no indication of exactly when he would come for you, so we must be ready."

He escaped to the back parlour and brooded alone. Even Agatha was too busy to entertain him. Stupid to feel neglected. He did not belong here when all was said and done. He'd been nothing but a burden from the first, turning the place upside down and causing no end of inconvenience to everyone.

At least now he could make shift for himself. He no longer needed Jack's arm, though the footman continued to act as his valet. As well, for he proved to have only a small wardrobe at his disposal. Presumably the greater part of it had been sent ahead with his actual valet in the coach.

He would miss Jack. He'd grown fond of the man, listening with a good deal of fellow feeling to his disappointments. The bough of mistletoe had been of his making, in hopes of luring Jemima into an engagement. He'd stolen a kiss, but failed to gain her consent. Lance could not but feel for him, his own equally unsuccessful foray big in his mind. And his gain was Jack's loss, for Jemima was to be of the party going to Ravensthorp.

Which reminder effectively drove all thought of the footman from his mind. Ravensthorp. His name and his destiny. Of which he no longer felt a part. How was he to bear it?

The sound of bustling outside the door drew his attention. The door opened and Agatha rushed in, her cap a little askew and a flush mantling her cheeks.

"A coach! Chloe said to fetch you at once to the drawing-room, my dear lord. I fear Lord Enderby has come for you!"

Trepidation whittled at Lance's senses as he waited, and he had all to do to keep hold of them. He could feel his mind slipping out of his grasp.

"Sit down, Lance. This pacing is making me nervous too."

He halted his steps, staring at the corner where the holly should have been. "You've taken down the garlands."

"They were wilting. Sit down."

He turned on Chloe. "Sit down? Why? I'm going to be sitting in a carriage for hours."

"Because you are fidgeting yourself to death. And me too."

It was her nurse voice. He let out an overwrought breath and passed a hand across his brow. Glancing at Miss Flook, perched in her usual chair, he saw agitation. "You too, Agatha?"

"Indeed, my dear lord. I fear we are all of us overset."

"Overset? I feel like a prisoner awaiting the hangman!"

"Come, this won't do, Lance." Chloe was at his elbow, her hands urging him towards the sofa. He went without protest.

"See how I need you?"

"There, that is better."

Was it? Seated, he had a view of the ornate wooden case clock on the mantel. He watched the second hand creep around its face, his pulse fluttering against the rhythm.

The doorbell jangled. Lance shot out of his seat. Chloe's hand grasped his arm again, yanking him down.

"Sit!"

He sat again perforce, letting out a hysterical laugh. "Am I a dog?"

She gave one of those exasperated sighs of hers. "Be patient. You are allowing your mind to be overborne and there is no need."

"I hate Jasper!" He knew he sounded childish, but the turmoil needed some outlet or he feared he would utterly lose his senses as he had in the early days.

He could hear Agatha tutting and Chloe's grip tightened on his arm. "He is only a man, Lance. He cannot harm you. You are your own master."

He had never in his life felt less so. The thought stilled in his head. Did he remember that far back? Perhaps there was hope.

There was a murmur of voices in the hall, a sound of movement and steps approaching. Lance held his breath, willing himself to remain rigid in the seat. The door opened and Basil entered the room, opening his mouth to announce Jasper's arrival.

"Captain Ravensthorp."

Lance gazed, stupefied, at the man walking into the drawing-room. Recognition slammed into his head and he leapt to his feet. "Hargrave!"

CHAPTER THIRTEEN

Chloe watched, dumbstruck, as Lance and the young man who had entered embraced. The air was full of joyful protestations and laughing acknowledgements.

"Is it you indeed? Where did you spring from?"

"Ravensthorp, of course. It's Christmas, old fellow."

"My God, I never thought! Are they all there?"

"None but your Aunt Adelaide now. Mama couldn't stand it. Place is like a blasted tomb without you, coz!"

"But you here? Where is Jasper?"

"At Enderby Court. I've come in his stead. Would've come sooner had I known." The captain stood back, looking Lance over. "Good God, what have you been doing to yourself, coz? You look like a damned corpse! Why didn't you send to me? Must know I'd have come at once."

Lance grasped his hand between both his own. "I know you would, but I couldn't. I was too ill. Besides, I remembered nothing. I wouldn't have known to send to you. And Chloe had no notion of anyone to send to." He turned, consternation in his face, and threw an apologetic glance at her. "Forgive me! My manners have gone begging. Hargrave, let me make you known to my saviour, Mrs Quilter."

The young man came up smiling as Chloe rose to greet him.

"How d'ye do? I heard of you from my cousin Rosaline. I gather you've had this horrible hound on your hands for weeks."

Chloe heard Lance's mild protest in the back of her mind, preoccupied with the disturbing thought that Lady Enderby had no doubt already dripped her suspicions into this young man's mind. His friendly manner gave the notion the lie.

"How do you do, Captain Ravensthorp?" She turned to include Agatha. "This is my companion, Miss Flook."

"Yes, we must not forget dear Agatha," said Lance in a tone at so much variance with his earlier discomfort that Chloe was startled. "She has been at pains to entertain me as well as sharing the burden of nursing me when I was wholly incapacitated."

He had moved to Agatha's side as he spoke, a gesture inviting his cousin to shake hands with her. Chloe watched the exchange, her eyes on this Hargrave as he made suitable noises punctuated by Agatha's protests delivered in the half-sentences to which she was always reduced when self-conscious. A personable man, the captain bore a slight resemblance to Lance. He had not his cousin's looks, but he had a similar cast to his countenance and the same light hair, worn long in the military style with an old-fashioned queue. He was an inch or two taller with a rangy figure and he moved with athletic energy.

"You must forgive my early appearance, Mrs Quilter," he said, turning once again to Chloe. "Jasper said he was not expected until January, but I was too anxious to wait."

"I am not surprised. Will you sit down?"

He disposed his long limbs in the chair opposite, but Lance hovered until his cousin told him laughingly not to stand over him like a hawk. "What the deuce is the matter with you, coz? Was never used to crowd a fellow like that."

Reseating himself beside Chloe, Lance sighed. "I don't know what I was used to do, Hargrave. I can remember very little."

A frown creased the captain's brow. "What, nothing at all?"

"Snippets. Odd images. Bits and pieces only."

The frown did not abate. "Rosaline said something of it. Didn't realise it was as bad as that. But you knew me, coz."

Lance grinned. "Yes. You're one of the people I did recall, you scamp!"

The captain's face broke into laughter. Chloe suspected it was never very far away with him and remembered Lance speaking of his cousin as something of a rascally care-for-nobody.

"Should I be flattered, old fellow?"

"Yes, you should," Chloe cut in swiftly. "I can assure you, sir, his memories are few and far between."

The captain sobered. "Shocked to hear you say so, ma'am, but it seems hardly credible he could forget everything."

"Not everything. To begin with, he did not even know who he was. But it is coming back to him, little by little." She smiled. "Indeed I am glad you came. It is as I hoped. Seeing how Lance greeted you, I am confident he will find familiarity triggers his memories more quickly than can be the case here."

The captain nodded, twinkling at his cousin. "Then the sooner we get you home, coz, the better."

Chloe looked quickly round and found Lance predictably disturbed.

He met her eyes and grimaced. "If it must be, I'd rather it was Hargrave than Jasper."

"Well, that's what I thought," said the captain on a bracing note. "You don't want his Friday face sending you into gloom, and so I told Rosaline."

"You said so to Lady Enderby?"

Agatha's scandalised tone expressed Chloe's sentiments. But Captain Ravensthorp laughed. "Oh, Rosaline knows what I think of her spouse. Prosy old bore. What's more, I've told him to his face more than once. It's nothing to what he calls me, I assure you, ma'am."

This was said with an engaging insouciance that could not but draw Chloe's sympathies. It would do Lance good to be in this man's company. "Do you intend to remain with his lordship at Ravensthorp?"

"Long as I can. I've put in for leave of absence. Sent an express to my colonel to tell him I'd got to post down here to fetch my cousin back home. I'm in hopes he'll allow me a few weeks' grace. Fortunately, we've not been called to Spain as yet."

Lance's urgent under-voice caught Chloe's ear. "But that does not mean you are released from your promise."

The mutter evidently reached the captain's ears for he sported a quick frown and looked from Lance to Chloe. "Rosaline said you meant to come, ma'am. Is it so?"

"She's coming because I demanded it."

The captain's brows rose. "No need to snap my nose off, old fellow. I've no objection." His mouth twisted. "Wouldn't pay me any heed if I did. Nor anyone else. Never knew such a fellow for going his own way."

Intrigued, Chloe hoped for more, but the captain got up.

"I'd best see if I can take a room in your village, ma'am. Sir Lancelot here won't wish to set off today. Is there a suitable inn?"

She noted the odd address in passing, but it did not need Lance's questioning look to loosen Chloe's tongue. "Certainly not, Captain Ravensthorp. We will have a room prepared for you here."

"No wish to impose, ma'am."

"Pray don't be ridiculous, sir. You are not imposing, and I won't hear of your staying in the village. Besides, I can't abide the innkeeper's wife. She would make you horridly uncomfortable."

He burst out laughing. "In that case, ma'am, I'll be grateful for your hospitality."

Chloe nodded, turning at once to Miss Flook. "Give order for it, will you, Agatha? If Basil has not already attended to the matter." Glancing at Lance, she changed her mind. "No, we will go together. I have much to do if we are to be ready tomorrow."

Captain Ravensthorp threw up a hand. "Good God, no, ma'am! At your leisure. I should not dream of hurrying you."

"Thank you, but I believe we are well ahead in our preparations already. Perhaps a day or two then." She looked at Lance. "Or you may be able to persuade your cousin to go on ahead with you and we will follow."

"No!"

A rueful look crossed the captain's face. "Decisive and forceful as ever, coz. I'm at your service, not the other way about, never fear."

"Then don't make suggestions designed to throw me into gloom."

The captain whistled. "Phew! As you command, oh, knight of the realm!"

That made Lance laugh and he looked a trifle sheepish. "Sit down and be quiet, scallywag!"

Chloe had to smile. "Well, now that the niceties of social etiquette are in order, I shall leave you together. Basil will bring in refreshments. I dare say you have a great deal to talk about."

With which, she followed Agatha from the room, feeling a good deal more hopeful. It was evident Lance and his cousin were on the best of terms. This Hargrave clearly knew him well. Could she hope to learn of him what might be of use to herself?

Left alone with his cousin, Lance at once felt oppressed. He hankered for his refuge and rose. "Let's go to my retreat."

"Retreat?"

"The back parlour. It has become peculiarly my own. I'm comfortable there." He led the way through the hall, encountering Jack on the way, armed with a tray of decanters and glasses. "Is that for us? The back parlour, if you will, Jack."

"Right you are, sir."

The footman followed as he ushered his cousin through the arch and along the short corridor that led to his sanctum. Once there, he threw himself down onto the daybed and gestured to the chair by the fire.

"Sit there."

Hargrave's brows went up as he surveyed the daybed. "No longer wonder why you like it in here. Cosy, ain't it?"

The footman set the tray down by the chair. "Thank you, Jack. My cousin will do the honours." He nodded dismissal and Jack left the room. Lance lifted his legs onto the daybed and lay back against the scrolled end with a sigh of satisfaction. "That's better. Now we can talk in peace."

"What's this? Madeira?"

"Yes and it's good."

"Suits me, whatever it is. I'm parched." Hargrave poured and came to hand a glass to Lance, standing over him and surveying him with a critical eye.

Lance balked. "Now who's being a hawk?"

His cousin pushed his legs aside and perched on the daybed beside him. "Taking a look at you, coz. Like a blasted scarecrow. What happened?"

"Didn't Rosaline tell you?"

"A rigmarole. You know what she is. Couldn't make head nor tail of it. Much rather hear it from you."

Lance gave him as accurate an account of his accident as he could. "I remembered nothing of it. Chloe told me, and I've had flashes of it myself since."

His cousin eyed him in a ruminative fashion. "What's all this Chloe business? Ain't like you at all."

"What isn't?"

"Well, to be so familiar with a wench."

"She isn't a wench!"

"Female, then. Usually run as fast as your legs will carry you."

This was of instant interest. "Do I?"

His cousin's lopsided grin appeared. "Never seen anyone who could put off a matchmaking tabby quicker. Been doing it ever since I've been on the town."

Yes, he recalled that much. "I remember. Some of it. I know I haven't looked at any woman in the way of marriage before. Not since Clarissa."

"So it's true, then!"

Shock and irritation claimed Lance. "What's true? Is this Rosaline's work? What has she been saying to you?"

"Lord, I don't know! Woman's a regular gabster."

"But you do know," Lance insisted. "Is what true?"

Faint colour came into Hargrave's cheek. "Well, if you must have it, she seems to think you've been snapped by the ankles. And this Chloe of yours is the culprit."

Lance's irritation increased, along with remembrance of his grievances. "Nothing of the kind. If you must know, the boot's on the other leg, only she won't have me. At least, not yet. But I'm going to marry her for all that."

Unholy glee entered Hargrave's eyes. "That'll set the cat among the pigeons. I wish I may see Rosaline's face when you tell her. Or Aunt Adelaide's, come to that. Though she's as batty as a crow these days, so I dare say she won't say much. Had a fit when Rowley got back to Ravensthorp without you, by all accounts. Thought you were at death's door."

Lance slumped back. "I might as well have been."

"How so?"

"I couldn't remember a thing. You don't know, Hargrave. It's been a nightmare. It still is on occasion. If I hadn't had Chloe, I think I would have lost my mind altogether." A look that was abruptly familiar came into his cousin's face, one that spelled the sympathy of intimate friendship. Lance spoke without thinking. "We're close, you and I, are we not?"

Hargrave's brows flew up. "You mean you can't remember that?"

Sighing, Lance took a sip of his wine. "In a fashion. I don't recall why or how, just that it is so." Puzzlement wreathed his mind. "Strange. You are years younger than I."

The other's peculiarly lopsided grin put his serious look to flight. "Well, if you've forgotten how I hero-worshipped you as a boy, I count that a triumph."

An image jumped in Lance's mind. "I taught you to ride!"

"You did, and a more bumbling effort I wish I may never see. Worst teacher in the world!"

Lance bridled. "You can ride, can't you?"

"No thanks to you."

"Rascally ingrate! I don't know why I wasted my time on you."

"Because you thought yourself a master, full of your own importance because you'd succeeded in teaching Clarissa to drive, with the result she went careering all over the county like a hoyden. How the mothers scolded!"

He was laughing, but Lance, beset with a plethora of images breaking through the barriers of his mind, heard it only vaguely. "Lord, Chloe is right! You're throwing me into the past. And I don't much like it. I'm not sure I want to remember."

Was he truly a creature of such arrogance? Before he could say any more, Hargrave grasped his free hand, holding it hard.

"Don't you dare say that! You're a good man, Lance. You know I can't resist plaguing your life out, but we need you. I need you. Nothing I want less than to step into your shoes, you know that. At least you will know it when you remember, if you don't now."

"I do know that. I told Chloe as much, I think."

"Well, you marry her and beget a string of infants. You have my blessing."

"In that case, I need have no qualms," returned Lance, with a flash of humour.

Hargrave grinned as he released him. "That only was wanting."

"Yes, I'm doubtless in the habit of consulting you before I take a step, young saucebox."

"Well, of course. Only make a mess of things without the benefit of my advice."

Lance had to laugh. "I'll admit it's doing me the world of good to have you here. Thank the Lord you told Jasper to go hang!"

"Always tell Jasper to go hang. Can't bear his prosing. What's it to him in any event if you choose to marry a —" He stopped, reddening.

Lance felt his bristles rise. "A what?"

"Oh, Lord! Slipped out. Didn't mean anything by it. You know what a rattlepate I am."

"A what, Hargrave?"

The other's discomfort increased, but he capitulated. "If you must have it, Jasper called her a harpy." He waved an impatient hand. "No need to look daggers, I didn't say it. I can see she's nothing of the kind. Strikes me as an eminently sensible creature."

"She's an angel. Harpy! My God, I could throttle him! Or is it Rosaline who set him on? She was asking all manner of questions in her letter."

"You know what she is, always the big sister where you're concerned."

"Yes, but I don't know. At least, I suppose I have an idea of it. But is she so high in the instep? Why should she take exception to Chloe?"

"The wonder is you don't take exception yourself. Ain't Rosaline who's high in the instep. Who is it who refused to look at any of the debutantes of lesser rank than an earl's daughter?"

Everything in Lance protested. "But I didn't want to marry anyone. And how was I to replace Clarissa with a female who couldn't match up?"

"No one could, according to you, coz. Could have thrown the handkerchief any time these nine years. Can't say I'm surprised Rosaline has despaired of you. She's paraded uncounted beauties before your eyes and you've turned your nose up at the lot. And then you go and lose your head with an impecunious and nameless widow, of all things. Can't blame her for panicking."

Lance was forced to recognise a modicum of truth when he put it like that. He was shamed by the thought of his own conduct. In his current state, it struck him with disgust. That his old self might have thought of Chloe in such terms was anathema. He was privy to such of her past as must shock his sister to the core. Yet he did not give a tinker's damn for it. He had not the slightest interest in the family Rosaline had been trying to dig out. Indeed the only point of contention was her marriage to Oswald, a man old enough to be her grandfather. And she'd admitted she'd agreed to it for her own advantage. Not that he cared for that. He balked at the thought of such a fellow bedding his Chloe, and that was the long and short of it. But as to her suitability to be the wife of a peer of the realm, he cared not a jot.

His wandering attention was recalled by his cousin, a more serious note in his voice. "What did you mean about nearly losing your mind?"

He met the other's concerned eyes, the agonizing moments of disorientation hovering in his head. Wary, he held back a moment. Yet somehow he knew he might trust Hargrave. "You at least would not have me confined, I'm persuaded, but Jasper —! If he'd witnessed one of my moments of — what shall I say? — oh, craziness, distortion, confusion, utter madness!"

Hargrave tossed off his wine and leaned to set the glass back on the tray. "Explain, coz, for I don't see it."

Lance sighed. "The worst, I think, were the wanderings in the night when they found me near collapsing in the corridor. I didn't know where I was, Hargrave. And for minutes together I didn't know who they were. Once I was sitting on the stairs in a kind of terror. I swear I became almost unhinged after Jasper sent to say he would fetch me home."

"Why should that trouble you? Are you not anxious to come home?"

"You don't understand." He set down his glass. "I don't know my home! I can only visualise parts of the place. I dread having to meet a houseful of persons I don't remember. As for management, you'd make a better job of it than I could at this present. And if anyone was to see how my mind sometimes betrays me, jumping from one thing to another without making sense — I still slip into thinking Chloe is Clarissa on occasion."

"Ha! I'll warrant she likes that not one jot. Females can't stand comparisons of the kind."

"She doesn't complain, but she thinks I still hanker for Clarissa."

"Do you?"

Brought up short, Lance stared at him. Did he? He no longer knew. Chloe had become so much a feature in his life he could not separate the two. "I don't know. Perhaps I never shall. Sometimes I think I am doomed to remain in this state, only partly privy to my life before this time."

Hargrave stood up, becoming brisk. "Then the sooner we restore you to Ravensthorp, the better. And if you fear to seem odd to your retinue, think of Aunt Adelaide. Can't be worse than she is if you try."

Lance shook his head at him. "Are you never serious?"

"But I'm perfectly serious, old fellow. Between the two of you, the servants will be driven into frenzy. Do them good. Getting far too complacent. Daresay half of them haven't even noticed your absence."

Exasperated, Lance picked up one of his cushions and threw it at his cousin. "The only one likely to drive anyone into frenzy is you. If I'd known I'd be plagued with a half-baked officer of the Guards, I'd have taken refuge in forgetfulness."

Hargrave burst into laughter. "Now you're sounding like your old self. Feel free to throw a few more insults around, coz, but I warn you I'll give as good as I get."

"You always do, scallywag." Surprising himself, Lance realised he did remember. He swung his legs to the floor and sat up, grinning up at the man. "You're doing me the world of good. For God's sake, don't dump me at Ravensthorp and go off, Hargrave. I need you."

CHAPTER FOURTEEN

It would have suited Chloe a deal better to have travelled separately, arriving perhaps a day or two behind the males of the party. But Lance, though his melancholy had vanished with the advent of his cousin, would by no means agree to this arrangement.

"I'm not leaving without you, so don't think it."

Chloe sighed. "Are you afraid I won't come?"

"Yes! No! I don't know."

"I won't break my word. I gave you my promise."

They were alone in her study where she'd asked him to come for a brief colloquy. Lance did not hesitate to catch her by the shoulders, his grip near frenzied.

"You're trying to palm me off on Hargrave! He's a good fellow, but I need you, Chloe. Hargrave hasn't seen me at my worst. He wouldn't know how to bring me out of it."

Chloe seized his wrists. "You're hurting me, Lance!"

He relaxed his grip but he did not let go. "Chloe, please!"

She could not but recognise the latent terror in the back of his eyes. She adopted the calm tone he responded to. "There is no need to fret, Lance. We will do it your way. Release me, if you please." A long breath escaped him as at last he removed his hands from her shoulders. She smiled at him. "Come now, you must not give in to your demons, Lance. For my part, I think your worst is behind you."

"Yes, if you are with me. Without you, I dare not think of where my mind may go."

She was dismayed, though she hid it. Captain Ravensthorp's presence had developed in him so much lightness of heart, she'd been drawn into thinking he'd come out of the darkness that sometimes enveloped him. A premature belief.

In deference to Captain Ravensthorp's convenience, the cavalcade set off earlier than planned, on the second day of the New Year. Chloe, perforce, accompanied the gentlemen in the Ravensthorp coach while Miss Flook and the maids occupied the other. She had toyed with asking her stepson to lend her the Quilter family coach, but the less she was beholden to Bernard the better. Her expenses had mounted with housing Lance, but quarter day had left her in funds again and the hire of a coach would be offset by the economy of living instead at Lance's expense for a time.

Not that her absence would go unnoticed. She had sent a note to Matilda to apprise her of her intention and the reason for it, fearing that rumour would place an undesirable construction on her activities. Thank the lord she had insisted upon bringing an entourage.

Captain Ravensthorp, at her secret request, beguiled the tedium of the journey with a fount of reminiscences. He was sitting forward and addressed himself in a cheerful fashion towards his cousin with "Do you remember when…?" producing some antic of his youth or a tale of mischief in which Lance had been involved. As Chloe had hoped, some of the tales sprung memories and Lance was kept in a ripple of amusement as he joined here and there in the telling. If he did not himself propose any incidents, at least it kept him from brooding on the coming ordeal.

They stopped for a meal at Bedford, and stayed the night at the Fox & Hounds in Northampton at Chloe's insistence. "I wrote to bespeak rooms."

"But we're close enough to make the rest of the journey in an hour or so," protested the captain at a moment while Lance was using the facilities of the house.

"I dare say, but I don't wish to arrive at nightfall. No one at Ravensthorp knows I am arriving, and with a retinue at that, and they will need time to prepare."

"I suppose there is that. But won't Lance be the better for getting home sooner?"

"He may fret a little tonight, but he'll be less disturbed if he arrives at his home in daylight. It will give him time to become accustomed."

"Before he must go to bed without having you within call?"

Startled by his shrewdness, Chloe laughed. "Exactly so. I'm afraid he has become too dependent."

"And you think to wean him off? You are baying at the moon, Mrs Quilter, if you'll forgive me for saying so."

A ripple of alarm went through Chloe. "Why do you say that?"

His lopsided grin was rueful. "Where his heart's involved, ma'am, he's as tenacious as bedamned."

She eyed the man, hovering between doubt and elation. She opted for prevarication. "He told you?"

"He's never reticent with me. The reverse is true too. It's been years since Clarissa died, but he's been steadfast. I don't scruple to mention it for he told me how he mistook you for her."

"Yes, he did," said Chloe with asperity, "and I have told him I cannot and will not replace her."

Captain Ravensthorp looked startled, but there was no time for more as Lance returned, interrupting them with a request to know at what time Chloe proposed to dine. She was obliged to give him her attention, but the exchange rankled. Had she not known it? If anything had been needed to convince her that her instincts were not at fault, Captain Ravensthorp had supplied it. Steadfast? Tenacious? But for whom?

He implied that Lance loved her as he had loved Clarissa, but Chloe was by no means convinced he had not merely transferred his affections from one to the other. Wean him off? Did the captain suppose that was her hope? All she hoped for was some sign that Lance indeed cared for herself, for what she was. Either that, or she would see his allegiance shift as he sank back into his old life, as his memory recovered and he was once more who he had been. In some ways, she regretted the necessity to accompany him. A clean break might have been easier to bear.

Her first sight of Ravenscroft on the morrow at once provided justification for Lance's fears. The place was massive. In the limited view afforded from the coach window, she descried a high ornate frontage across a wide expanse of building. Realising Lance had grown silent beside her, she turned to find him staring across her out of the window, his hands clenched on his knees. She set her fingers on the nearest fist.

"Come now, Lance, there is no need to fret. Your people are well disposed towards you and they know of your trouble. No one will expect too much of you."

He said nothing, throwing her an eloquent look in which she read the beginnings of panic.

"Just so, Mrs Quilter. And if they do, coz, they'll have me to reckon with," said Captain Ravensthorp on a bracing note. "I'll warn Potticary not to disturb you until you're ready."

Lance's brow furrowed. "Potticary. It rings a bell."

"Steward. He's been holding the fort. Capable fellow. He can very well keep his hand on the reins a bit longer."

By this time the carriage was slowing. As it swung into position before the vast columned portico, a swarm of people came hurrying out and Lance leaned forward, alarm in his eyes as he scanned the faces. "Good God, who are they all?"

"Your anxious household, coz. They've missed you."

The coach stopped. Someone opened the door and Captain Ravensthorp pushed forward and jumped down as the gathering crowd surged forward. "Hey! Give room there! Give room! Yes, yes, your master is here at last, but you're like to crush him to death! Shift along there!"

Lance was looking horrified. Chloe touched his arm. "Take it as a sign of their care of you, Lance. It is obvious you are well loved."

"I wish to God I had not come!"

"There is nothing to fear."

"Yes, there is. I don't know who they are."

"You will have time enough to find out. Your cousin will see they don't overwhelm you at this moment. Courage!"

"You first, then."

By this time the steps had been let down and someone was waiting to hand Chloe out. She recognised Lance's groom and smiled as she prepared to alight. "Rowley? It is good to see you again. How do you do?"

"I'm well enough, ma'am. How is master?"

He sounded eager, and Chloe turned back towards the coach. "You may see for yourself. Lance, here is Rowley, ready to assist."

But Lance was already exiting the coach. Rowley touched his forelock and grinned. "You look a sight better than when I last saw you, me lord."

Lance's gaze was travelling over the sea of faces, but he looked round at the groom and a faint smile came. "Thank you. I am better, in body at least."

The captain, who had evidently succeeded in persuading the horde of servants, if that was what they all were, to move aside and leave a pathway towards the house, returned at this moment to his cousin's side. He lowered his voice. "Let us go in, coz. No need to greet everyone by name. Just smile and nod and they'll be satisfied. Will you take my arm, ma'am?"

But Chloe, who had seen the second carriage draw up, had no intention of entering the house without her retinue. "No, I must first see to my people. If you will direct the housekeeper to come to me, I think it will be simpler if Lance goes in with you."

Rather to her surprise, Lance made no objection to this proposal. Perhaps he was still too overwhelmed, for his eyes were once more scanning the faces of his household as if he were trying to recall the individuals staring his way.

"Come, old fellow."

Captain Ravensthorp took his arm and led him forward. There was a concerted movement in the gathering, but an elderly fellow held up a hand, moving forward and bowing. "On behalf of the staff, my lord, may I say how happy we are to welcome you home again?"

Lance halted. "You're the butler."

Chloe waited for no more, but hurried back towards the hired coach, where the two maids were already on the ground and Miss Flook was just descending with Jemima's help.

A voice spoke behind her as Chloe reached them. "Begging your pardon, ma'am."

She turned to find a stout dame in bombazine, round-faced and wearing a prim cap, bobbing a curtsey. "I am Mrs Howmore, his lordship's housekeeper, at your service."

"Ah, how do you do?"

Chloe introduced herself and her retinue. Mrs Howmore acknowledged the maids with a nod and gave a curtsey to Miss Flook. Then she turned once more to Chloe.

"May I offer you my heartfelt thanks, ma'am, for all you've done for his lordship? Rowley told us how you took him in and brought the doctor and cared for him and all."

Not a little relieved and rather touched, Chloe smiled. "Anyone would have done the same."

The frills on Mrs Howmore's cap rippled as she shook her head. "No, ma'am, not as Rowley told it." Her voice dropped to a hush. "Is it true he's lost all recollection of his past?"

"It is coming back to him, piece by piece. I hope that being at home may bring it back the quicker."

"Lordy, I hope so, ma'am! It's very good of you to come back with him."

This was entirely unexpected and Chloe warmed to the woman. "Thank you. I'm afraid his lordship would not leave my home without me. You must understand that I and my people have become something of a point of stability to him."

The housekeeper looked a little puzzled. "Indeed, ma'am?"

Chloe sighed. "It is perhaps difficult to understand that his lordship's present life began again when he woke up from his accident. It is all he is sure of. But I am confident he will very soon become accustomed to you all again."

Mrs Howmore was nodding. "I see, ma'am. I admit it was a shock to realise that he did not know me just now."

"He will remember, you'll see. Give him time."

"All the time in the world, ma'am. There isn't one of his household who wouldn't wish his lordship well."

"That is good to hear. Meanwhile, I hope our unexpected arrival will not incommode you?"

"Not in the least, ma'am." An air of efficiency overtook the creature. "I'll arrange for rooms to be prepared, but allow me to lead you in. I dare say you'll all be glad of an opportunity to rest and refresh yourselves."

"In fact we have only been travelling an hour. We lay at Northampton, for I thought it would inconvenience you less if we arrived early in the day."

"Well, it makes it easier, ma'am, of course, but it would have been no trouble if you'd arrived last night. If you'll follow me, ma'am."

Refraining from informing her of her real reason for the delay, Chloe beckoned the others and began to accompany the woman towards the entrance to the mansion. She was relieved to see that the crowd was rapidly dispersing. But Lance and his cousin had vanished inside, and Chloe was chagrined to realise she felt stupidly neglected. Worse, she was bereft. The weaning had already begun.

Impressions rushed at Lance at every step, bewildering, yet with here and there a thrust of familiarity. The juxtapositions kept him intent as he murmured responses to the greetings, bobbings and bowings.

The butler Kenninghall, as his cousin muttered in his ear, accompanied his progression through the persons who had gathered to greet him. Lance was grateful for his keeping them at bay, but would have wished the man had known enough to re-introduce these individuals by name. Or perhaps not. He would never remember so many.

He was glad to be free of them as Hargrave ushered him into the huge hall with a chequered floor that he at once recognised.

"Her ladyship will have been fetched by this time, I believe, my lord. They will wheel her to the Green Saloon."

"He means Aunt Adelaide," Hargrave said in his ear.

Lance nodded and followed where the butler led, wishing only for the whirling kaleidoscope of faces still in his head to disappear. As he passed through one room after another, it struck him that the pattern felt right. There were few poky corridors here, unlike at Derry Lodge. The place was big, but not intimidating to him.

The moment the party reached the Green Saloon, he was beset with the oddity of déjà vu. He stood still, looking from one wall to another as the phenomenon struck at his mind. He saw it anew, but knew it already.

"Pettipher, at last! Good heavens, boy, where have you been all this time?"

The querulous voice was at once familiar and the oddity in his mind vanished. He turned to the wizened creature in the wheeled chair. "Aunt Adelaide?"

She beckoned with a bony finger. "Come here and let me look at you, boy."

He approached with caution, eyeing the lined face under its lacy cap and the escaping wisps of white hair. A gimlet eye bored into him. "Ye don't look to be in prime twig, but I dare say ye'll do. What possessed you to go turning yer carriage over?"

Thankfully, Hargrave came to his rescue. "It was not done by design, ma'am. And my cousin has suffered enough without enduring one of your scolds."

The old lady's gaze did not leave Lance's face. "They tell me ye've lost yer memory. That true?"

He cleared his throat. "Mostly. At first it was everything, but it is coming back in fits and starts."

"Well, ye'd best stop with the fits and starts and get it all back quick. Can't have the head of the house with addled wits."

Had he not known it? But before he could protest, his cousin was in again.

"That's what he hopes by being at home, Aunt, where familiarity may do the trick. Meanwhile, our good Potticary here will keep everything running smooth, won't you, sir?"

He was gesturing forward a man of middle years with a pleasant face and a deferent manner. This must be his steward. Lance recognised concern in the man's gaze. And was it affection? He struggled for recognition, but it did not come. He took the steward's hand and felt it grip hard.

"I'm relieved to see you home again, my lord."

"Thank you. Potticary, is it?"

A shadow passed across the man's face and his tone became puzzled as he released his hold. "That's right, my lord."

Lance essayed a smile. "You'll have to forgive me. I can't force remembrance. It comes upon me suddenly and I regret I have no control over it."

A frown gathered on the steward's brow. "I'm dismayed to hear you say so, my lord." He added with a flicker of a smile, "I stand ready with whatever assistance I can render. We may go over anything you need when you are ready."

If he ever was. But he must not say so. He barely had a chance to thank the man before his aunt claimed his attention.

"Where's this hussy ye've got in tow?"

The gust of rage took him unawares. In the periphery of his vision, he saw Hargrave about to speak, but he forestalled him, ice in his tone. "I am indebted to Mrs Quilter for my life, ma'am, and if you again refer to her in such insulting terms, you may look elsewhere for a benefactor."

The elder dame's sharp eyes widened and Lance became aware of an uncomfortable silence around him. A flurry attacked his pulse and the thump of his chest was loud in his ears. What had he done? Dear Lord, where was Chloe to settle him and smooth it over?

But a sly grin twisted the elderly dame's mouth. "Ye've not changed as much as ye'd have us believe, boy. Though you needn't come the earl with me."

A hideous suspicion burgeoned. The words came rapidly, without volition. "Are you saying that is a typical remark? To make such a threat? Is that the kind of creature I am? Or was?"

His aunt frowned. "What d'ye mean? An earl, ain't you?"

"Only by accident of birth. I didn't know who I was when I regained consciousness, Aunt."

"Well, you know now. And it's to yer credit you behaved like one. Needn't think I'll take it in snuff. Take more than yer rantings to unhorse me, young saucebox!"

He was both relieved and alarmed. It would not do to go upsetting people the minute he entered the house. On the other hand, he did not much care for the glimpse of his former self. He recollected having spoken to Chloe in a similar fashion when she enraged him. Which thought reminded him of his aunt's question. Where the devil was she?

Hargrave was giving Aunt Adelaide and Potticary an account of his accident, repeating what Lance had told him. Had she asked then? He'd been too preoccupied to hear. His attention slipped to his surroundings and he wandered across to the side wall to examine a painting that hung there. It was of a young woman dressed in the fashion of an earlier time. His mother? Or was it Rosaline?

He turned, interrupting without ceremony the low-voiced conversation going on near the fireplace where his aunt's wheeled chair was standing.

"Who is this?"

Both men turned towards him, and his aunt positively glared. "Don't you know?"

"I wouldn't ask if I did," he snapped.

"It's your mother," said Hargrave, coming across to join him.

"I thought as much." He turned back to the painting. "Though it might have been my sister."

"She is, or was, very like your mama at this age. Rosaline is plumper now. Which reminds me." He looked back. "Potticary, will you send to Lady Enderby to tell her his lordship is here, if you please? She is anxious to see him, I know."

"Oh, my God! How many more?"

Hargrave grinned, laying a hand on his shoulder. "Don't worry, she won't bring Jasper."

"Thank God!" Lance blew out a breath. "Where is Chloe?"

"I sent Mrs Howmore to her, so I imagine her comfort is being seen to, coz. I dare say she will be brought here presently."

"Damn it, I need her!"

"Patience, coz! She's come as you asked. She can't be at your beck and call in the same way here, you know."

Was that how Hargrave saw it? Was he so demanding? Yes, he had been. He'd importuned her dreadfully, commanding her presence whenever he needed her. Lord above, but he was a selfish creature!

At this opportune moment, Kenninghall re-entered the room, armed with a tray of decanters and glasses.

Lance moved swiftly towards him. "What have you there?"

"Claret and sherry, my lord," the butler recited, setting down the tray on a convenient sideboard inlaid in a pattern of coloured woods. "Which would your lordship prefer?"

His stomach revolted. "None. I want coffee. Is that possible? May I have coffee?"

The butler was pouring sherry into a glass, but he bowed at that. "Certainly, my lord. Let me serve her ladyship and I will go and arrange for it at once."

"I'll serve her. Give it to me." Kenninghall paused on his way to the wheeled chair and Lance seized the glass. "Go! I need that coffee."

He was about to take the glass to his aunt but Hargrave took it out of his hand, a faint frown on his forehead. "You'd best sit down, coz. And keep your hair on! No sense in getting het up."

Lance found himself pushed into a chair opposite his aunt, and watched while Hargrave handed her the errant glass. Her eyes were on him in a look he recognised. Yes, she was formidable, was she not? Had always been so. It came to him that snapping arguments between them were frequent. A cantankerous old dame, she interfered quite as much as Rosaline, her manner even more irritating than his sister's rambling discourse. It struck him that he knew this without needing to attach specific memories to support the notion. Did he know then more than he realised? Was it only the lack of incidents with images that impaired his memory?

He felt battered with the impressions he'd already undergone. Just as well he was not plagued with a plethora of remembered pictures too.

Longing overtook him for Chloe's calm nurse voice to soothe away his agitation. And for his back parlour hideaway, where he could relax and recoup his failing strength. As of instinct, he looked towards his steward, who was hovering with a glass in his hand.

"I need a room of my own. Is there one?"

Potticary came across at once. "Your apartments, my lord? Is that what you mean?"

"What apartments? I mean, of what do they consist?"

"Your bedchamber, my lord, an adjoining dressing-room and a parlour."

"A parlour? I have a parlour of my own?" Eager now, he looked up at the man, trying to visualise the rooms. All that lingered in his mind was his bedchamber at Derry Lodge and the back parlour he'd appropriated there.

"What's this?" His aunt's black eyes were snapping. "If you think to hide away from the world as ye've been doing up to now, Pettipher, you can think again. Ye'll have the whole county about yer ears before long."

Hargrave, who had taken up a stance near the mantelpiece between them, threw up his hands. "Don't tell him that, ma'am, for the Lord's sake! Bad enough as it is for the poor fellow running the gauntlet of the household."

"Poppycock! If he's come home only to brood, he can go away again."

"Ain't a matter of brooding, ma'am. Needs time to settle, that's all."

"Settle? Settle what?"

"His mind, ma'am. Got to understand he received a severe crack on the head."

The harsh voices were taking their toll. Lance gripped the arms of his chair to stop himself seizing his head in the wild gesture he knew would be misinterpreted. If only Chloe were here! He shut his eyes tight, struggling to control the onset of panic.

At length, his frantic breathing slowed and he became aware of silence about him. A cool hand was at his brow and a welcome low murmur came to his ears. "There now, all will be well." His lids slid up and he found Chloe leaning over him. She smiled. "Better?"

"It's you!" It came out as a relieved gasp and he groped for her hand. "Thank God!"

Her fingers squeezed his and then let go. "Here is your coffee. Now you may be easy."

For a moment he thought himself back at Derry Lodge and comfort seeped into his heart. Then he saw his aunt's astonished face, Hargrave still standing by the mantel and Potticary, a concerned look in his face, off to one side. "Oh, God, I'm still here!"

Chloe had shifted out of his line of sight, but she came back at this and presented him with a cup and saucer. "It's black. You have only to ask if you wish for cream or sugar."

He seized the saucer and grabbed the cup, lifting it to his lips like a dying man desperate for water. The bitter taste was balm for the first few sips, the hot liquid both calming and comforting. And then it became unpleasant. He set down the cup. "There's no sugar in it."

Chloe signalled and his butler appeared with a tray. She took up the tongs and dropped two lumps of sugar into the cup. "Cream too?"

"Yes, if you please." He watched her put in the cream and stir, and then tried the brew again. Satisfaction claimed him. "That is much better."

The ritual had a beneficial effect, for the panic had left him and he was able to look around at the assembled company without a resurgence of dismay. Chloe was here, and that made all the difference.

At this moment, she looked at Hargrave. "Captain Ravensthorp, would you be kind enough to introduce me?"

He shifted away from the mantel. "Of course, ma'am. This is Mrs Quilter, as you may have gathered, ma'am. Lady Adelaide Ravensthorp."

What? Had Chloe not yet met his aunt? Then how had she taken charge of him as she had? She was standing over Aunt Adelaide, holding out her hand.

"How do you do, my lady? I trust you will forgive me for barging in as I did and enjoining you all to silence."

Is that what she did? His aunt was looking both suspicious and puzzled. But she took the hand and glinted up at Chloe.

"Seem to be a woman of resource, Mrs Quilter. But it was young Hargrave here who bid me leave you to handle my nevvy."

Chloe's smile looked mechanical to Lance, and her tone was cool. "His lordship is used to me, ma'am, that is all. I have been his principal nurse, you must know."

Aunt Adelaide's brows rose. "That's how it was, eh?"

"Perforce, ma'am, since his accident occurred within a stone's throw of my home. He was too ill to be moved, even had I been unchristian enough to wish to eject him when he was in need of care and support."

Lance could be silent no longer. "You'd never do that, Chloe, no matter who I was. She's a charitable creature, Aunt."

Chloe threw him a warning look. "Your aunt is understandably puzzled as to why you should insist upon my presence. I am merely trying to explain."

"Well, you needn't try," snapped the old lady. "I've eyes in my head and I can see what's what."

Lance would have burst out at this, but his cousin's eyes were on him in a warning look. He glanced at Chloe and found her tight-lipped. She directed an enquiring eye at Hargrave and gestured slightly towards his steward.

Hargrave laughed. "I do beg your pardon, Mrs Quilter. This is Potticary, Lance's steward."

Chloe held out her hand and addressed the fellow in her friendly way. "Ah, you've been holding the fort, I gather?"

To Lance's approval, he shook the hand and bowed, returning the smile. "Thank you, ma'am, yes. It is not more arduous than usual, however, except for needing his lordship's approval on a couple of matters and his signature on one or two documents. He is frequently in Town and I am used to handling matters on his behalf."

"I am relieved to hear it. His lordship has been troubled about having to attend to matters he may find difficult at the moment. But I see he need have no qualms."

Relief swept over Lance. Trust Chloe to ascertain at once how matters stood. And she'd handled his aunt to perfection. But how soon could he get her to himself? Must he do the pretty for long? Impulse threw him into speech. "Chloe, where have they put you? Are you near my apartments?"

She turned an admonishing face upon him, her colours flying. "I have no notion, my lord. I don't know where your apartments may be. But you need have no fear. I am comfortably situated and Miss Flook is next door. We shall do very well."

Her tone was repressive and he frowned. And she'd called him my lord. Was this designed to fool his aunt? A vain hope. Aunt Adelaide would divine his feelings in a trice. He'd never been able to hide anything from those penetrating eyes. Even now they were sneaking from one to the other, like a pair of curious ferrets.

Had he embarrassed Chloe? She was acting with reserve towards him, except when she'd used her nurse voice. He wanted to ask her at once, but it was too public. Only how would he find her? How, in this barrack of a mansion, keep her close enough? Unless he could persuade her to visit his parlour? Or would that give particularity to the meeting?

Not that he cared. He would willingly shout his wishes to the world. But he knew Chloe would balk. Her attitude, as Hargrave set a chair for her and she sat down, was that of a stranger. Which she was here. He must remember that. She was not yet mistress of Ravensthorp. He must not expect her to behave as if she was.

"I think it is time to show my cousin to his quarters."

Hargrave moved to his chair and Lance looked up, setting aside his empty cup. "You're coming with me, I hope."

"Would I desert you, coz? If you're feeling rested, we may leave Mrs Quilter with your aunt, since she is best placed to answer any question concerning your health."

Not pleased to be losing Chloe so soon, Lance demurred. "But she may not wish to remain." He seized a question from the air. "Where is Miss Flook? She is supposed to be chaperoning you."

"She is unpacking. Mrs Howmore will bring her to find me presently."

Hargrave was standing over him. "Come, coz. You've to face your destiny some time. Might as well be now."

"You only say that because you don't want to step into my shoes." But he rose nevertheless.

"I don't. Wouldn't fit me."

Potticary was suddenly flanking them. "Do you wish me to accompany you, my lord?"

Hargrave waved him away. "No, no, man. You may get about your business. Don't doubt you've enough on your hands. I'll see to his lordship."

Potticary bowed and turned his gaze on Lance. "If you should need me, my lord, or wish for information on any matter, pray do not hesitate to send to me."

"Thank you, I will."

Hargrave's hand at his elbow forced him to move and Potticary stood aside to let them pass. The moment they were out of the room, his cousin released him and grinned. "Now you may be grateful to me for getting you out of there, coz. Don't want you starting up your old warfare with the dreaded aunt."

Incensed, Lance halted in the massive saloon they were passing through. "But you don't care if Chloe has to sit through a damned catechism."

"She can hold her own, coz. She won't let the old besom browbeat her, be sure. Besides, if you want her to approve of your Chloe, you'd best give her time to get to know her."

He was urging Lance onward and he set his steps in motion again without thinking about it. "I don't care if she approves or not. She's not the arbiter of whom I choose to marry."

"Ain't she just! Don't you think Rosaline reports to her on every female you deign to stand up with at a ball? The two of them have had their heads together about getting you married off for years."

"Well, they'll be disappointed if they have any idea of dictating to me on the subject."

"Yes, I can see you've become even more intransigent than you were before," said Hargrave with a comical grimace. "Hot at hand, Sir Lancelot, that's what you are!"

"You can talk, scallywag!"

His cousin laughed. "That's better. Sounding more like yourself. We'll have you back to normal in no time."

A prognostication that threw Lance back into dismay. If "normal" meant the arrogant creature he suspected, he had no desire to return to that state.

CHAPTER FIFTEEN

Left with the formidable invalid in the wheeled chair, Chloe accepted with real gratitude the wine pressed upon her by Lance's steward. She needed to fortify herself.

She had acted on instinct upon entering the room to find Lance in one of his confused fits, muttering into his chest, his hands clenched on the arms of his chair and his aspect as rough as she had seen it several times. She had put a finger to her lips, holding her other hand palm up. Thankfully, the captain had understood and nodded, moving to the elderly lady's chair while Chloe went directly to Lance.

He had responded to her voice as she'd known he would, but the episode dismayed her. She had half hoped, in the flurry of settling into the allotted rooms and arranging for the accommodation of the maids, that her presence might soon be dispensed with. That Lance had gone off with his cousin without even looking for her had been both balm and hurt. But it had proved a temporary respite. It was obvious she was still going to be needed.

"Leave us, Potticary."

Chloe's heart sank and she took a fortifying sip of her Madeira as the steward bowed.

Lady Adelaide waited only until he had disappeared into the next room before turning to Chloe. "Now then, girl, ye'd best give me a round tale."

Chloe set down her glass on a convenient table and turned her chair a little so that she might more comfortably confront the creature. "What do you wish to know, my lady?"

"Ye can leave off addressing me in that formal manner for a start. Can't abide toadies."

Meeting the snap in the keen eyes, Chloe raised her brows. "I beg your pardon, ma'am. I had no intention of toadying."

"Then stop putting on an act for my benefit. What's your name? Chloe, did he say?"

"Yes, ma'am."

"Chloe then. You can cease this pretence. You ain't his nurse, nor nothing like."

A faint pulse started up in Chloe's breast, but she maintained her air of calm. If Matilda could not break her, this old dame most certainly would not be permitted to do so. "You are mistaken, ma'am. A nurse is precisely what I have been to his lordship."

"And what more?"

Chloe set her teeth. "His hostess, Lady Adelaide."

"Hostess! Yes, I know well enough how that goes."

Fury rippled through her but she held it back. She could not help the clipped tone. "You are offensive, ma'am. Yet if you insist upon frankness, I will give tit for tat."

"Well, thank heavens for it, girl! My generation ain't mealy-mouthed. Say what you will to me, but don't hand me a mouthful of lies, for that I can't endure."

Despite herself, a ripple of amusement ran through Chloe. The creature was as candid as Oswald. She dropped her reserve. "You sound just like my late husband, ma'am. He was a good many years my senior, you must know, and was apt to invoke plain speaking."

The old dame's belligerent manner lessened a trifle. "Was he so? How many years older?"

"A good many. My stepchildren are my seniors by several years."

"Pah! No wonder you grabbed at Pettipher!"

"I did not grab at him and I resent your accusations! If you must know, he mistook me for his late betrothed and conceived a wholly unsuitable passion for me. But if you suppose that I either acted upon it or took advantage of his error, you have entirely mistaken my character."

She was subjected to a concentrated stare for a moment. Then Lady Adelaide let out a rasping laugh. "I believe ye, girl."

Chloe blinked. "You do?"

"Oh, yes. Yer don't live to my years without learning to judge yer fellows. However, you won't bring Rosaline round as easily. She thinks yer scheming to be countess here."

Chloe hesitated. If she withheld the truth, would this penetrating old lady see through her?

The sharp gaze narrowed. "Out with it."

A laugh escaped Chloe. "You are too shrewd, ma'am."

"Well?"

She sighed. "Lance thinks he is in love with me. He wants me to marry him."

"But you won't?"

"Not unless I can be certain he is not trying to resurrect his dratted Clarissa in me."

Lady Adelaide regarded her in silence for a space. "Ye have a look of her, it's true. Flighty little thing she was. Always thought it an excellent thing she died before she could ruin young Lancelot's life."

Astounded, Chloe stared at her. "You are too cruel, ma'am. As far as I can make out, he's been wearing the willow ever since."

"Cruel perhaps. She'd have made him a shocking wife nonetheless. Expensive too." The old eyes snapped. "Besides, he ain't been wearing the willow, as you put it. Too picky to choose another, that's all. Had plenty of high fliers in his train, so you needn't think he ain't found consolation."

"High fliers?" Chloe's tone became dry. "And you supposed me to be another. I thank you, ma'am."

"Well, what else was I to think when I had Rosaline fretting and fuming in my ear? No reason to suppose otherwise. Pretty widow. And my great-nephew is handsome enough. Had him at yer mercy. What could be more natural?"

"It is scarcely natural in me to be jumping into my patient's bed," snapped Chloe with asperity. "In his condition it would have been a ridiculous thing to do in any event. You have no notion how bad he was."

She came once again under scrutiny. "Tell me."

Chloe sighed again. "I doubt he would wish me to reveal the worst of his sufferings."

"What d'ye suppose I care for his wishes? Tell me straight and no holding back."

Thus adjured, Chloe gave her an account of Lance's first days, not omitting his wild fits and the confusion under which he still laboured on occasion. "That is why he wanted me here, ma'am. He is afraid of being thought to have lost his reason when he has one of these episodes. He fears you, or his brother-in-law, will seek to have him confined."

"Poppycock!"

"So I thought, but I could not persuade him otherwise. He was insistent upon my coming because he trusts me to bring him out of it."

"And he fancies himself in love with you," said the other in her sapient way.

Chloe smiled. "That too. But I believe if he had been confident of remaining stable, he would have come home without me. After all, if he truly loves me, there is nothing to stop him returning to claim me."

"Except his sister's objections. And mine, if I chose to exert myself against him."

Chloe had to laugh. "You don't know him, ma'am, if you think he would listen to either of you."

The elder lady's thin brows shot up. "Indeed? When I've known him from the cradle?"

A riffle of unease crept through Chloe. "He's changed, I think. He speaks of — of misliking who he supposes he was before his accident."

"Does he indeed? Well, he'll soon find his feet again, I don't doubt."

Chloe did not share her confidence, but she refrained from saying so. Instead, she put a question of her own. "What was he like, ma'am? Before, I mean."

Lady Adelaide shrugged. "How am I to answer that?"

"As frankly as I've answered you, ma'am," said Chloe with asperity. "It cuts both ways."

A sly laugh came. "I like you, miss. You don't fear to speak yer mind. Good for young Lancelot. Don't do for young men to be given too much their own way. Need ruling, the lot of 'em."

Chloe could not help laughing. "Yet, as I understand it, ma'am, you never married."

"Not with these hips of mine." She gestured downwards. "Started when I was a young 'un and my doctor said I'd never bear children. Decided then and there I'd stay single." Another sly look came. "And make a nuisance of myself to my nephews and nieces."

"I don't doubt you've succeeded in that ambition."

The rasping laugh sounded. "In spades. They all tremble when I send for 'em. Except young Lancelot. Gives as good as he gets."

"And you like him for it." Chloe gave a wry smile. "Yes, I can see you take pleasure in creating brangles, ma'am. Well, you won't do it with me. I dislike brawling and prefer a soft approach."

"Then you'd best tame Pettipher if you want a quiet life. Temperamental young scamp he's always been. Led us all a dance as an infant and went on from there. But he's got charm in abundance and can twist anyone round his little finger if he chooses."

Yes, that she had seen. His mischievous look never failed of its effect. But temperamental? She thought of his occasional outbursts of panic. She spoke the thought aloud. "I had not supposed as much, but it may be his wild fits are a manifestation of his character. If, as you say, he has a temper."

"He don't rant and rave, if that's what you mean. He's like quicksilver. Goes up and down in a bang. One moment one thing, the next another. Unpredictable, that's young Lancelot."

A surge of hope swept into Chloe's breast. "Then he is not so very different. I thought it a result of his accident that he is so mercurial." Remembrance tempered this reasoning. "At least, I still believe his inability to hold himself in the present is due to his condition."

The old lady's brows drew together. "What d'ye mean?"

Chloe blew out a breath. "It is less apparent now, but sometimes he slips into the past. He talks as if he is there rather than recalling an incident. He still calls me Clarissa on occasion."

"Ah, you said he was disorientated at the first."

"Still now sometimes. I think his memory plays him false. Or the memories come too fast for him and he can't control them. It makes him desperate and he panics."

Lady Adelaide regarded her with that penetrating stare, tapping one hand against the wooden arm of her chair. Then, with sudden energy, she sat up. "Ring the bell, Chloe. I need my maid. And we'll call for yer chaperon. Ought to be with you."

Not a little relieved to be released from her ladyship's catechism, Chloe got up and went to tug on the bell-pull. The feeling of being out of place returned. A guest in the house, she knew not how she would occupy her time. The trouble was she was too used to running a household. And here she would not be in attendance on Lance.

The thought caused a hollow to open up in her chest. An idyll, barely recognised, had come to an end.

The knocking penetrated unquiet dreams. Chloe sprang awake, caught between fading images and the stifling cocoon of the bed-curtains.

"Mrs Quilter! Mrs Quilter!"

A man's voice. Recognition filtered into her head as she scrambled from the bedclothes, tugging aside the curtains and calling out. "I'm coming, Captain!"

The knocking ceased. Even in the disorientation of sudden waking, Chloe knew why he'd come and urgency climbed into her bosom. Fumbling for her slippers, she pushed her feet into them and groped in the dimness for the dressing-gown she'd left on the chair by the bed. She was tying the belt as she wrenched open the door, blinking in the sudden light provided by Captain Ravensthorp's candle.

"Is he bad?"

Relief made his features sag. "I didn't know what to do. Nothing I say will quiet him."

He was moving as he spoke, leading Chloe along the wide upper corridor that let onto the principal bedchambers.

"Was he wandering? Where did you find him?"

"Oh, he was in his rooms all right. Finch called me."

"His valet?"

"Yes. He'd taken the precaution of sleeping in the dressing-room."

"You mean you advised him so to do."

The captain turned his head, the worry visible in his countenance even in the candlelight. "Lance told me what happens to him sometimes, and after he'd had that wild fit…"

"Wise of you. Is he very bad?"

"He didn't know me. I could think of nothing better than to lock the door and come for you."

Chloe's anxiety accelerated and she quickened her steps. "You locked him in? Dear Lord, we must hurry!"

"Was that wrong? He's got Finch in there."

"It's what he fears most coming here. That he'll be confined."

Captain Ravensthorp cursed and she said no more. He was not to know. Her thoughts winged to Lance. He would be climbing the walls!

The captain turned the corner of the gallery and went to the first door, producing a key as he passed the candle to Chloe. "Hold this for me."

She took it, mentally willing him to hurry as she heard muffled thumps from within. The door opened and she thrust the candle back at the captain and pushed into the room. There was plenty of light to illuminate a scene of distress.

Lance was on the floor, a forlorn heap, hitting with his fists upon a chest situated at the end of a large four-poster bed. Groans issued from somewhere inside, his face hidden by his hair. He was in his nightgown, but someone had thrown a shawl across his shoulders.

Chloe noticed in passing the hovering form, wringing his hands and looking distressed. The valet? She paid no heed, but moved quickly to Lance and sank down beside him, setting her hands on his to still them. She spoke with authority, and in the nurse voice he knew. "Come now, this won't do. Look at me!"

His fists were shaking under her hands, but he stopped trying to beat at the wood. His head came up.

"See? I am here. There is nothing to fear."

He stared at her, despair in his face, the green eyes anguished.

Chloe smiled and brought his hands from the chest and down between them, chafing at his fingers. "You'll take cold sitting here, you know."

She could not tell if he yet knew her and dared not give him her name in case he was transported back in time and would think her Clarissa again. His fingers began to respond, moving on hers as she rubbed. His breath was coming in spurts, catching in a near sob. His voice came at last, low and fearful.

"Where were you? I looked for you."

"I am here now. There is naught to fear. All will be well."

The tone seemed to soothe him and he sighed. "You always say that."

"Because it is true. Nothing can harm you now."

"Not if you are here, I remember that."

His fingers curled around one of her hands and Chloe let it lie there. "Did you dream?"

He shook his head. "I woke inside the curtains. I didn't know where I was."

"Do you know now?"

A faint echo of his mischievous smile came. "I'm with you."

The upset was dissipating. Chloe was aware of the captain, silent and sensibly remaining still a little way off. The valet had retreated a step or two. She glanced at him and made a move to get up.

"Come, Lance, it will not do to be sitting on the floor. You must allow Finch to help you up."

He did not object and she signalled to the valet to come forward. Lance permitted the man to assist him, but he kept his eyes on Chloe. "You won't leave me?"

"No, I will stay. But you must get back into bed." She had released his hand and went to draw back the curtains. "See, we will open it up so you may see where you are." She looked across at the captain. "Your cousin will help, will you not?"

Captain Ravensthorp sprang forward, setting down his candle on the dresser. "Certainly I will."

Lance watched the operation, eyeing the movements as she and the captain pulled back all the curtains surrounding the bed. She ought to have thought of it, she reflected. Lance had never had the curtains closed in his room at her home. But was he yet wholly back to himself? She could not tell.

Finch was guiding him to the bed and he got in, making no objection when the pillows were banked behind him and the covers, which were in considerable disarray, re-arranged about his person. His eyes remained on Chloe throughout, as if he feared she might vanish again.

She addressed the valet when he completed his task. "Have you a chair you may set for me beside the bed, if you please?"

From behind her, the captain's voice came in a whisper. "You intend to remain with him?"

"Obviously I must do so," she returned in the same tone. She turned to look at him. "Are you thinking of the proprieties?"

He grimaced. "Well, yes."

"It will not be the first time I've sat with him at night, I assure you. But we will tell Finch to keep the door to the dressing-room ajar."

He flicked a look at Lance, who was now resting against his pillows with his eyes closed. "Perhaps he will sleep soon."

"Unlikely, without a draught of some kind. He has not needed it for some time and we brought none."

"Should I get something? Laudanum?"

Chloe threw up a hand. "No! He was taking a milder powder before. And we don't want to wake any more of the servants. I'll talk him to sleep."

"Do you wish me to stay?"

"You must do as you choose, Captain." Suspicion burgeoned. "Ah, you think it will be less improper if you are here?"

A trifle of colour was visible across his cheekbones and he grinned. "Well, you must admit my presence must improve things."

"I dare say it may, but are you prepared to stay all night?"

He cursed under his breath. "That long?"

"Possibly. He may settle presently."

His eyes strayed to his cousin's still form. "He looks settled now."

The valet came in with a straight chair and hovered by the bed, holding it as he cast a questioning glance at Chloe. She nodded and moved around the bed to take her seat, nodding dismissal to Finch. Not much to her surprise, Captain Ravensthorp moved to perch on the far corner of the bed, leaning against the post there.

Silence reigned for several moments. Lance remained unmoving and Chloe wondered if he had indeed dropped off. His breathing was shallow, which argued otherwise. The name came murmuring through his lips.

"Clarissa?"

Chloe's heart sank. She'd been tempted into belief, and here it was again. Should she correct him? If she never did, would he ever learn to distinguish between them? She hesitated too long. His lids fluttered and lifted. He stared at her for a long moment. Then a smile came and a comfortable sigh.

"Chloe!"

He put out a hand. Her heart swelled. She took the proffered hand and felt his frozen fingers curl around hers. "Dear Lord, your hands are cold! Give me the other." He did as she bade him, and she set both hands in her lap, rubbing them briskly on the back and then turning them so she could rub the palms. She was aware throughout of his gaze, concentrated on her face. Equally of the silent spectator on the other side of the bed.

"There. Now tuck them inside the covers."

She pushed the hands back, let go and pulled the bedclothes over them, tucking them over his chest. Without thinking, she leaned close and brushed his tangled hair away from his face.

Lance tossed it back, grinning. "Next you'll be brushing it for me, nurse of mine."

She laughed. "I would if I had a brush. Though I'm sure you can manage it for yourself."

"I like to have you care for me."

"No doubt. But I have no mind to become your valet as well as your nurse. Besides, you have Finch."

Mischief glinted in the green eyes. "Finch is not nearly as alluring."

Heat swarmed into Chloe's cheeks. As if he was wholly unaware of the presence of his cousin! "I wish you will be quiet, Lance. Go to sleep!"

"I would sleep better with you beside me."

"That will do. If you won't behave, I shall return to my room and leave you to your cousin's ministrations."

She gestured as she spoke and saw the startled look in his eyes as they fell upon the captain's still form. "Hargrave! Where did you spring from?"

"I've been here all along, coz."

"I didn't see you." A frown creased his brow and he brought one wavering hand from within the covers, setting it to his temple. "No, wait!" He turned a puzzled look upon Chloe. "Did I have one of my turns? Is that why you're here?"

There was no point in concealment. "Just so. Your cousin fetched me."

He groaned, dropping his hand. "Damnation! I thought I was done with all that."

Chloe set her fingers on his. "Don't fret. The place is still alien to you. I dare say it is inevitable you will become disorientated once or twice. Indeed, I have myself today."

That caught his attention. His fingers turned, grasping hers. "You? How so?"

"Oh, the sheer size of this place, I think. And the plethora of servants." Unguardedly, she spoke aloud of the troubled thoughts that had kept her awake a while. "Memories have been surfacing I thought long buried."

His fingers tightened on hers. "Memories? Of what? You've not lost memories, Chloe. Have you?"

Discomfort rode within her, but she had said too much to withdraw. "Very early ones. I've not forgotten precisely, because they've been rising all too readily since I've been in this mansion of yours."

"But of what? When?"

"My early childhood. I've been reminded of my grandparents, of their home. It was — it was a substantial place, like this one." She forced a smile and shook off the discomfiting images crowding her mind. "It's all rather vague now."

Lance was regarding her with frowning bewilderment. "You've never spoken of this before."

"I prefer not to speak of it."

"Well, do so now. I thought you spent your childhood abroad."

"Only the latter part. From little more than an infant I was at Mayberry House. My recollections are scanty, but I know my grandparents were remote figures. Perhaps that gave me a distaste for the place. Had I been better acquainted with them, I might have chosen to remain."

Lance's puzzled expression did not abate. "But why were they remote? You are the cosiest person I know, Chloe. How could anyone not wish to be close to you?"

She knew she was blushing. "Cosy? Is that how you see me?"

He gave a laugh and shook her fingers. "You know what I mean. One is comfortable around you. All your people are. Anyone can see that. You generate so much warmth, Chloe. It's what I love in you."

Her heart was buzzing. "Is it? Truly?"

"One of the things I love about you. But don't fob me off, for I can't see how you became as you are with these remote grandparents."

"I did not learn from them, but from Mama. She and I were exiled together. I shared her disgrace."

Realising where her words were tending, she cast an anxious glance towards the captain. His head was nodding on his chest.

"He's fast asleep," Lance said, lowering his voice.

"As you should be."

"I won't sleep until I know the answer to this puzzle. Why was your mother in disgrace?"

Chloe sighed. "Can't you guess? She eloped with my father. His status was inferior, but he had an abundance of charm. Only he was feckless and irresponsible, as I have good reason to know. My mother left him when she discovered her mistake and threw herself upon the mercy of my grandparents."

"It does not sound as if they were very merciful."

"No, but they took her in. She could not go into company, of course, because of the scandal. My father tried time and again to retrieve her, and I think she would have gone back. But my grandparents would not permit it."

The memories were rife now, teeming in her head. Her fingers still rested in Lance's and she let them lie, grateful for his comforting hold. Yet he was not done with questions.

"But they let you go, did they not?"

"They could hardly stop me. My father had a legal claim and he used it. He would not have forced me, though. He gave me the choice."

"And you took it."

"Yes." Reminiscence made Chloe smile. "He did have a great deal of charm. And he painted an attractive picture. The reality proved less so, but I believed him at the time."

Lance released her fingers. "But these grandparents. Who were they?"

She stiffened. "I never speak their name, Lance. My grandfather told me if I went with my father, I might consider myself dead to that family. My grandmother was no better. She turned her back on me when I said goodbye." The memory still had power to hurt. She crushed it down. She could not smile, but she kept her tone even. "That is why I am plagued here with memories I would rather not recall."

Lance's fingers found hers again. "I too. I don't want to be here either. Can't we go home?"

Her heart twisted. "This is your home, Lance. You will become accustomed."

"Not if you won't marry me. I couldn't bear to be here without you."

Her pulse skittered. "We will discuss it when you are more settled."

"That's what you always say. Why won't you say yes, Chloe? Why do you deny me? Don't you love me?"

"Lance, don't! Don't ask me that. I can't — I can't commit to you. Not yet. I must be certain…"

"Of what? Isn't it enough that I need you? That I love you? And I don't believe you don't care for me. You wouldn't do what you do for me if you did not."

"Of course I care for you! Only I can't yet be sure… And your sister thinks I am an upstart schemer. If I agree to marry you, she will be certain of it."

Annoyance crossed his face. "It's nothing to do with her. And clearly you are no sort of upstart, if your grandparents inhabited the kind of establishment you've just been talking about."

Chloe pulled her fingers out of his. "Merely because I was born into that sphere does not make me worthy. The Kittisfords are nobodies, even if the Mayberrys are of the peerage."

Triumph lit in Lance's eyes. "Mayberry! I knew it rang a bell. Then your grandfather is Lord Nevin, isn't he?"

"You remember that?"

"I do now. You can't refuse me on the score of being unworthy, Chloe. You haven't a single reason to reject my suit." He paused, sudden consternation in his face. "Unless … unless you don't wish to marry me. Is that it?"

Chloe had no words. She could not say what was in her heart. Nor could she confirm an untruth. She'd told him once, in anger. She did not want to repeat it. He would vehemently deny any allegiance to Clarissa's memory. At least insofar as it could interfere with his feelings for Chloe.

Anxiety was in his face as he searched hers. She must speak. "I can't answer you, Lance. Not now. Give me a little time."

He sank back upon his pillows, sighing out a frustrated breath. "I hoped you would marry me at once. I was going to send Hargrave to procure a special licence. Then you could marry me and cuddle me to sleep every night."

A gust of fury washed through Chloe and she got up. "Is that all? That's why you want me to marry you? Then the answer is no, Lance! I knew you were prone to think only of your own comfort, but I had not supposed you to be utterly selfish!"

She grabbed up one of several candlesticks alight on the dresser nearest the bed. As she turned to go she saw that Captain Ravensthorp was wide awake and looking severely shocked.

"I will leave the nursing to you, captain. Goodnight!"

She heard Lance speaking behind her, but she paid no heed. She needed to get to the refuge of her bedchamber before she succumbed to a distress too intense to be borne.

CHAPTER SIXTEEN

Lance stared through the shadows at Chloe's vanishing form. The door closed with a snap and she was gone. Confused and bereft, he looked at his cousin.

"What in Hades just happened? What did I say?"

Hargrave came around the bed and plonked down into Chloe's vacated chair. "You're a fool, coz. Don't you know anything of women?"

"Of course I do, what are you talking about?"

Hargrave shook his head at him, a rueful smile appearing. "She's right, you know. You are selfish as bedamned."

Hurt rode Lance. "You too? How am I selfish? Does she think I don't value her enough?"

A hard note entered his cousin's voice. "She thinks, and rightly, that you need her for your own comfort."

"That's not true!" A thrust of guilt made him revise this. "Well, not entirely true."

"Nothing you've said encompasses Mrs Quilter's needs or wishes. You don't listen to what she says and you don't care either. You expect her to do what you want because it will save your bacon. And to crown all, you still seem to think she's your blasted Clarissa."

Brought up short, Lance stared at him. "Did I call her Clarissa again?"

"Not directly. But you named Clarissa. Your first thought was of Clarissa. It's obvious you still confuse them and I can't think why. To my way of thinking Mrs Quilter bears only a passing resemblance to that creature."

"Don't call her a creature," snapped Lance, firing up. "Clarissa was a diamond!"

"And a bundle of mischief and disobedience, by all accounts. I was too young to recognise it at the time, but I well remember her careering all over the countryside on that wild horse of hers and without even a groom. It's a wonder she didn't break her neck."

"No, she broke the ice instead!" He threw the words at his cousin before he realised what he'd said. They replayed in his mind and he groaned as recognition hit, throwing his hands to his head. "Dear God, you're in the right of it! Will the little witch never leave me alone? All these years…"

Hargrave's voice came again, less heat within it, but still accusatory. "Yes, years and years of regret and guilt. You can't forget because you won't let yourself forget. There was nothing you could have done, Lance. Everyone said so. You've said it yourself. It's not Clarissa who won't leave you alone. She's long gone, coz. It's you who won't let her go."

His heart churning as well as his mind, Lance nevertheless protested as his hands dropped. "That's not true. It's only since the accident she's been on my mind."

"How in the name of Satan do you know if you can't remember?"

"I remember that."

"Yes, very selective is this memory of yours," his cousin said on a derisive note.

Stung, Lance hit back. "I can't help that. I only have what comes to me. Are you suggesting it is all pretence?"

Hargrave sighed. "I don't know. Seems to me you're using your condition to coerce that poor woman into going against her conscience."

"Chloe? I wouldn't do that. I love her."

"To the point of forcing her into marriage? You call that love?"

"Hargrave!" Anguished, Lance stared at the implacable look in his cousin's face. From nowhere, the fear flooded him and he spoke it aloud. "I can't bear to lose her! I'm afraid if I let her go, she'll vanish."

Hargrave's face changed. He reached out and laid a hand over Lance's unquiet fingers. His tone gentled. "Chloe is not Clarissa, coz. She's not going to vanish. You'll only lose her if you won't set her free."

Unquiet dreams plagued his night, despite his cousin's snoring form beside him. Hargrave had snuffed the candles and climbed in, declaring his intention of going directly to sleep. Which he had.

Lance had lain wakeful for some time, turning over his cousin's words. He was glad of his presence, relieved he had not left him alone, though he would infinitely have preferred to have Chloe in his place.

He was forced to admit some truth in her accusation. He'd insisted on her coming with him to Ravensthorp without thought of the inconvenience, the disruption it must make in the pattern of her life. Odd of him, because he had thought of how his presence in her home was a trouble to her and her household. At first. Latterly he'd allowed it to trouble him less. Because he'd appropriated Chloe as his own?

Damnation! She'd been so much to him. His nurse, his solace and his hope. He'd taken it as his right. Had he? How arrogant if he had!

Yes, she spoke truth. As did Hargrave. He was selfish. Was this the real Lancelot Ravensthorp? Did a man change his character because he lost his memory? Well, he could change.

He must, if he wanted to keep her. Doubt shook him. Was it Chloe he truly wanted? Or, as Hargrave said and she suspected, was it Clarissa for whom he yearned still?

He tried to recall Clarissa, other than the fell images of her tragic demise. She eluded him. What had Hargrave said? She careered all over the countryside without a groom. Could he see her riding? A vague picture surfaced, of a girl with bright hair loose in the wind, waving a whip. When he tried to focus on her face, the picture was instantly replaced with one of Chloe: her hair tumbled about her shoulders, a blanket about her nightgown as she sat in the chair by his bed looking like a sleeping angel.

His guts clenched. Chloe had been with him tonight and he'd driven her away. She'd come at once, heedless of the proprieties. She'd soothed him and seen him back to his bed and prepared to sit with him, all night if need be. And then she'd spoken of her childhood, opened her secret to him and he'd seized on the one thing pertinent to himself and taken instant advantage of its portent.

Dear God, but he was a crass fool! Selfish? He did not deserve her. Nor her love — if he had it.

Doubt caused a thumping to start up in his chest. She had not said it. She would not say it. She admitted she cared for him, but that was as far as she would go. What did it mean? Care? She cared for her people. Chloe had a big heart. But had he won the warmer feeling, the affection he craved?

If not, he could scarcely blame her. He had done little to attach her. The opposite, if anything. No wonder she shied from his proposals!

He fell asleep resolving to do better and dreamed of Clarissa and his futile attempt to save her. Waking to an empty space where his cousin had been and his valet's arrival with a cup of hot chocolate, Lance groaned in the fog of despair, his doubts reviving.

Sleep had been a long time coming. Her temper cooled fast and Chloe fought the inevitable desire to go back and mend the rift. She could not afford to give in. While Lance knew nothing of her background, it was ammunition in reserve. She'd known deep down that if she ended by marrying him as he wished, she could confound the condemnation of his relatives. But now she'd lost the advantage.

Trust Lance to seize upon it for his own ends. Her own doubts surfaced the more. She recalled her frank discussion with Lady Adelaide. She'd thought Lance must be changed, but from his aunt's discourse it appeared his moodiness was characteristic. Could she endure to be tied to such a temperamental creature? A tiny choke of amusement lightened the gloom. With whom, pray, had she fallen in love?

The thought stilled in her head. She had not before admitted it, even to herself. She probed the notion, with caution. It was novel, if it was so. She'd had affection for her mother, even for her feckless father. And for Basil of course. She had developed fondness for Oswald over the years and she cared about her people. But *love*? Was it this constant attention on his welfare? On him, if she was honest. Not a waking thought — or a sleeping one if it came to that — but Lance was part of it. Had he become so much a feature of her world to make it revolve around him? Was this love?

Setting aside the urge to touch him, to feel his fingers curl around her own, and the scarcely acknowledged burning in her woman's depths… Could she set all this aside? Should she? Was that not part of it? To be moved in physical ways as well as in her heart?

Her ignorance chafed. She'd been shielded from romantic entanglements. Not by design, but by the sheer isolation of her life, first in her unsettled existence on the continent and then in the security of her marriage. Oswald had never inspired in her the sort of feelings Lance had done and did. He'd troubled her little, though she'd accepted his caresses as a duty.

How little Lance realised the reactions he provoked when he spoke of his need to have her beside him in his bed. It was no wonder she'd reacted in fury, if the truth be told. The very notion of it had the power to sweep her with unbearable heat. If he'd spoken of his desire to bed her, he might have received a different response. Of course she would still have refused, but in confusion, not anger. But he did not say that. What he'd said was her presence was needed to soothe him to sleep. *His* needs again. Which had nothing to do with Chloe.

She might have borne it better if his need had been centred in his desire for her, for her womanly attributes. For her kisses, her tender curves. Dear Lord, anything but the implication that his nurse must cuddle him to sleep! As if he was a baby in need of a breast.

He did not love her. He was obsessed with the notion of keeping her close because he was afraid of being overtaken by his condition. And she, fool that she was, had encouraged him in this. She had been at his beck and call, ready to run at the first hint of trouble, making herself indispensable to him, but in the wrong way. Such love as he professed to have for her was a farcical copy of his passion for Clarissa. An old passion, which ought to have burnt itself out by now in the absence of its object. But it had not, had it? He was still ridiculously attached to a memory, to a ghost. And she, Chloe Quilter, must needs have a look of the creature.

Lord, but she loathed the very name! Clarissa. Clarissa, the beautiful, bold, mischievous, disobedient, headstrong creature who had disappeared through the ice and turned Lancelot Ravensthorp into a melancholic travesty of a lover. *Clarissa, Clarissa, Clarissa.*

A mewl of frustration escaped and Chloe turned in the bed, burying her face in her pillows where the muffled protests would not be heard outside the curtains of her bed.

Out of the tangled, roiling thoughts came one blatant fact. She was jealous.

Chloe stilled, frozen for a moment on the implication. Jealous of a dead woman?

Flinging herself about, she lay in the darkness, staring up at the dim shape of the tester. Jealous? Of the girl who'd had his true love, his constancy and his dreams. She'd taken his youth and buried it in the tomb with her. And left a skeleton of a heart for Chloe to pick up and toy with, like a plaything which did not belong to her, to which she had no right.

He was obsessed? *No, Chloe Quilter. You are obsessed.* She was so morbidly teased by the thought of his love for a dead girl, she dared not believe in his affection for her.

Ridiculous. Who was present? Who cosseted and cared for and soothed him in his debilitating condition? Who had power over him now?

Lady Adelaide's words crept back. "You must tame him." And she could. Oh, she could. So readily. If she could only conquer the creature who stood between them. Rid him of Clarissa once and for all. She slid into sleep on vengeful thoughts and dreamed of wandering through Venice in search of a lodging and coming upon waterways instead of streets, where rags in the narrow canal floated with spreading hair.

Waking to Jemima arriving with the luxury of hot chocolate, Chloe sat up as the cogitations of the night slipped back into view. Shuddering a little, she thrust them away. She would not think of all that now. She must have been mad, or half asleep, to be thinking as she had. Instead, she enquired into the welfare of her maid and Little Tibby.

"Has Tibby settled a little more, Jemima?"

The maid, who was preparing Chloe's clothes for the day, paused to grimace. "She's scared as a kitten, mistress. And them others look at her leg and it makes her stumble."

Chloe's heart went out to the girl. "I should have left her to Mrs Vaughan."

"Oh, no, mistress. She'd have been miserable."

"It sounds as if she's miserable here."

Jemima became bracing. "She'll do, mistress. I've got me eye on her, never fear."

But Chloe remained troubled. Not only for the child, for all of them. Here she was contemplating a future within these walls and disrupting the lives of every one of her comfortable little household. Oh, so comfortable it had been, until the advent of the dratted Lord Pettipher. How much did he know of, or indeed care for, the comfort of his servants? She would swear she already knew more than he did. After Lady Adelaide had been wheeled away yesterday within moments of Miss Flook's joining them, Chloe had swept them both back to her allotted chamber and summoned the maids with the intention of ensuring Jemima and Tibby were comfortably situated, despite Agatha's protests.

"The servants here will think it so odd of you, dear Mrs Quilter."

"Let them think me eccentric, if they wish. I could not reconcile it with my conscience if I did not check."

"Then let me go. Mrs Howmore will not suppose my venturing there peculiar."

Chloe, with her two maids hovering at her bedchamber door, Little Tibby hopping about from foot to foot, brushed this aside with impatience. "I am going, and to the devil with Mrs Howmore or anyone else who chooses to question my actions. Wait here, Agatha. Now, Jemima, if you please."

The little attic room given over to the use of the maids was adequate, if a trifle cold. A cot bed big enough for the two of them, a makeshift curtained corner with pegs for their clothes and a stand with basin and jug constituted the furniture. A mat on the floor promised little in the way of protection for bare feet.

"Are all the servants' rooms like this?"

Jemima shrugged. "I don't know, mistress. The upper servants have rooms on the floor below, I think."

"Do they indeed? Well, I suppose it must serve for the present." She felt the thickness of the blanket. "I'll have Mrs Howmore find you a quilt."

Little Tibby banged on the bed. "Mattress is hard as hard, mistress. Not like mine at home. When can we go home, mistress?"

"Hush, Tibby!" Jemima lowered her voice. "She's not happy, mistress."

Chloe put an arm about the girl's shoulders. "Come now, Tibby, it won't be for long. You'll become accustomed in a day or two, and Jemima will take care of you."

"Will I do the fires in all the rooms, mistress?"

She had to laugh. "Of course not. You won't do the fires at all here. You are to wait upon Miss Flook and that is all."

Little Tibby brightened. "Like Jemima does for you?"

"Just like that."

She left the girl delighted with her new status, but found herself resolving that if ever she did become mistress here, one of her first tasks would be to improve the quarters allotted to the servants. Oswald had been a stickler in such matters. None under his roof should be housed in little better than a hovel. Chloe, having endured pitiful accommodation in many an inferior lodging as she traipsed in her father's train, embraced this dictum with enthusiasm.

By contrast, her allotted bedchamber was palatial. She doubted if Lance had the faintest notion of how domestic affairs were managed in his household. And not on account of his accident. It was obvious he'd been brought up to think of little but his own comfort. It was common to the aristocracy, as she knew from her childhood, just as she'd foolishly blabbed to him last night.

Oh, enough. She would not think of it. She must get up, although for what purpose, she had no notion. What in the world would she find to do in this barrack of a house?

She sipped her chocolate while she waited for Jemima, who had gone off to collect Tibby and fetch up jugs of hot water for washing, but her mind obstinately returned to Lance. She could not help a faint rise of apprehension at the thought of their inevitable meeting. After the way she'd left last night, it was bound to be awkward. She sighed in defeat. She would have to apologise, for her loss of temper if nothing else. Despite her affection, she found the necessity galling. Really, he had deserved her censure. He was altogether too concentrated on what he wanted and she would be stupid indeed to think of marrying the creature.

Breakfast at Ravensthorp was served in the smaller dining parlour, to which the butler Kenninghall led Chloe. Accompanied, very properly, by Miss Flook, she made her entrance in a little trepidation only to find the place empty except for a couple of footmen waiting to serve them.

"Where is everyone? Lady Adelaide does not take breakfast?" She took the seat Kenninghall was setting for her as she spoke.

"Her ladyship has her breakfast in bed, madam. She does not in general come down much before eleven. And Mr Potticary broke his fast an hour ago."

"Also his lordship?"

"No, madam. Lord Pettipher went out riding with Captain Ravensthorp. It has ever been his habit to take his exercise before eating, madam."

"I see. Well, I dare say he is well enough to resume the habit. Are the gentlemen still out?"

"I believe they came in to change about fifteen minutes ago, madam."

Then Lance would be down presently. Her heart pattered. She'd half hoped he might have been in here and gone already. She could not help wondering if a ride was wise. It might tire him too much. On the other hand, he ought to resume his normal life as soon as possible.

The butler had begun enumerating the viands on offer and she was obliged to turn her attention to food. She chose scrambled egg and a warm roll, and accepted a cup of coffee. Recalling Lance's inability to remember how he liked to drink it, Chloe was swept with an instant flush of annoyance. That was what set him off yesterday morning after their arrival. Was she going to be drawn into an immediate resumption of her role?

The notion chafed at her nerves. What if she ignored it? Pretended not to notice. Or left it to the captain to sort out. Yet for what purpose? What was she trying to prove?

Agatha, seated beside her, leaned to speak in a low tone. "Are you quite well, dear Mrs Quilter? You seem a trifle agitated."

Chloe cursed inside. "Is it so obvious?"

"Only to me," said the other with haste. "I know you too well, dear Chloe." She paused a moment, setting her cup to her lips and drinking, but her eyes were still on her employer. "Is it this place? I confess I find it a trifle overwhelming too."

Chloe seized on this. "Quite so. I do find it disturbing. Especially with nothing to occupy me."

Miss Flook tittered. "Perhaps we should look upon it as a holiday, dear Mrs Quilter."

A holiday? Good heavens! It was anything but restful. But she could hardly speak of her troubled heart. Especially to Agatha, who was likely fretting on her own account. She could wish she might reassure the woman, but she could not bear to refer to the possibility of transferring her life to this place, even obliquely. The whole business was too fraught with question and distress. She prevaricated.

"For my part, I must be doing something. Perhaps we may explore the gardens later, if it is not too cold out."

Miss Flook agreed to this and Chloe applied herself to her breakfast. She was hungry, but the apprehension she could not dismiss spoiled her appetite. The moment she heard the murmur of male voices approaching the parlour door, the food in her mouth turned to a ball of cotton wool. She seized her cup, swallowing the hot coffee in a bid to force it down.

"— and I shall insist upon riding the young horse tomorrow," Lance was saying as he entered the room.

Chloe looked up as she set down her cup and saw him stop short at sight of her, a frown drawing his brows together. Despite the unruly behaviour of her pulse, which was jumping in an unpleasant fashion, she forced a smile, her gaze encompassing the captain.

"Good morning, gentlemen. I trust your ride was enjoyable."

Captain Ravensthorp thrust into the room, his tone jovial. "What, with this ingrate complaining throughout merely because I persuaded him to take a quiet ride on old Brutus? For his own safety, mark you."

"I'm perfectly capable of riding any horse in my stables, I thank you, young scapegrace. Kenninghall, give me a jug of ale, would you, so I can empty it over this fellow's head."

"Give him some coffee, Kenninghall," retorted the other, taking a seat opposite Chloe. "It might mend his temper. Good morning, ladies. Forgive my cousin's ill manners. His wayward memory, you know. He can't remember the basic courtesies of life."

Glancing at Lance to see how he took this sarcasm, Chloe saw his lips compress as he gravitated to the head of the table and pulled out his chair. He nodded towards her, avoiding her eye and instead letting it fall on Miss Flook.

"Good morning. I trust you are comfortably bestowed, Agatha?"

"Oh, yes indeed, my dear lord, perfectly comfortable, I assure you. Quite overwhelmingly so, I declare. I have never been in such a chamber." Consternation leapt in Agatha's eyes as they shifted to Chloe's face. "I don't mean to imply I am not perfectly comfortable at Derry Lodge, dear Mrs Quilter..."

Chloe set a hand on the fluttering one beside her and squeezed it slightly. "I never supposed otherwise." She was hard put to it to think of anything sensible to say. Afraid of meeting Lance's eye, she concentrated on the captain. "Where did you ride?"

"Through the woods. There's a bridle path leading to a patch of greensward where we were able to let the horses have their heads." He was obliged to give his attention to the footman who had placed a platter before him and was now lifting the covers on two of the silver dishes. Helping himself to a quantity of ham and eggs, he resumed. "Nothing like a hard ride to work up a good appetite. Do you ride, Mrs Quilter?"

"Indifferently. I prefer a brisk walk."

Out of the corner of her eye, she saw the butler serving Lance with a little of the ham although he waved away the eggs. Instinct urged her to intervene to encourage him to eat a more substantial amount, but she suppressed it, conscious of the dismaying rift between them. She took refuge in requesting a refill of her cup and indicated the half-eaten remains on her plate.

"And take this away, if you please. I've had enough."

The butler poured coffee for her and moved up the table with the pot. "Coffee, my lord?"

Lance nodded. He had not yet touched his meal and Chloe found herself fretting for him. Her tongue betrayed her. "You must eat, Lance!"

His head came up and his eyes met hers briefly before dropping to his plate.

Chloe's heart jerked. He looked more troubled than angry. She'd hurt him!

But then he picked up his fork and dug it into a piece of ham. She watched the fork hover. But he set it down again and reached for the coffee. On instant tenterhooks, Chloe waited for the complaint as he drank of the dark brew. It did not come.

She became aware of the silence, broken only by the scrape of utensils on plates and the clink of cups. Her own cup was in her hand but she'd not sipped at the coffee, to which she'd added a little cream and sugar without thinking.

To her relief, as she drank, she saw Lance begin to eat. She cast about in her mind for some innocuous remark, but it dwelled obstinately on last night. The quarrel, if one could so call it, replayed in her head, along with the rising memory of her thoughts about Clarissa. There could be no doubt Lance had his attention on what had passed between them. She yearned to know his thoughts. The awkwardness of this meeting at breakfast was too hideous to be borne.

At last the moment was rescued by Agatha addressing the captain. "Mrs Quilter and I had thought of taking a turn in the gardens, sir, if the weather holds. Is it too cold, do you think?"

Captain Ravensthorp swallowed down his mouthful and waved towards the windows. "The sun was beginning to break through as we came in. If you are well wrapped up, I imagine it might be quite pleasant."

"Oh, well, in that case…"

She faded out and awkwardness fell over the table again as the captain applied himself to his breakfast. Chloe could think of nothing beyond the urgent necessity to talk to Lance alone. Matters could not be left thus. As things stood, she could not even be sure he would wish to speak to her.

The matter was taken out of her hands as Lance cleared his throat. "I hope you ladies may find a way to amuse yourselves. I aim to be closeted with Potticary today. It is high time I caught up."

His tone was dismissive, with nothing in it of the Lance she had come to love. Was this the earl taking back control? If so, she must be glad she'd refused to entertain his suit.

She rose. "If you are ready, Agatha, we might take that walk now. I had best don boots and a cloak, I think."

"Yes, indeed. How very wise, dear Mrs Quilter."

With a nod to both men, Chloe swept from the parlour, the shreds of her dignity vanishing with the swell of distress in her bosom.

Lance had the greatest difficulty refraining from turning his head to watch her leave. For the first time in their dealings, he'd not known how to address her, nor what to say to overcome the breach. How had it become impassable? And so fast.

All through the morning's ride, though managing his horse had provided a distraction, at the back of his mind had floated the question of what he was to do, how he was to set things right between them. He'd half-hoped and half-feared to meet Chloe at the breakfast table. With reason. Her distance chilled him.

"Potticary will be over the moon if you mean to attend to business, coz," his cousin observed.

Lance merely grunted. He'd invented the excuse on impulse, at once regretting it. Not wishing to respond, he forked ham into his mouth and resolutely chewed, though it felt like eating string. He caught a penetrating look from Hargrave and sedulously avoided his eye.

Silence reigned for a space. His cousin broke it as he sat back, leaving an empty plate. "Well, if you're going to busy yourself with estate affairs, you old sobersides, I'll take myself off to Northampton."

"Do as you please, coz."

Hargrave flicked a glance at the servants waiting by the sideboard and lowered his voice. "Surly as a bear this morning,

Sir Lancelot, and I can guess why. Why don't you mend it, you fool?"

Lance looked up. "How can I? You've seen what she's like." Remembering they were not alone, he dropped his voice to a murmur. "I'm not going to sue for forgiveness if that's what you mean."

"You'll get nowhere without talking."

"That might be for the best."

Hargrave's lightness vanished. "You don't mean that."

Despair gripped him. "I don't know what I mean."

"Talk to her, man!"

Lance seized his cup and drank deeply of the bitter brew. Why the deuce had Kenninghall not sweetened it? He set the cup down. "Sugar! Where's the sugar?"

The butler stepped forward even as Hargrave shoved the silver sugar bowl across the table. "Here. Put some in yourself. It won't kill you to pick up the tongs."

Lance glanced at him, puzzled by his cousin's impatience. Was it meant for a reproof?

Kenninghall was hovering. Lance waved him away and reached for the sugar bowl. Did Hargrave suppose he was incapable of doing the least little thing for himself? Was this another accusation of selfishness? He dropped a couple of lumps into his cup, beset by an uncomfortable reflection. Had he not fussed about the coffee any time it was not to his satisfaction? Chloe always made it right when he did that. Had he relied on her even for such a trivial thing?

Absently he drank, finding it a trifle too sweet. Damnation. Chloe knew just how he liked it. With his cousin's ironic eye on him, he felt obliged to drink it down. He was not going to give Hargrave more ammunition to be making him out even more selfish than he truly was.

He set down the cup and rose. One of the footmen was instantly there to shift the chair out of his way. Dear God, was this what his life was like? Was he to be dogged at every step by underlings? As he went towards the door, which opened in front of him, he remembered dressing this morning. Finch, left to himself, would have had him stand while his valet did all. Having grown used to Jack, who had only helped with what Lance was as yet unhandy enough to do, he'd found it irksome. His conscience all too raw, he'd refused to allow Finch to do anything but hand him his clothes and brush his coat once it was on. If Chloe supposed him incapable of acting for himself, she would soon find out her mistake.

"Hold up, coz!"

Hargrave had caught him up as he was about to mount the stairs. Lance grasped the bannister and turned. "What is it?"

"If you intend going to Potticary, you're going the wrong way."

Lance frowned. "Hasn't he a study?"

"He's taken to working at your desk in the library. And his study is on this floor. Have you forgotten the layout of the house?"

Lance hesitated. "Some of it."

Hargrave's brows rose. "You weren't going to Potticary, were you?"

Some of the tension left him and he sighed. "I don't know where I was going. My mind was elsewhere."

"On Chloe?"

Obviously. But he preferred not to say so. There was no avoiding his cousin's speculative eye. "For heaven's sake, Hargrave, let me be! I can't think straight and I'm sick of discovering unpleasant truths about my character."

Hargrave grasped his arm with a strong hand, urging him up the stairs. "Come, we'll go to the den. You're in no fit state to be trying to get back in the saddle."

"What den?"

"It's by way of being your private sitting room. You and I always retreat there when the women become too importunate, don't you recall?"

Allowing himself to be shepherded up the stairs and along the gallery, Lance tried to remember such a room. It proved to be a comfortable parlour on the second floor, situated at one corner of the house with an excellent view over the front lawns. It felt both familiar and alien as Lance stood at one of the first of two large windows, gazing out. The atmosphere was warm from a lit fire, where Hargrave had already appropriated one of two deep wing chairs set either side.

Lance had not before had a chance to take in the grounds from this angle. They were extensive and his eye roved the terraces leading to a massive lawn dotted with little copses. Two figures came into view, walking slowly along a gravel path leading around a fountain on the lower terrace. Chloe! It must be. She'd had the intention of walking in the gardens with Agatha. Riveted, Lance watched her slow progress, the glimpse of gold hair under the hood of her cloak becoming more visible every moment.

At this distance it struck him she might indeed be Clarissa. Had she been much of a height with Chloe? Did she in fact resemble her so closely? He had never properly examined the phenomenon, forgetful of the miniature in his possession when he had the replica in person within his orbit.

Replica? Was she indeed so? Had he, as she'd several times accused him, tried to resurrect Clarissa in Chloe?

A protest rose up in his breast. It could not be so, for when he tried to recall Clarissa's face, all he got was Chloe's. They could not be identical. Impossible. They were not twins, or even of the same blood. There must be differences.

On impulse, urgent suddenly, he turned and trod quickly across to where Hargrave sat. "Is there no portrait of Clarissa? Had I only the miniature?"

His cousin's brows drew together as he looked up, a stony expression coming into his face. "Why should you want to see it now? For what purpose?"

Disregarding this, Lance seized on the implication. "Then there is one. Where is it?"

Standing before the portrait, Lance felt as if he stared at a stranger. The girl depicted was a waif, though bright-eyed and smiling in a sweet innocence that had nothing to do with the Clarissa he remembered in the snatches of imagery left to him. Of more significance, her only resemblance to Chloe was the tumble of golden hair worn loose in the fashion of the day. She was devoid of Chloe's curves, Chloe's assurance, Chloe's warmth. Yet for years he'd apparently left her up here on his library wall where his eyes must necessarily fall upon her every time he looked up from his desk.

Embarrassed at the sentimentality thus betrayed, he was relieved Hargrave had requested Potticary to leave them. He needed no other witness, for he could no longer doubt his cousin's assertion. He'd refused to let go of the memories. If he'd been haunted, it was by his own contrivance. Or, if he had been, it was in his other life, the one he was no longer living.

"Well, coz?"

Hargrave spoke from behind, but Lance did not immediately turn, his attention still concentrated on the thoughts revolving in his head. He answered without reflecting on what he said. "I'm not the man who caused this thing to be placed here."

"Oh? Who else, then?"

Lance glanced round. "I don't mean that. I'm not who I was then, Hargrave. Who I was until a few weeks since." He flourished a hand at the image. "Look at her. She's scarcely more than a child."

Hargrave joined him, his eyes going to the picture. "You go too fast for me, old fellow. Of course she's young. It was painted a year or so before she died, wasn't it?"

"I have no notion. I don't recall much beyond a patchwork of the time. Except for the accident. I remember that." The familiar shadow crossed his heart, but its power was diminished. A thought occurred and he did not hesitate to give it voice. "In an odd way, my accident mirrors hers. Oh, I don't mean her demise. But who I was then was lost. I may be Lord Pettipher, but I don't know him any longer." He found Hargrave's frowning gaze upon him. "Can you understand at all?"

His cousin's mouth twisted. "No. But then I've never had my memory fail me."

"Count yourself lucky." A faint and rueful laugh escaped him. "Though why I say that I don't know. I've a feeling I may have cause to be grateful for the lack."

He received a buffet in the shoulder. "Don't be so hard on yourself, coz. You're not as bad as all that."

"That's not what you said last night." Remembrance threw a shaft of anguish into his chest. "And Chloe has reason to think the worst of me."

"Don't be ridiculous! Do you think she's ceased to care for you?"

"I don't know that she does care for me."

"Because she ranted at you? She wouldn't have done so if she was indifferent, you fool."

"I didn't say she was indifferent. But last night —"

"She lost her temper with you, and why not? You behaved like an idiot. But that doesn't mean you're wholly irreclaimable. You never were, coz. What idea you have in your head I know not, but you're no monster. Your people wouldn't care for your welfare if you were, and they do. And Aunt Adelaide thinks the world of you, whatever she may say to your face."

Amusement lightened Lance's burgeoning gloom. "What, when she clearly thinks me next door to a moonling?"

Hargrave laughed. "You didn't hear her defending you to Jasper and Rosaline before we knew what had happened to you. And no one was more distressed than she when Rowley brought the news, for Potticary told me so."

"It's good of you to try and comfort me, coz, but it's plain I've been an arrogant and thankless creature, too apt to ignore the claims of others."

"Well, if that's true, you may blame your upbringing."

"Of course it's true. You said as much last night. And how the deuce I'm to persuade Chloe otherwise I can't imagine."

But Hargrave was looking past him and dropped his voice to a murmur. "Well, now's your chance, coz, for here she is."

Shock spun him to face the door. Chloe was standing in the aperture, regarding him in frowning silence. An unaccustomed thumping started up in the region of Lance's chest and he hardly heard his cousin's parting words.

"I will leave you, coz. I'm persuaded you will do better without me." He cast a smile at Chloe as he went towards the door. "If you'll excuse me, Mrs Quilter?"

Chloe moved to allow the captain to pass, but her gaze remained on Lance. Vaguely in the background, she heard the door close. She gathered her shredded nerves, ignoring the jumping of her pulse.

"Mr Potticary told me you were in here."

His instant frown dismayed her. "You were looking for me?"

She swallowed. "Yes. Yes, I was."

Her courage failed and she looked away, her gaze falling on the polished mahogany desk, the matching cabinets about the walls stuffed with books and the alcoves at the windows with cushioned seats below.

Lance said nothing and she faced him again, amazed to discover apprehension in his face instead of the brooding look she'd anticipated. Was it apprehension? Her nerve snapped.

"Oh, this is silly! How am I so shy of you? After all we've endured together."

She heard him draw a snatched breath and his expression changed. "Chloe … Chloe, we've much to discuss."

A slight smile escaped her despite her inner agitation. "It's what I came for." She took a couple of steps towards him and the corner of her eye caught on a flash of image. She turned her head. A wash of dismay engulfed her as she took in the full impact of the angelic creature smiling from the wall. "Oh, my God!"

"Chloe, don't! It's not what you think."

His quick denial confirmed her instant thought. "It's her, isn't it? It's your Clarissa."

He shifted as if he would insert himself between her and the portrait. Chloe thrust him back with some violence.

"Let me look!" With a sigh, he gave way and she moved to confront the picture full on. Her heart sank as she took in the golden head, the delicate tint in the youthful cheeks, the pretty pouting lip and the soulful eyes. "She's beautiful."

His voice came, flat and unemotional. "Yes, she was. But she's not nearly as beautiful as you."

Chloe jumped, her eyes flying to his. "What? Don't lie!"

His eyes blazed suddenly. Chloe found her shoulders gripped as he held her there, her back to the portrait. "Stand there! Don't move!"

He released her and Chloe, her heartbeat loud in her ears all at once, watched his face as he moved back, looking from her to the picture and back again. "I was right. There is no resemblance other than the hair. I saw it at once when I came here on purpose to look at the thing."

She eyed him, hope hovering beneath the frantic racing of her pulse. But a hint of irritation thrust through. "Well, there is one sure difference. I'm alive!" Lance looked as if she had struck him. Chloe was at once remorseful. She put out a hand. "I should not have said that."

He looked at her with eyes hard as agates for a moment. Then they softened and he sighed. "Yes, you should. You must always say what you wish to me. Don't try to spare me, Chloe."

A tiny sob escaped her. "I can't help it, Lance. I'm sorry… I was cruel last night."

"You had every right to say what you did."

He made a move towards her but Chloe threw her hands palm up. "No, don't. Let me say it all." She turned a little so she could gesture towards the picture. "She is not the difficulty, Lance. It's not her fault. I realised something after — after we quarrelled."

Pain crossed his face. "Was it only a quarrel? I thought you had left me forever. Hargrave told me if I wanted you to stay, I must set you free."

Her smile felt twisted. "But you won't."

"I can't. If it's selfish of me, I'm sorry for it, but I want you so badly, Chloe."

"You mean you need me."

"That too. But it's not all." He eyed her with a hint of uncertainty. "Shall I be truthful?"

"I wish you would. If we can't even be honest with each other, we have no chance at all, Lance."

"Then know that I've been guilty of wishing to have you in my bed almost from the first."

Shock claimed her. "What?"

He laughed, though his cheeks darkened with colour. "You were sleeping in the chair in your nightgown, with just a blanket around you. I watched you. If you will have it with candour, I followed every curve with lustful eyes. If I could have dragged you into the bed with honour, I would have done it without compunction."

Chloe's mouth was dry. Why she should find the recital of his disgraceful thoughts so alluring, she could not tell, but an answering flush made her grip her thighs together. She tried for a light note. "Shocking, my lord!"

His lips twitched. "Is it not?"

An uncomfortable thought intruded. "Is that why you kept asking me to marry you?"

Consternation flitted across his face. "I don't know. Perhaps. I know it began one way and ended as truth. You became all in all to me."

"As your nurse, yes."

"No, you don't understand. How should you? I didn't understand it myself until last night."

Confusion swept her. "What are you talking about? Because of what I said?"

"Because you left me." She saw him catch his breath and sigh it out. "I was afraid — I've been afraid all along that you would disappear … like Clarissa."

She struggled with resentment, but it seemed Lance was not done.

"It's not because I still love her, though I think I must always feel some tenderness for her memory. That I can't help. It's because I love *you*. And because I lost her so abruptly. I'm afraid you'll be whisked away from me, just as Clarissa was whisked away. Can't you see, Chloe? It's not that I think of you as Clarissa. You are not in the least like her in character. And very little in your features now that I've looked at the portrait. It's just … it's just that I care so much, I want you so much, and I'm afraid of losing you, don't you see?"

Chloe's heart was behaving like a trout on a string and she could barely get the words out of her mouth. "And I was so foolish as to be jealous of her!" She swept the portrait with an arc of one hand. "She seemed to have so much power over you…"

He caught the hand she'd used and brought it to his lips. The touch of them on her skin sent a flitter through her veins. "Chloe, she no longer has that power. That's why I came down here. I wanted to see if you truly did look alike."

"And?"

"It's as I said, and more. She was a child, Chloe, while you —" His eyes roved her figure. "You are all woman."

She could not speak. He came a step closer, his hand running along her captured arm to draw her towards him. Without will to resist, Chloe came.

His voice dropped to a low caressing murmur, husky as his face hovered close. "You are beautiful, desirable and everything I could ever want." She thought he was going to kiss her and waited, half melting in anticipation of the remembered explosion from that mistletoe embrace. But instead, his fingers traced her features. "I've said I love you so many times, but never with as much truth as I do now. I love you, Chloe Quilter, for everything you are."

Her lips trembled on a smile and she could not help the husky note as her throat ached with the lump rising there. "And I love you, Lance Ravensthorp. There, I've said it. You must know I never would have left you…"

Her words vanished under his mouth as his lips found hers.

Time wasted away. Presently, her senses returning, Chloe found herself side by side with Lance on one of the window seats with his arm about her and her hand nestling in his. A murmur escaped her. "This is comfortable."

His hold tightened briefly. "It won't be for much longer."

She pulled free a little so she might look round at him. "How so? Can't we just stay here for a while?"

Lance sighed. "There's still my wayward memory and my wild fits. It won't stop, Chloe, only because we've settled things between us."

"Have we?"

The green eyes met hers, a slight look of apprehension rising within them. "Haven't we?"

It was Chloe's turn to sigh. "There's so much to sort out. And don't speak of licences and haste."

"Why not? Why wait? You are going to marry me, aren't you?"

"Yes, but with due form and ceremony, Lance. There are my people to consider. I have to provide for them. Bring them here if they wish for it, but perhaps Basil won't. Agatha, yes. Jack and the maids, but of the others, I don't yet know."

"All these things may be —"

"And I must see my lawyer, for there are settlements in question. Oswald provided for a second marriage. Not that I ever anticipated…"

She was silenced with a kiss. Lance left her breathless again, but spoke as she pulled away. "None of this is important. Besides, you don't need any of it, Chloe. I can provide for you. Why must we wait?"

She shifted so that she faced him. "You're doing it again, Lance!"

A grimace crossed his face. "Being selfish, you mean?"

"That's exactly what I mean. I have a life you've interrupted. I can't drop everything at your whim. There is a great deal to arrange."

"Can't it be arranged after we are married?"

Chloe eyed him with frustration, not unmixed with amusement now that she had surrendered her heart. "Why am I even bothering to argue with you, impossible creature?"

The mischievous look appeared. Chloe's heart did a little flip. She'd not seen it since they'd come to Ravensthorp.

"Because you're determined to reclaim me, nurse of mine. I wish you joy of the battle, but I won't yield."

"No, you expect me to. I must insist at least upon sending for my lawyer first. Then we shall see." She smiled at him. "We will find a compromise, my dear one."

His expression changed at once and Chloe was touched as his eyes filmed. His voice went low and husky. "You've never said that before. Am I your dear one? Truly?"

Her heart melted. She reached up her fingers to caress his cheek, no trace there now of the gauntness she'd seen in the early days. "I stroked your face when you were in need. I cosseted you, and comforted you and nursed you back to health. How could you not be my dear one?"

He caught her to him, holding her so tightly she could scarcely breathe. "Chloe, Chloe! My love, my precious life, my darling…"

Her doubts crumbled into dust as her affection blossomed full and free. There were shoals ahead, changes to be accommodated, people to pacify and settle. But she could weather it all now. The ghost of Clarissa had been laid to rest.

A NOTE TO THE READER

Dear Reader,

This is the second amnesia trope I have tackled. There were many years between the two and by the time I wrote this one, I had a much better idea of the effects of memory loss. My mother had been suffering from Alzheimer's for several years and I had been a close witness of the phenomenon before she went into a home.

I did not consciously model Lance's experience on my mother's, but with hindsight I see that there were similarities of which I must have been aware. Of course it's not the same thing. As we age, we all experience a little of the phenomenon when a shutter comes down between what we want to express and what the mind will present. Dementia though is a gradual process, while sudden amnesia is a great deal more shocking and complete.

Yet the change manifests in ways that are recognizable. Shifts of attention. The inability to maintain concentration. Confusion of past and present, including bouts of hallucination. Concepts slip away before they become fully formed ideas. Names of ordinary things as well as people disappear from the mind. It's unsettling and scary.

My mother could not bear to be alone and this is understandable. Everything is unfamiliar and the points of stability have to be grasped hard. Those few faces recognised, even if you can't put a name to them. Surroundings that remain the same – any change of space is worrying. It's as if the person has to hang on to whatever remains constant, and even then can't be sure it will not vanish.

The condition is trying indeed for those who become the point of stability, in this case Chloe. Worse, as her emotions become involved. Lance needs her, that is seen. But does he love her?

Fortunately, since this is a romance, I was able to bring our hero enough out of his affliction to be able to start to distinguish his own feelings and to make sense of them in relation to the dichotomy of Chloe and Clarissa.

However, I could not in conscience suggest that everything will be roses from here on out. It won't be. It can't be. Memory loss, however acquired, is not readily recoverable. As Chloe realises, there will be shoals ahead, years of intermittent bouts of confusion and upset. Yet love, real and true, heals all things and enables one to overcome the worst as well as enjoying the best. We leave Lance and Chloe in hope.

If you would consider leaving a review, it would be much appreciated and very helpful. Do feel free to contact me on **elizabeth@elizabethbailey.co.uk** or find me on **Facebook**, **Twitter**, **Goodreads** or my website **www.elizabethbailey.co.uk**.

Elizabeth Bailey

Sapere Books is an exciting new publisher of brilliant fiction and popular history.

To find out more about our latest releases and our monthly bargain books visit our website: **saperebooks.com**